ST. MARTIN'S

MINOTAUR

MYSTERIES

"[*The Hunting Wind*] is to the same standard . . . [as] Hamilton's Edgar-winning *A Cold Day in Paradise*."

—*The Boston Globe*

WINTER OF THE WOLF MOON

"This is a most entertaining tale, peppered with wry humor and real, amusing characters."

—*Publishers Weekly* (starred review)

"This is the kind of book you climb inside and when you're forced to leave, you wish you could stay a little longer."

—*Booklist*

"[Hamilton's] protagonist is likeable as well as durable, his raffish cast sharply observed and entertaining. Moreover, he knows how to pace a story, something of a lost art in recent crime fiction." —*Kirkus Reviews*

"The isolated, wintry location jives well with Hamilton's pristine prose, independent protagonist, and ingenious plot."

—*Library Journal*

A COLD DAY IN PARADISE

"Hamilton unreels the mystery with a mounting tension that many an old pro might envy."

—*Kirkus Reviews*

"Combines crisp, clear writing, wily colorful characters, and an offbeat locale in an impressive debut."

—*Publishers Weekly*

"Hamilton can write . . . [A] nicely crafted debut that makes you look forward to his next book."

—*The Orlando Sentinel*

"There's plenty of great UP atmosphere here . . . [A] brooding, caustic, well-plotted and tightly written thriller."

—*The Detroit Free Press*

"Chilling as the November wind. A must for PI and suspense fans."

—Charles Todd, author of *Wings of Fire*

ALSO BY STEVE HAMILTON

The Hunting Wind

Winter of the Wolf Moon

A Cold Day in Paradise

AVAILABLE FROM
ST. MARTIN'S/MINOTAUR PAPERBACKS

NORTH OF NOWHERE

AN ALEX McKNIGHT MYSTERY

Steve Hamilton

St. Martin's Paperbacks

NORTH OF NOWHERE

Copyright © 2002 by Steve Hamilton.
Excerpt from *Blood Is the Sky* © 2003 by Steve Hamilton.

Library of Congress Catalog Card Number: 2001058552

ISBN: 0-312-98381-6

Printed in the United States of America

St. Martin's Press hardcover edition / May 2002
St. Martin's Paperbacks edition / May 2003

St. Martin's Paperbacks are published by St. Martin's Press, 175 Fifth Avenue, New York, NY 10010.

10 9 8 7 6 5 4 3 2 1

To Dad

Acknowledgments

I want to thank, yet again, all of the usual suspects—
Bill Keller and Frank Hayes, Liz Staples and Taylor
Brugman, Bob Kozak and everyone at IBM, Bob
Randisi and the Private Eye Writers of America, Ruth
Cavin and everyone at St. Martin's Press, Jane Che-
lius, Jeff Allen, Larry Queipo, former chief of police,
town of Kingston, New York, and Dr. Glenn Hamil-
ton from the department of Emergency Medicine,
Wright State University. Thanks also to Dave Swayze
for sharing his knowledge of Great Lakes shipwrecks,
and to Bill Webb for helping me with the history of the
Royal Navy.

More than ever, I owe everything to my wife, Julia,
who puts up with my daydreaming and my late
nights. And to Nickie and to Toni, who make every
day a miracle.

Chapter One

That summer it was all about secrets.

It was the summer I turned forty-nine years old, which made me start thinking about fifty and what that would feel like. Fifty years with not a lot to show for them. One marriage that was so far in the past, it was like something you'd dig up out of the ground. My baseball career—four years of minor league ball and not a single day in the majors. And my career as a Detroit police officer, which ended one night with me on my back, watching my partner die next to me. That's what I saw when I looked back on my life.

On the plus side, I was getting a lot of reading done that summer. And, though I didn't know it yet, I was about to meet some interesting new people. I wouldn't get to see any fireworks on the Fourth of July, because I'd spend most of that evening lying facedown on a stranger's floor, a gun held to the side of my head. I would wait for one final blast, maybe one final blur of color. And then nothing.

I already had one bullet inside me. I knew I didn't have room for another one.

More than anything else, it was the summer in which I had to make a big decision. Was I going to rejoin the human race or was I going to keep drifting until I was too far away to ever come back? That's what the summer was really all about. That and the secrets.

Jonathan Connery, AKA Jackie, owner of the Glasgow Inn in Paradise, Michigan, raised in Scotland, alleged second-cousin to Sean Connery, and in his opinion anyway, just as good-looking—this is the man who took me to that house on that Fourth of July evening. The Glasgow Inn is just down the road from my cabins. I live in the first cabin, the one I helped my old man build back in the sixties and seventies. The other five I rent out. My customers are mostly hunters in the fall, snowmobilers in the winter. In the summer, they're families who want to do something a little different. They come up here from the Lower Peninsula to Paradise because it's the most out-of-the-way place you can go to without leaving the state—hell, without leaving the country. After driving forever on I-75, they think they're almost there when they cross the Mackinac Bridge. But it's another hour through the emptiest land they've ever seen until they finally get close to Lake Superior. Even then they still have to circle around Whitefish Bay, driving deep into the heart of the

Hiawatha National Forest. By then, they're wondering to themselves how anyone could actually live up here, so far away from everything else in the world. When they finally hit the town, the sign says, "Welcome to Paradise! We're glad you made it!" They go through the one blinking light in the middle of town, keep going north along the shore a couple of miles, past Jackie's Glasgow Inn, until they get to my cabins. When I see their faces as they get out of the car, I know how it's going to be. If they look around like they just landed on the moon, they're in for a long week. There's not much to do up here, after you go to the Shipwreck Museum one day and then to the Taquemmenon Falls State Park the next. If they get out of the car, close their eyes, take a deep breath, and smile, I know they'll like it here. They'll probably come the year after, too. And the year after that.

Which is why I have mostly repeat customers now—people with standing reservations who come up here the same week, every year. In the summertime I don't have to do much for them. They don't use much firewood, maybe just a little when the winds off of the lake cool things down at night. They sure as hell don't need me to tell them what to do or where to go. They're just as happy to never see me.

I was spending a lot of time alone that summer. It's what I had to do. There was a time when a certain lawyer had talked me into becoming a private investigator. I tried it and got my ass kicked. Then I met a young Ojibwa woman and tried to help her out of a jam, and got my ass kicked even worse. I got my ass kicked in ways that nobody's ass has ever been kicked before. Then an old friend from my baseball days came back, thirty years after I had last seen him, and asked me to help him find somebody. I agreed to help him. You'd think I would have known what was about to happen. Although this time I got my head kicked along with my ass.

Enough of this, I said to myself. This I do not need. Ever again.

When the summer began, I was finding excuses not to go to Jackie's for lunch. Or for my afternoon beer, even though I knew he'd have a Canadian on ice for me. Or dinner. When I did stop in, he'd ask me where I'd been. I'd tell him I'd been busy, cleaning out the cabins, fixing things. He'd give his famous look, like he could see right through me.

By the end of June, I was spending most evenings in my cabin, reading the paper, and as many books as I could get my hands on. I had never read so many books in my life. Whatever the tiny Paradise library had, or the couple of gift shops that sold paperbacks—thrillers, mysteries, some of the classics even—that's what I read. The books I craved the most were true crime. You'd think that would've been the last thing I wanted to read, with eight years as a cop and a year or so of trying very hard not to be a private investigator, and with everything that had happened to me. But for some reason, true crime books were comforting to me. Maybe because I was reading about all these people getting their asses kicked and for once it wasn't me.

By the time the Fourth of July rolled around, I don't think I had even seen Jackie's face for a solid week. He knocked on the door. I opened it and saw him standing there. It would have been a surprise no matter what the circumstances, because he never came to my place. The Glasgow Inn had the television and the food and the Canadian beer. So there wasn't much reason for him to come my way.

"Jackie," I said. "What's going on?"

"Alex," he said. He stepped past me and looked around the place. I think Jackie was sixty-five that summer. Over the years, his face had felt a lot of cold wind off the lake. He had a certain sparkle in his eyes, though, that told you he could take whatever the lake gave him. When the snow melted, he'd be there smiling.

"Is everything okay?" I said.

"Everything's fine," he said. "Just dandy." He picked up the book on my kitchen table and turned it over to read the back.

I stood there watching him. I wasn't sure what to say.

"Okay," he said, putting the book down. "Here's the deal. I brought a tent with me. It's practically brand new, one of those space-age nylon things. Doesn't weigh more than thirty pounds, but it's plenty big and it keeps the wind and the rain out. It's beautiful. Along with that, I've got a good portable propane stove. A sleeping bag that'll keep you warm to forty below. A backpack. You know, the kind with the frame that keeps the weight on your hips instead of your shoulders. A lot of other little stuff. Water purification kit, first aid kit, some mosquito netting. Oh, and I almost forgot, a couple of great fishing rods. I mean the best."

"Why are you telling me this?" I said. "Where are you going?"

"I'm not going anywhere," he said. "You are."

"What are you talking about?"

"You'll need a good rifle," he said, "You'll have to get that yourself."

"Jackie . . ."

"I'll draw you a map of this place. It's up in the Yukon Territory. If you drive, it'll take you a hell of a long time to get up there. I hope your truck is up for it."

"Jackie . . ."

"If I were you, I'd sell the truck and fly up there. Tell you what, since I'm giving you all this equipment, just leave the truck with me. It's what, about twelve years old?"

"Jackie, will you kindly tell me what the hell you're talking about? Since when am I going to the Yukon Territory?"

"I'm just trying to help you out, Alex. I thought you'd appreciate it."

"By sending me to the Yukon? That's helping me?"

"Think of it, Alex. The guy who told me about this place, he says you could set up camp there. Fish the rivers for food, maybe shoot some small game once in a while. There's a little town a few miles away if you really need it, but aside from that, no human contact at all, Alex. You could go a whole year and never see another person's face."

"You're trying to be funny, right? This is a joke."

"I'll look after the cabins," he said. "I promise. Now get your stuff together."

"Okay, I get it," I said. "This is your cute little way of telling me I haven't been coming around much lately."

"Yeah, it's been killing me," he said. "Nobody to tell me I'm doing everything wrong. Nobody to make dinner for whenever he snaps his fingers. It's been a real nightmare."

"I was gonna stop by tonight," I said. "Really."

"The hell you were," he said. "Look at you. Look at this crap you're reading. 'A heart-stopping tale of murder and revenge.'" He picked up another book and then plunked it back down. "'A true story of deception and naked greed.' If this is what you'd rather do than come harass me all night, so be it. It doesn't bother me one bit, believe me. Not until everybody starts asking me questions. 'Where's Alex, Jackie?' 'How come Alex doesn't come in anymore?' 'What the hell's wrong with Alex, Jackie? I said hello to him at the post office and he walked right by me like he didn't know me.'"

"Who was that?" I said. "Who said hello at the post office?"

"It doesn't matter," he said. "You don't care. You don't need us anymore. Any of us. This is the goddamned loneliest town in the whole country, and you still have to hide in your cabin. So I figured, what the hell, there's only one thing to do with him. Send him north! Let him live with the bears!"

"Are you about done?"

"No, I'm not," he said. "I came here to give you an ultimatum. I'm not leaving until you choose. Either I take you to the airport and put your ass on a plane to Moosehide, or you come play poker with me tonight."

"Poker? Where, at the Glasgow?"

"No, in the Soo. At this guy's house. You haven't met him."

"Since when do you go out playing poker?" I said. "Who's gonna run the place?"

"We usually play at the bar," he said. "Not the old crowd you used to play with. This is a new thing. You'd know that if you ever came by. Win wants to show off his new poker table, so I figured I'd let my son look after things. It's called a night out, Alex. It's what sociable people do sometimes."

"Jackie, I really don't feel like playing poker with a bunch of guys I don't know."

"Too much of a strain, I understand. Okay, I'll help you get packed."

"Knock it off. I'm not going to, where you'd say? Moosehide? Is that really a town in the Yukon?"

"I told you, Alex. One or the other. I'm not leaving until you pick one."

"None of the above, Jackie. Thanks for the offer."

"You're gonna have to forcibly remove me," he said.

"Since when do you use words like 'forcibly'?"

"Poker or the Yukon, Alex. I'm waiting."

What else was I going to do? I sure as hell wasn't going to the Yukon, and I didn't feel like forcibly removing him. So I chose poker. It seemed like the easy way out.

Little did I know.

Jackie has a silver 1982 Lincoln Continental that he supposedly bought for three hundred dollars in 1990. Since then he claims to have put on another 200,000 miles on top of the original 150,000. But then Jackie has been known to exaggerate. No matter how much he had paid for it, and how many miles he had gotten out of it, somehow he kept driving it every year, even in the dead of winter when four-wheel-drive vehicles were sliding off the road all around him.

"I don't see any camping equipment," I said when I got in the passenger's side.

"It's all in the trunk," he said. "This thing has a huge trunk."

"Uh-huh. I'm sure that's where it is."

"I hope you brought some money," he said. "The stakes might be a little higher than what you're used to."

"This feels like a mistake already," I said. I watched the town roll by as we headed south down the main road, past the Glasgow Inn. It felt strange to be passing it without stopping. As we paused at the blinking yellow light, I looked at the new motel they had put up on that corner. The gas station was across the street, then another bar. There were two gift shops on the west side of the road, then another little motel. For a moment I wondered if maybe Jackie's Yukon idea wasn't so bad after all. If Paradise, Michigan was starting to look too busy for me, maybe it was time to head into the woods.

A half-mile south of town, we crossed over a thin, curving strip of land that separated the lake on one side from a pond on the right. It always made me feel like I was driving on a tightrope when I came this way myself. Jackie kept one hand on the wheel and kept his speed up all the way around the bend. Never mind that one false move and we'd slide right into Lake Superior.

The sun was just beginning to set when we hit Lakeshore Drive. It's a twenty mile stretch along the southern rim of Whitefish Bay, maybe the emptiest road I've ever been on. In the wintertime you'd be a fool to try it, but on a summer evening it was the only way to go.

We drove in silence for a while. "You really missed me, didn't you," I finally said.

"If you want to live like a hermit, that's your business," he said.

"Admit it. You missed me."

"Get over yourself, Alex." If Jackie had stayed in Scotland, he might have ended up one of those old caddies who carry bags all day and then head to the local pub. Instead he came here to the Upper Peninsula and eventually opened up his own pub, complete with the overstuffed chairs and the fireplace. He had been here over fifty years, and yet you could still hear the hint of a Scottish burr in his voice. On the rare occasions when he talked about his childhood in Glasgow, that old burr seemed to grow even stronger.

"Reason I asked you," he said, "was because we needed another player. Swanson couldn't make it, which would have left us with five. You know how much I hate poker with five players."

"Yeah," I said. "You can't play high-low or all those other horseshit games you like to call."

He just shook his head at that one.

"Swanson," I said. "Do I know him?"

"You've seen him around," he said. "He's a lawyer in the Soo."

"A lawyer," I said. "My favorite."

"He's not so bad," Jackie said. "Just because he's a lawyer . . ."

"Yeah, yeah, I know."

"There are good lawyers in the world."

"Yeah, three of them at last count."

The road was deserted, as always. We wouldn't see a single car until we got to Brimley. There was nothing but pine trees all around us. And the lake. There's always a wind of some sort coming off the lake, but tonight it was almost calm.

"Where are we playing again?"

"Win Vargas's," he said. "I don't think you've met him. You'd remember if you had."

"Uh-oh. This doesn't sound promising."

"He's good for a few laughs," he said. "Among other things."

"What's that supposed to mean?"

"You'll see," he said. "I just hope you don't mind expensive whiskey and cigars. I may have mentioned your little obsession with Canadian beer, too. I wouldn't be surprised if he had a case waiting for you. If he does, remember to make a big deal about it. He likes to impress people."

"Beautiful."

He kept driving. The sun went down. We finally came to an intersection, and there in the shadows of the pine trees sat an abandoned railroad car from the Soo Line. It was an old passenger car, half the windows covered with wood, the other windows dark with grime. A sign taped to the door read "No Trespassing!"

We passed the lighthouse at Iroquois Point, and then we hit the northern edge of the Bay Mills Reservation. We drove by the community college, then the little Kings Club, the casino that started it all, and then the much bigger Bay Mills Casino. Just past that was the new golf course. It looked almost finished now. From the road we could see a half-dozen bulldozers and excavators, sitting motionless in the dying light, their work done for the day.

"They're really tearing up the pea patch here," Jackie said. "It seems like they just started this thing last week."

"What are they calling this thing again?"

"Wild Bluff," he said. "What do you think?"

"I don't know," I said. "You'd think they'd come up with an Ojibwa name at least."

We crossed the bridge over the Waishkey River. We were on Six Mile Road now, heading due east toward Sault Ste. Marie. But just as we passed the entrance to the Brimley State Park, Jackie hung a left onto an unmarked dirt road.

"Where are we going?" I said. "I thought we're going to the Soo."

"Sunset," he said. He didn't have to say anything else.

The road went north through the pine forest. The trees were close on either side, close enough to hear the pine needles hitting the windows. A mile and a half in, the road ended. There was an old boat launch there, with a wooden dock left to rot in the cold water. Jackie stopped the car six feet from the shoreline.

We got out of the car. We both stood there on the edge of the water, looking west toward the setting sun. The clouds were painted a hundred different shades of red and orange, the sky itself a color of teal blue I have never seen anywhere else.

You have to be outside to appreciate it. You have to feel the wind on your face, smell the freshwater scent in the air.

It is the largest lake in the world. It is terrifying, and deadly. There is no silt at the bottom, no soft bed to sleep in, no weeds to hide in. It is a lake lined in pure granite, a great rock crater carved into the ground by glaciers, filled with pure, sweet, cold water and not much else. A few whitefish. The splinters of broken wooden hulls. The silent steel walls of the *Algoma*, the *Sunbeam*, the *Edmund Fitzgerald*. The bones of the dead. The ghosts.

It is beautiful. God help me, on a summer night when the sun is going down, it is the most beautiful place on earth. This is why I'm here. This is why Jackie is here.

This is why we live through the long winters, the brutal cold, the blizzards that dump three feet of snow overnight, the incessant whining of the snow-mobiles. The long slow melt in the spring, the black flies in June, the mosquitoes in July and August. It is over so quickly, and then the air is cold again and the lake turns back into a monster.

For some of us, it is enough. We stay, year after year. Nowhere else would feel right to us. Nowhere else would be home.

In that summer of secrets, this was the biggest secret of all. Those of us who live here all kept the secret. We guarded it closely, and shared it with those few people who could not live here for whatever reason, but still chose to come back here whenever they could.

I couldn't have guessed that even this secret would be in jeopardy that summer. I couldn't have imagined it. How could one man ever threaten such a thing? One man.

We got back in Jackie's car and drove to our poker game. I was about to meet that man.

Chapter Two

The house was on the east side of Sault Ste. Marie, on the banks of the St. Marys River, right next to the old golf course. It was a big house, one of those contemporary things, all windows and angles. Every light in the house seemed to be on, including a huge chandelier that you could see through the window over the front door.

"Why are we here again?" I said.

"To play poker," Jackie said. "And to drink his whiskey, eat his food. Like I told you. And smoke his cigars."

"Whatever you say."

"There's another reason, as well. It's a little thing we do. When we get to it, just play along."

"Get to what? What are you talking about?"

"You'll see," he said.

As we stood at the doorway, an evening breeze came in off the lake. We could have gone to the Locks Park instead, taken a walk along the edge of the water and then gone to the Ojibway Hotel, had steaks in their dining room. Instead we were here. When Jackie pressed the doorbell button, it didn't just go ding-dong. It went through eight long notes, like church bells ringing the hour.

"Do we get to see the changing of the guards now?" I asked.

"Don't get started," Jackie said. "Give the night a chance at least."

"Okay," I said. "You're right." I liked playing poker, after all. Tonight, maybe it would get me out of my own head for a couple of hours. It might be just what I needed.

We heard a dog barking on the other side of the door. Then it opened. The man who opened it was bald. That was the first thing I noticed. He had that bone hardness that some bald men have, that extra tough bad-ass mystique. It makes you think of a bald biker who sits patiently at the end of the bar, waiting for the right time to stand up and hit you in the face with a pool cue.

"Miata, stay down," he said. Which wasn't asking much, because the dog was only about eight inches tall to begin with. I would have guessed Chihuahua, with the short hair and the bug eyes, but in the back of my mind I remembered the old urban legend about the couple who went to Mexico and brought back a dog, only to find out it was a rat. This might have been that animal.

"I forgot to warn you about the dog," Jackie said.

"You must be Alex," the man said. He shook my hand with a firm grip just this side of painful. "I'm

Winston Vargas. Win for short, because that's what I do. Right, Jackie?" He gave Jackie a wink.

Jackie rolled his eyes and stepped past him. The dog kept dancing around us and barking, its little legs moving at hummingbird speed.

"Don't mind him," Vargas said. "He thinks he's a Doberman. Hell, maybe he was in his last life."

"What did you say his name was? Miata?" I bent down to offer my hand. The dog showed me its teeth. Okay, bad idea.

"My wife named him after her car," he said. "Of course she's not here so I get to look after him all night. Again."

"Well, thanks for having me over," I said. I was giving the night a chance, like Jackie said. I really was.

"I'm glad you could make it," he said. "Let me show you to the table."

He led me through the house to the poker room. I guess it would have been called the entertainment room most of the time. There was a home theater set up along one wall, with a screen that had to be seven feet across. A wet bar dominated the opposite wall, with enough bottles on the shelves to restock Jackie's place. The back wall was all windows, looking out over the river. In the center of the room, beneath a great Tiffany lamp, was one of those six-sided poker tables with the green felt in the middle and the little compartments on each side.

"What do you think?" he said. "I just got it."

I was thinking he'd need the green visor and the

red garter on his sleeve to go with it. "Quite a set-up," I said.

There were a couple of men already sitting at the table. I recognized Bennett O'Dell, an old friend of Jackie's who'd stop by at the Glasgow every now and then. He was another tough old bird like Jackie, although a hell of a lot taller, and at least seventy pounds heavier. He was in the bar business, too, with a place called O'Dell's over on the west side of town. Bennett's father had opened it up back in the thirties, and it had been run by the family ever since. I remembered a story Jackie once told me about running around with Bennett when they were in high school, practically living in that bar, doing their homework at one of the tables every night. When Jackie was ready to open up his own place, he didn't want to take any business away from the O'Dell family, which is why he bought a place out in Paradise.

"Alex," Bennett said. "What the hell are you doing here?"

"I see you know Bennett," Vargas said. "This here is Kenny, one of my business associates. I guess you could say he's my right hand man." Kenny had long straight hair tied back in a ponytail. I shook his hand. Kenny looked like he was pushing forty, which meant that he had a tough choice coming soon. Unless you're a hairdresser, you can't have a ponytail and call yourself Kenny when you're forty. Not in Michigan, anyway.

"We're still waiting on Gill," Vargas said. "You

know how it is. Indians don't operate on white man's time."

"Take it easy, Win," Bennett said, giving me a quick wink. "You don't want him to scalp you, do you?"

"Nothing here to scalp, my friend." Vargas ran his hand over his bald head and laughed. The night was already looking longer. "Alex, I'll show you the house," Vargas said. "While we're waiting."

"Good idea," Jackie said as he sat down next to Bennett. "Go take the tour."

Vargas spent the next twenty minutes showing me around his house. We started in the kitchen. It had the professional-quality gas range, the island in the middle with the second sink. The butler's pantry. "This is what I specialize in," he said. "Top of the line appliances. Viking ranges, custom cabinets, you name it. Your wife wants a dream kitchen, I'm your man. Are you married?"

"No," I said.

"You were married. Once?"

"Yeah," I said. "A long time ago."

"I got married again a few years ago," he said, "after being on my own for a long, long time. Nothing like getting it right the second time around." He ran his hand along the countertop. "It's too bad you won't get a chance to meet her tonight. Next time, huh?"

"Sure."

From the kitchen we went out onto the back deck. The edge of the water was just below us, not thirty feet away. There was a freighter heading south down the river, moving slowly, away from the locks.

"Where's that from?" he said. "What's that flag? That's Brazil, isn't it?"

There was a light on its flagpole. You could just make out the blue globe on the yellow diamond on the field of green. "I think so," I said.

"Those boys are a long way from home." He waved to the ship. We could see a couple of crew members standing on deck, but they didn't wave back.

"I've got a little dock down there," he said. "Not big enough for my boat, but I do have a couple of jet skis. You ever been on a jet ski?"

"Never been," I said. "I imagine I'd like it about as much as a snowmobile."

"Yeah, I've got one of those, too. I don't know how much time I'll be spending up here in the winter. We've got a place in Boca. But you never know."

We went back inside. The light hurt my eyes, made me want to go back out to the darkness. "I'll show you upstairs, Alex. There's one room you've really got to see."

I followed him up the staircase. The house had a beautiful staircase, I had to say that much. The treads themselves were all hardwood, with a matching rail and thin wooden posts. My old man the self-taught carpenter would have been impressed as hell.

"These are guest rooms down here," he said, "and this is the master suite." There was a king-size bed, all made up in white with lavender trim. "It probably goes without saying, but my wife did the decorating.

Here's the bathroom in here. What do you think?"

I looked in and saw a raised whirlpool tub, a separate shower, two vanity mirrors, two sinks. The fixtures gleamed like pirate treasure. "This is something else," I said. I had already been thinking to myself that the bedroom was bigger than my cabin. Now I was wondering if the bathroom was bigger, too.

"We carry these tubs now," he said. "You wouldn't believe how expensive they are. Go ahead, take a guess."

"I wouldn't even know," I said.

"Ah, never mind," he said. "That's tacky. Here, I want to show you the best room of all now."

He led me to the end of the hall and opened the door. It took a moment for my eyes to adjust—this was the only room in the house that wasn't as bright as an operating room. He turned up a dimmer switch so I could see where I was going. There were floor-to-ceiling bookshelves on two walls, some nautical maps on another wall. By the window there was a telescope on a tripod. "I call this my 'lake room,'" he said. "Here, come look."

He turned the dimmer back down as I looked through the telescope. It was pointed to the northwest. As I moved it, I could make out the Soo Locks and the International Bridge. During the day I was sure you'd be able to see into the lake itself.

"God, I love this lake," he said. "Don't you, Alex?"

I looked at him. With the light still down, I couldn't make out his face, but his bald head seemed to glow.

"What's in here?" I said. There were glass cases running along the wall, beneath the maps.

He turned the light back up. "Some artifacts," he said. "I'm a collector."

There were some shipwreck artifacts in one glass case—a small brass bell, a metal comb, a mug made of pewter. In another case were what seemed to be Indian artifacts—an arrowhead, a wooden paddle that had practically disintegrated, a small metal bowl that was probably some sort of smudge pot. Everything had that particular reddish gray tint around the edges, the kind of wear you see when something's been left in fresh water for a very long time.

"How'd you get all this stuff?" I said. "I thought the salvage laws were pretty strict."

"On the Michigan side they are. Not so much on the Canadian side. What can I say, divers pick things up, sell them to people, who sell them to other people. If I end up buying something, it comes right up here to this room and stays here. My wife thinks it's kinda hinky, but I tell her, hey, when I die, every single one of these things goes to the museum. Either the Shipwreck Museum out on Whitefish Point, or the Indian museum at the community college."

It still didn't sound quite right to me, but I wasn't going to tell him that. I just nodded my head at him and hoped the poker game would be starting soon. If he was going to start offering me expensive whiskey like Jackie said, it was about time.

When we finally made it back down to the poker table, Gill LaMarche was sitting in his spot, calmly counting out chips. "Look who showed up," Vargas said. "You missed the tour."

"Been there, done that," he said. "Bought the T-shirt." Gill was a member of the Sault tribe, and lived here in town, right next to the Kewadin Casino. Like most Ojibwa in Michigan, especially the Sault members who had less restrictive blood lines than the other tribes, you didn't think "Indian" the first time you saw him. If you knew what to look for— a little fullness around the cheekbones, a slow and careful way about the eyes—you could just make it out.

"Let's get everybody set up first," Vargas said. Then came the trays of food from the kitchen, the drinks from the bar, the cigars. "What kind of whiskey do you drink?" he asked me. "I've got some Macallan twelve-year here . . ."

"Is that Jack Daniels I see over there?" I said.

"It is," he said. "If that's your preference."

"That'll do me fine. Save the single malt for somebody special."

"Jackie tells me you were a catcher," he said. "I should have known a catcher would take Jack Daniels over a Macallan. You can always spot a catcher."

I gave Jackie a look. He gave me an innocent smile.

"I played some ball when I was in the college," Vargas said. "And then in the Air Force, when I was stationed in Korea."

"Let me guess, first base," I said.

"First and a little third. How did you know?"

"You can always spot a first baseman," I said.

He laughed at that, brought my drink over and sat down. "Are we gonna play some cards here or what?"

So we did. Jackie was on my left, then Bennett, Vargas, Kenny, and finally Gill on my right. Vargas played the way I would have expected. He was aggressive in his betting, and he hated to fold. He wanted to be in every single hand. When he wasn't raising, he was fussing over the table itself, making sure we kept our drinks off the green felt and in the little coaster compartments. I had never known how much I hated fancy poker tables until that night.

Vargas also liked to talk. It was just a matter of time until he wandered back to his business. "When I got out of the Air Force," he said, shuffling the cards, "I decided to take over the hardware business from my father. He had a little store down in Petoskey. Now you're probably thinking, how does a little hardware store survive these days when you've got your Lowes's and your Home Depots all over the place? The answer is, you have to see the train coming before it runs you over. Those big hardware places? The best thing that ever happened to me. You know why? They destroyed my competition. All of them. They all got run over by the train, and I jumped off the track. I moved to a different market. A *better* market. If you want to buy a sink nowadays, or a toilet, or a tub, or a dishwasher, or a refrigerator, or kitchen cabinets, where do you go?"

Nobody said anything. We just waited for him to finish and deal the damned cards.

"Where do you go? Hmm? Where do you go?"

"Lowes," Jackie finally said.

"Home Depot," Bennett said.

"Exactly," Vargas said. "Now suppose you want a solid marble sink that's made in Italy? Or a Viking gas range like the professional chefs use? Where do you go for that? Not Lowes. Not Home Depot. They don't carry that stuff. There's no volume in it for them. You've got to go to a specialty store."

"Like yours," Bennett said.

"Like mine."

"Deal the cards," Bennett said.

He started dealing, but that didn't stop his spiel. "Me and Kenny, we make a great team. We go to somebody's house, and we split the couple up. Divide and conquer, right? Kenny takes the wife into the kitchen, really fags it up with her, does the whole interior decorator thing." Kenny didn't even blink. He just sat there with a serene smile on his face, like a man who is paid very well to play along. "While he does his thing, I'm hanging out with the husband. I'm saying, 'It's all over now, chief. Your wife wants the best, and you're gonna come through, or deal with the consequences. But don't worry, I'll give you a great deal.' If I don't get 'em when they build the house first thing, I'll get 'em a couple of years later. As soon as that wife goes to have coffee with the neighbor and sees *her* kitchen, she'll go to her husband and then he'll come to me. I always get 'em in the end."

"Queen bets," Bennett said. "That's you, Kenny." He let that one hang for a few seconds before realizing what he had said. "I mean, you've got the queen, Kenny. Your bet."

Kenny gave him a look that was nothing but cool, and then slid a buck into the pot. "The queen bets one dollar."

"I'm doing this house over in Canada," Vargas said. "On St. Joseph Island. You wouldn't believe what I'm putting in that kitchen. The floor alone, these tiles from Mexico. Problem is, they got these guys at Customs. Big old dumb Canucks sitting on that bridge, they're basically paying them to be in a bad mood all the time. See me bringing a refrigerator over, they take it personally. Like I'm taking jobs away from Canadians by bringing in an American refrigerator."

"Duty on durable goods," Bennett said. "Is that what they call it?"

"That's what they call it," Vargas said. "They *should* call it bend over and grab your ankles."

"I thought it ain't so bad anymore. You know, with this NAFTA thing."

"They don't worry so much about the small stuff now," Vargas said. "Up to a hundred dollars, something like that. But the big ticket items, hell, they still stick it to ya."

"The customer's gotta pay for this, right?"

"Yeah, I think it's safe to say that, Bennett. It sure isn't me."

"Who are these people?" I said. "Who's got this kind of money to spend on their kitchens?" I shouldn't have asked. I should have just shut up and played cards and drank the man's whiskey. That's what I should have done.

"There are a lot of people building houses in Canada," he said. "You'd be surprised. Of course, that's not where my bread and butter is . . ."

"Where would that be?" I said.

"Bay Harbor," he said.

The words went right down my spine. Bay Harbor. He might as well have said Sodom and Gomorrah.

"I made most of my nut right there," he said. "In Bay Harbor. Of course, that place is gonna be full one of these days." He looked at the cards he was holding close to his chest. He called Kenny's dollar and raised ten more. "Ain't that right, Kenny?"

Kenny folded his hand. "Too rich for me."

"The big question is, who's gonna build the next Bay Harbor?" Vargas said. "And where's it gonna be?"

Chapter Three

If you drive south, over the Mackinac Bridge, and then down M-31 along the Lake Michigan coast, the first town you'll hit is Petoskey. It used to be a sleepy little fishing village, now it's yuppie heaven. Keep going toward Charlevoix, another sleepy little fishing village turned yuppie heaven—about halfway there you'll hit Bay Harbor. Or rather, Bay Harbor will hit you. First thing you'll see is the Bay Harbor Yacht Club. There's a white building next to the road, all done up like a lighthouse. A guard sits at the gate, ready to check you over to make sure you're on his list. Further down there's the Bay Harbor Golf Club. Another white building right next to the road, another guard sitting at the gate. Across the street, on a hill that's as high as any hill in this part of Michigan, sits the Bay Harbor Equestrian Center. Anywhere else in the state, it's a horse farm. Here it's the Equestrian Center. Needless to say, there's another gate with another guard.

The houses are all on the lake side of the road, of course. You have to go through yet another gatehouse to get to them. There are condominiums, too, and a big hotel. There's even a little Main Street where you can try on some diamonds, maybe buy a painting, and then have a cappuccino. If you don't have a lot of money to spend, don't even bother slowing down. Just take a quick look at Bay Harbor, friend—be impressed, be envious, be sorry that you can't live here yourself. And then keep driving.

"The thing is," Vargas said, "the market has to level off eventually. You can only build so many top-of-the-line houses in one place. That's why I know there's gonna be another big boom somewhere else. There has to be. With Bay Harbor, I got a little lucky, because with the store in Petoskey it all happened right in my backyard. This time, I've got to be ahead of the curve, you know what I mean? It's all a guessing game. Which is what got me thinking . . ."

Vargas paused to roll the single malt around in his glass. If he was hoping for a spellbound audience, he wasn't getting it. Jackie called Vargas's raise, and then Bennett raised him ten more. Vargas slid his chips in without even looking at them.

"I'm thinking, why try to guess where the next boom is going to be, when I can help make it happen myself? Branch out of the custom kitchen business, you know, actually get in on the building itself, from the beginning, once we find the right place. That's one of the reasons I built this house here."

That one hit me like an ice pick. Jackie, Bennett,

Gill, they didn't even flinch. They must have heard this one before. Kenny just had a little smile on his face. He'd heard it before, too, and probably liked the sound of it.

"Of course, it's not all my own money," he said. "I don't have that kind of capital yet. I'm just the point man, you realize. We have investors in place, who prefer to stay in the background . . ."

"You're talking about shady money?" Bennett said. "You're talking about real kingpins here?"

"I can't discuss that," Vargas said.

"You already are," Bennett said. "You're discussing it. You'd better be careful, you're gonna end up sleeping with the fishes."

"Don't worry about me," Vargas said. "I'm a big boy."

I had to wonder. For every man who was really connected, there had to be another twenty who liked to sound like it, who liked to run their mouths off just like Vargas was doing.

"You have to admit," Vargas said, "as nice as Lake Michigan is, Lake Superior is the far better lake."

"It's the superior lake," Jackie said.

"Hell yes," Vargas said. "Hence the name."

"It's so far away though," Jackie said. "Even Bay Harbor was a stretch. It's four hours from Detroit."

"Who needs Detroit?" Vargas said. "Bay Harbor has the airport in Traverse City. We've got one right here in the Soo."

"I guess you could call it an airport," Bennett said. "Not many flights in and out."

"Least of our worries," Vargas said. "Hell, a lot of these guys have private jets."

"Still," Bennett said. "It's a lot different up here. The weather. The way people are. Everything."

"That's part of its charm," Vargas said. "You've still got the feeling of wilderness up here. Not to mention the best casino, thanks to Gill here."

Gill nodded. "Glad to help," he said. "That's why I built it single-handedly."

"You know what I mean," Vargas said. "You and your people. Those lousy little casinos down by Traverse City, they can't even compare to the Kewadin. You can really take care of the high rollers up here. And then there's the international thing. You've got something foreign and exotic right across the bridge there."

"Bennett," Jackie said, "did they move Hong Kong over there without telling me? Because last time I went over that bridge, I was in Canada."

"That's foreign," Bennett said.

"And exotic," Gill said.

"You know what I'm talking about," Vargas said. "It's *different* over there. They've got clubs over there, for one thing."

"Oh, so when you say exotic," Jackie said, "you mean exotic *dancing*. Why didn't you say so?"

"Let me ask you something, Alex," Vargas said. "You live out in Paradise, right? What's that, about a half-hour drive?"

"Something like that," I said.

Jackie cleared his throat. "On a good day. When there's no snow."

Vargas didn't even hear him. "You go right through Brimley, right? Where they're building that new golf course?"

"Yes."

"What's land going for out your way? On the coast, say out by Whitefish Point?"

"Well . . ." I didn't know what to say. I didn't *want* to say anything at all. I wanted to hit him over the head with something.

"Because I'm thinking," he said, "maybe we should be looking out that way instead. Here we were thinking it's nice to already have some infrastructure in place. Some good roads and services and all, not to mention the golf course, which needs a little work, I admit. But maybe we're thinking too small. If we got something going out on your side of the bay, we'd have a lot more land to work with. Plus we'd actually be on the lake itself. Here we're on the river."

Kill him now, I was thinking. Kill him now, cut up his body into little pieces and throw them to the fish.

"You don't want to be on the lake," Bennett said. He said this calmly, like he didn't want to kill the man at all. "The lake will wreck everything eventually. Here you've got some protection at least."

"Yeah, the weather," Jackie said. "It's even worse over there, believe me. I can't imagine trying to build anything over there."

"How are your black flies out there?" Gill said. "They can get pretty bad here in town. I'm imagining out there in the woods . . ."

"Oh God," Jackie said. "The black flies. Every June. Tell him about the black flies, Alex."

"Horrible," I said, which was a lie. The black fly season hadn't been that bad this year. Not bad at all. Especially when you got close to the water and the breeze helped keep them down. "People talk about mosquitoes eating you alive, they don't know about black flies."

"Mosquitoes are like surgeons," Bennett said. "They got those little needles, in and out. But black flies, those goddamned things just gnaw on your flesh like blood-thirsty little zombies."

Vargas shook his head as he got up to refill his glass. "It's something to think about, I guess." He was probably imagining a giant airplane dropping insecticide all over Whitefish Point.

Kenny looked us all over one by one, shaking his head. He knew what we were doing. This was what Jackie meant when he told me there was another reason why they played cards with Vargas, this whole idea of helping him rethink his development plans. But that look on Kenny's face seemed to say, "You can fight it all you want. But it's coming. If not this year, then next year. Bay Harbor is coming."

The phone rang while Vargas was pouring himself another shot of Macallan. He picked it up and said, "Vargas here." Then he excused himself, told us to deal him out a couple of hands.

We played without him. It wasn't quite the same. Too quiet, for one thing.

"Tell me, Kenny," Bennett finally said. "What's it like working for him?"

"Why do you want to know?" Kenny said.

"Just making conversation," Bennett said.

"I've got a house there myself," Kenny said. "In Bay Harbor. That's how it is to work for him."

"Fair enough," Bennett said. And that was the end of that.

When Vargas got back to the table, something had changed. He left his Macallan sitting untouched on the bar, took out a real glass and filled it with three fingers of Jack Daniels. "You had it right, Alex," he said. "This does feel like a J.D. night."

"Everything okay?" Gill said. "You seem a little tense all of a sudden."

"I'm an old first baseman," he said as he sat down. "I'm always tense. Right, Alex?"

"My deal," I said. "You know the game."

"Five card stud," Vargas said. "And speaking of studs, where's Mr. Swanson tonight, anyway?"

"Don't know," Bennett said. "He said he couldn't play tonight."

"He couldn't play last time either," Vargas said.

"He's a busy guy," Bennett said.

"Yeah, he's busy," Vargas said. His voice was getting colder by the second. "Fortunately, we've got Alex here to take his spot. I guess you're not as busy as Swanson is, eh Alex?"

"I asked him to play," Jackie said. "So we'd have six guys. Is there something wrong with that all of a sudden?"

"No, not at all," Vargas said. He emptied his glass, then got up for a refill. He brought the bottle back with him this time.

"It's a shame you didn't get a chance to meet my wife, Alex. Her dog you got to meet." He looked around the room. "Where'd that dog run off to, anyway?"

"He's under the table," Gill said.

"What's he doing down there?"

"He's licking himself."

"Okay then," Vargas said. "Now that we've established that . . ." He poured himself another triple, spilling some on his precious table. He didn't bother to clean it up.

"Maybe you should ease up on that," Jackie said.

"Always the bartender," Vargas said. "Don't worry, I'm not driving tonight. My wife took my car, anyway. She left me the little Miata, which she knows I hate. The car, I mean, not the dog. It's like driving a little tin cigar box."

"King high," I said. "It's your bet."

"Five bucks," he said. "On the king. You wanna know something funny, guys? You wanna know who that was on the phone just now?"

Apparently, nobody did. He told us anyway.

"That was a private investigator," he said. "Did you know that there's only one private investigator in the whole county?"

Oh no, I said to myself. Please, God, no. This will not be good.

"He struck me as kind of a goofball at first, quite honestly. But I gotta hand it to him. He's got some energy. Just give the guy a little money, point him in the right direction, and he's all over it."

Jackie was trying very hard not to laugh. I wanted to smack him.

"Do you want to know what this private investigator is doing for me tonight?"

Again, no takers.

"I'll tell you," he said. He took another hit off his glass of J.D. "He's watching my wife. He's been following her, in fact, for two weeks straight."

"Why are you telling us this?" Bennett said. "If there's something going on between you and your wife . . ."

"No, no," Vargas said. "Not between me and my wife. Between my wife and somebody else."

"Well okay," Bennett said. "But come on, you don't have to—"

"Oh, but I do," he said. "I most certainly do. I'll tell you why. I would like somebody at this table . . ." He gave Kenny a quick glance. "Kenny, you are excused from this question. I would like somebody else at this table aside from Kenny who has no fucking involvement in this matter whatsoever to tell me why our friend Mr. Swanson is not playing cards with us tonight."

"He said he couldn't play," Bennett said.

"Yeah, we got that part," Vargas said. "Tell me why he couldn't play."

"We don't know," Bennett said.

"You don't know. Okay. And last week, when he couldn't play, you didn't know why then either."

"That's right."

"Okay. So we play with five last week over at

Bennett's bar and the game sucks and we would
have played with five this week, but fortunately,
Jackie just so happens to have this friend Alex handy
who can fill in for Swanson."

"Leave Alex out of this," Jackie said. "I asked
him to play. So we'd have six. That's all there is to
it. We don't know anything about Swanson."

"What about next week?" Vargas said. "Is Swanson going to play next week? Or will Alex be sitting
in again? Because we certainly wouldn't want to
cancel the game, now would we? Because then my
wife wouldn't have an excuse to go have a night out
with the girls."

"Vargas . . ."

"Which apparently, gentlemen, doesn't mean that
she's actually doing anything with the girls like she
says she is, but instead is getting a little free legal
advice from our good friend the lawyer Mr. Swanson, Esquire, in room one-seventeen of the Best
Western Inn, even as we speak."

Nobody said anything. Vargas tried to pour himself another drink, dumping half the bottle into his
little chip compartment. He looked down at the
whiskey fizzing away on his brand new poker table.

The dog started barking. We just sat there watching Vargas, while his miserable little rat of a dog
barked its little rat head off.

"Miata," Vargas finally said. "What the fuck are
you barking about?"

We found out about two seconds later. Just when
I thought the night couldn't get any worse, the men
with the guns broke down every door in the house.

Chapter Four

"Everybody facedown on the floor! Move it move it move it move it!"

It all happened in a dreamlike unreality, something played out in slow motion, in another dimension where none of the rules apply. I had been in that place once before, the night my partner was shot and died on the floor next to me. I didn't think I'd ever have to visit that place again. But here I was. Here we all were.

"I said on the floor now! Are you deaf?"

I heard the sound of a chair being upended, a body hitting the floor. It was Kenny, I thought. Somehow, I was already on the floor myself. I was trying to stop my own head from spinning, trying to breathe again and to make myself think clearly about what was happening.

One man. Another there. Was there a third? Yes. Three men. Some of the lights went out. The Tiffany lamp above the table was still on, casting a bright circle in the center of the room. The dog was running around the place in a total frenzy, making more noise than a dog that size should be able to make.

"Nobody moves. Are we clear on that, gentlemen? One move and we start shooting. All of you."

Handguns. Three men with handguns. Glocks, I think—that sleek, black profile. I didn't see any faces. Why didn't I see any faces?

I was lying on the carpet, my face turned away from the table, away from the others. The other players must have been spread out behind me, I thought, all around the table in about the same positions as they were sitting.

One of the men walked by me. His shoes were covered with green fabric. Like they wear in the hospital. That's why I didn't see any faces. Just a flash of . . . Yes, of green. They were wearing surgical masks.

The dog took a run at one of them. I could see him tearing at the green fabric with his teeth.

"Goddamn miserable little rat! Get away from me!"

I needed to see the others. I needed to see Jackie, especially. I waited for the man to hop by me, trying to shake the dog loose. Then I flipped my head to the other side. I was facing Jackie now. His eyes were open.

"You! I thought I told you not to move!"

A gun was pressed to the left side of my head. I could feel the cold metallic sting of it. He pressed down on the gun, pinning me to the floor with it.

"I believe I asked you not to move? Did I not ask that?"

I didn't say anything.

"You move again and I'll shoot you in the head. Then I'll pick somebody else and shoot *him* in the head. Are we clear on that? You have permission to nod your head now."

I nodded my head.

"Good man."

The same man was doing all the talking. I could only see his feet as he moved next to Vargas and stood over him. "You," he said. "Is this your dog?"

"Yes."

"On your feet. But keep your eyes on the floor."

Vargas didn't move. His eyes were closed.

"I said on your feet." A hand reached down and grabbed him by the back of his shirt collar.

"Leave him alone," Bennett said. He picked his head up.

I saw the second man move toward Bennett. He kicked him hard, right in the ribs. Bennett dropped his head back to the floor, his face gone red with the pain. He fought hard to breathe.

"Okay," the first man said. "You've got ten seconds to get this dog off us and into a closet. Starting now."

Canadian, I thought. This one sounds Canadian. The other two, they haven't said a word yet.

Vargas came off the floor and grabbed the dog, who had gotten hold of one of the men's shoes again. "Come on, Miata. Take it easy." It took him a few seconds to pry open the dog's jaws. Then the dog started barking again. "Good dog, Miata. Good dog. Good dog."

I heard a door open and shut behind me, and then the muffled sound of the dog barking and trying to tear the door down with its teeth and claws.

"All right now, that's better. You're gonna go upstairs with this man here, and you're gonna open up your safe. Make sure you keep your eyes on the ground, eh?"

Keep your eyes on the "groond," eh? Definitely Canadian.

"We hear one funny noise, we start shooting your friends. Do you understand?"

They left the room. There were five of us on the floor now, with two men watching over us. They paced around the table, moving silently in their green slippers. Miata kept attacking the closet door.

I could see one shoe, where the dog had ripped the fabric. Old athletic shoes, a dirty shade of gray, with blue diagonal stripes. I couldn't guess the brand.

I looked at Jackie. He looked good, all things considered. He was calm. He returned my look, giving me a slight nod.

Bennett was still catching his wind, his eyes closed.

Kenny's eyes were wide open. He was shaking, and obviously scared out of his ponytailed head. I didn't dare say anything to him. Look over here, I thought. Goddamn it, hold yourself together. I willed him to look at me. His eyes didn't seem to be focusing on anything at all.

I couldn't see Gill's face, but his body was still. I'm sure Gill is just fine, I thought. It's Kenny I'm worried about.

And Vargas. I hope he's cooperating up there.

Maybe five minutes passed, though it could have been five hours. The two men kept pacing. I looked at their legs, tried to measure their stride. Both around six feet tall, I thought. The one with the athletic shoes a little heavier than the other. So let's say maybe 180 for Man Number One, the man who sounded Canadian. A little over 200 for Man Number Two, with a description of his shoes that wouldn't be much help to anybody. Definitely Glocks they were carrying, now that I got a little better look, and both identical. I tried to remember the most common model numbers—Glock 17, 21, 31 . . . I didn't know the gun well enough to say.

Man Number One went to the window. As he moved away from the table I got a better look at him. He was wearing blue jeans and some sort of black, shiny plastic coat.

No, a garbage bag. He had a black plastic garbage bag on. Along with the surgical mask, and the cap made from the same green fabric. As he turned around, I saw his eyes. I could see that he had fair skin, and eyebrows so blond they were invisible.

He looked right at me and saw me looking at him. I quickly looked away, but it was too late. I heard him come toward me, and then once again I felt the weight of the gun press against my left temple.

"Close your eyes," he said.

This is it, I thought. This is the last thing I feel.

The carpet against one side of my face, the gun against the other. A dog scratching at a door, the last sound I'll ever hear. Until the gunblast.

I waited for it. The gun didn't move.

"What's taking them so long?" the other man said, his first words. This man didn't sound Canadian. "Maybe one of us should go check on them?"

"Just relax," the man above me said. I felt the gun leave my head. "Give 'em another minute."

"I should have shot that dog."

"You don't shoot dogs."

"That one I would shoot. It's not even a dog."

"Thing's so small you would have missed it."

There was a sudden commotion from upstairs. It sounded like glass breaking.

"The fuck's going on up there?"

"It's okay. He told you to expect that."

"Sounds like he's destroying the place."

"You know what he's doing."

There was another crash, and then another. A few seconds passed, and then there was another crash that had to be a window breaking.

A minute later, the third man came back into the room.

"Where is he?" the first man asked.

There was no answer, not one that I could hear.

"Are we done?"

Again, no answer. Maybe the man was just gesturing with his hands, or nodding his head.

"All right, let's get the hell out of here then," the first man said. "Gentlemen, here's what you're going to do. I see a very fancy oven in that kitchen. I'm sure it has a timer on it. I'm going to set it for fifteen minutes. During that time, you will not move, eh? Do you understand me? You will not move a muscle. I hope you appreciate the fact that we didn't shoot anybody. In fact, you'll notice that you still have your wallets, your watches, your wedding rings. Please don't make us change our minds. It would really spoil the evening, don't you think?"

On that note, they left. We heard the door close. A vehicle started up in the driveway and then drove away. We all kept lying there on the floor. There was no other sound except the dog in the closet.

"Like hell I'm staying here for fifteen minutes," Jackie said.

"How's everybody doing?" I said. "Bennett? You all right?"

"I think so," he said, sitting up.

"Get down!" Kenny said. "Didn't you hear what they said?"

"Kenny, if they come back," Bennett said, "I'll be sure to tell them not to shoot you."

"Where's Vargas?" Gill said. "I don't think he came back down."

We all looked at each other—not including Kenny, who still had his nose buried in the carpet. "Why don't you guys make sure they're gone," I said. "And call the police. Jackie and I'll go see about Vargas."

"You got it," Bennett said. "C'mon, Gill."

Jackie rubbed his legs as he stood up. "I'm too damned old for this," he said. "You reach a certain point in your life, you shouldn't have guns pointed at you."

"I can't argue with that," I said. We went up the stairs.

Jackie stopped midway up, leaned over with one hand on his knee, the other on the rail.

"Jackie, are you all right?"

"Is this what it felt like, Alex? When you were a cop and that man was pointing the gun at you?"

"Yeah, it was," I said. "Right up until he shot me."

"Do you think they would've shot us if they had to?"

"I don't know," I said. "I'm glad we didn't have to find out."

"Which room is he in?" Jackie said, pulling himself back up. He went to the first door and pushed it open. "He's not in here."

"All that glass breaking," I said. "I've got a feeling he's down here . . ." I led him to the last door in the hallway. It was closed. I gave Jackie one more look, and then I pushed the door open.

Vargas was on the floor, his hands on his face. The rest of the room was in a complete shambles. All the maps had been torn off the walls. The display cases had been broken, every single one of them. The window overlooking the river was shattered.

"Vargas!" I said, bending down next to him. I put my hand on his back. He was alive.

"Oh God," he said. "Oh God oh God oh God."

"Are you all right?" I helped him up. He got halfway up and then sat back down against the wall. He looked at me, and then at Jackie, and then at what was left of his room.

"What happened downstairs?" he finally said.

"Everybody's fine," I said. "They just left."

"The dog's still in the closet?"

"Yes."

"Anybody call the police yet?"

"Bennett's probably doing that right now," I said.

"He put the gun on the back of my neck and said, 'Open the safe, or this bullet will come out right between your eyes.' When I opened it, he made me get down here on my knees and cover my face with my hands. And then he started smashing everything. I was afraid to look."

"You did the right thing," I said. "Nothing else you could've done."

"He knew about the safe," Vargas said. "He even knew what room it was in."

I turned and saw the open safe on the far wall. It had been hidden behind one of the maps.

"Why destroy the place?" Vargas said. He pushed himself up against the wall until he was on his feet. "Why did he do that?"

"Look down here," Jackie said. He was standing by the window.

Vargas crunched through all the broken glass, picking his way across the room. When he got to the window, he stood next to Jackie and looked out. A breeze brought the damp smell of the river into the room.

I went to the window, making the same sounds as Vargas on the broken glass. Peeking over their shoulders, I saw the wreckage on the ground below. One of the maps was halfway out of its frame, a corner flapping as the wind picked up. Vargas's telescope lay a good thirty feet from the house, right on the shoreline, half of it on land and half in the dark water. A thousand shards of glass twinkled in the light from the back deck.

Vargas looked out for a long moment. Then he looked at Jackie and me again. "They knew where the safe was," he said. "That's the thing. How did they know that?"

I didn't think it was a question we were supposed to answer, so I didn't even try.

"How did they know that?" he said again.

"Come on," Jackie said. "Let's go downstairs."

He took Vargas by the arm. Vargas didn't seem to want to move at first, but finally he did. We all crunched our way out of the room and down the stairs. Kenny had finally gotten off the floor, God bless him, but he still looked like somebody needed to slap the color back into his face.

"Win!" he said. "What the hell happened up there?"

"He made me open the safe," Vargas said. "Then he smashed the window and every fucking thing in the room."

"Police are on the way," Bennett said. "Gill is outside."

"Where's my dog?"

"They broke one of your doors," Bennett said. "I guess the other two must have been unlocked."

"Yeah, I didn't figure on getting invaded," Vargas said. "If they hurt that dog . . ."

The shock was wearing off, I thought. I've seen this before. Now it's time for him to start getting mad . . .

"Come here, Miata," he said, opening the closet door. The dog came bolting out into the room, ready to kill somebody. He ran out into the kitchen, legs skittering all over the place, and then back into the poker room, the living room, every room in the house, barking himself hoarse.

"Is that the bravest little fucking dog you've ever seen or what?" Vargas said. "At least *somebody* put up a fight."

"I seem to recall Bennett taking a nice shot for you," Jackie said.

"When was that?" he said.

"For God's sake," Jackie said, "when they pulled you off the floor, he told them to leave you alone, remember? They kicked him right in the ribs."

Vargas looked at Bennett, and seemed to be playing the scene back in his mind.

"Doesn't matter," Bennett said. "It was stupid, anyway."

Vargas kept looking at him, and was about to say something when Gill came into the room. "No sign of the police," he said. "They should be here by now."

"Did you call the Soo police?" I said. "Or the state troopers?"

"Soo," he said. "I mean, that's where we are, right?"

Vargas picked up the bottle of Jack Daniels from the poker table and took a hit off it. Then he went to the sliding door, opened it, and went out onto the deck. The thought of fresh air must have appealed to everyone at that point, because we all followed him.

I was the last one out. By the time I was on the deck, Vargas had already walked down the steps to the river. He picked up the telescope from the shoreline and held it in his hands.

Kenny went down and stood next to him. The rest of us stayed on the deck, watching over them. "What did they take?" Kenny said.

"They cleaned out the safe," Vargas said.

"What was in it?"

Vargas looked at him, and then up at us. "You all know what was in the safe," he said.

"How much money was in there?" Kenny said.

"When the police get here," he said, "let me talk to them about the safe. Everybody got that?"

Another freighter came moving down the river. It was at least seven hundred feet long, moving too quietly for something that big. Bennett, Jackie, and Gill all leaned against the rail and watched it pass. The flag was American.

"What else did they take?" Kenny said. "Anything?"

"It looks like they just threw all this shit out the window," Vargas said. "Some of it made the water. The rest of it . . ."

"Here's something from your display case,"

Kenny said, picking up a small bell. "These maps are kind of ruined, though."

"This was a thousand-dollar telescope," Vargas said. With one sudden motion he coiled it back around his body and then sent it spinning out into the river. It hung high in the air and then landed with a splash a hundred feet out.

"That might have been evidence," Kenny said.

"Excuse me?" Vargas said. He looked like he very much wanted to throw Kenny out there with the telescope.

"I'm just saying," Kenny said. "I mean, never mind."

"They didn't touch the jewelry," Vargas said. "All those diamonds I buy my wife every fucking Christmas. They went right to my room, right to *my* secret safe, and then they did this to me. Anybody have any ideas?"

Nobody said anything, but I had a feeling this was all tied to what he was getting at before the robbers broke in—this whole business with Swanson and his wife.

And good God in heaven, the private eye he had apparently hired to follow them. In all the excitement, I had almost forgotten about that little piece of news.

"Anybody?" Vargas said. "Don't be shy."

We heard the sirens then. It sounded like three cars, maybe four, all hitting his street at once.

"You know something?" Vargas said. "The man who took me upstairs, I got a real good look at his eyes. If I ever see those eyes again, I'll know 'em in a second." He snapped his fingers to emphasize his point.

We heard a voice from inside. "Hello! Who's here?"

"Remember," he said, coming up the steps, "I'll do the talking about the safe."

We ended up with four Soo police officers in the house, plus the on-duty detective. I kept expecting the police chief himself to arrive on the scene. He and I had a bit of a history, after all, and everything else that could have gone wrong that evening had already happened. So I figured a visit from Chief Roy Maven was inevitable.

"Where's the chief?" I asked the detective. "I kinda figured he'd be here by now."

"He was downstate today," the man said. "I don't think he'll be back until tomorrow."

"There is a God," I said. "That's the first good thing that happened all night."

He didn't argue the point. He worked for Maven, after all, so he knew what I was talking about. I told them everything I knew—the partial descriptions of the two men who had stayed downstairs, the heavier man in the athletic shoes with blue stripes, the fair-haired man who sounded Canadian. The Glocks. It wasn't much, but he wrote it down and thanked me.

It was well after midnight when they finally finished with us. I knew they'd be back the next day to do a good daylight search of the place. The investigation would be the center of Vargas's life for the next few days, but the rest of us were through with it, or so I hoped. I had had quite enough of this house. I wanted very much to never see it again. Or its owner.

"Let's go, Jackie," I said, as soon as the police left. "We've gotta get you home. You must be exhausted."

We left Vargas sitting there at his bartop, next to the poker table. All of the chips and cards were still lying there. Nobody bothered to settle up.

Jackie let me drive his car. He sat in the passenger's seat, looking out the window. I went back the same way we came, across town to Six Mile Road, all the way out to Brimley, past the two Indian casinos with their signs glaring in the night and their parking lots full, the golf course with the heavy equipment sitting all together under a single security light mounted high on a wooden pole, and then out to Lakeshore Drive. There was a half moon, reflected in the lake. There were no clouds.

The old railroad car was there on the corner, in shadows so dark you wouldn't notice it if you didn't know it was there. For some reason, that railroad car felt like the perfect thing just then. It felt like I could stop the car right there and go open the door and climb inside. For me, the door would open. I'd go to sleep on the bare floor next to the rats and raccoons and God knows what else, in an abandoned, useless old railroad car that would never go anywhere ever again.

I don't know what made me think this way. I don't know what made me imagine going to sleep in that old railroad car and never waking up. It was a hell of a thing to think about on your way back from an armed robbery.

"Well," Jackie said, finally breaking the silence. "At least I got you out of your cabin tonight."

"You did," I said. "I can't wait to see what you've got planned for tomorrow night."

"What were you thinking?" he said. "When we were lying on the floor?"

"With the guns pointed at our heads?"

"I seem to recall them pointed a little more at your head than at mine, but yeah, what were you thinking then?"

"You know the old expression about your life flashing before your eyes?"

"Yeah?"

"Turns out it's true," I said. "That's exactly what I was thinking about. My whole life."

"And?"

"And what?"

"What did it all add up to?" he said. "Your whole life, I mean."

"You really want to know?"

"I really want to know."

"Not a hell of a lot," I said. "What about you? What were you thinking?"

"Same thing, more or less. But mine had a happier ending."

"How's that?"

"I was thinking," he said, "that if this was my last night on earth, then at least I don't have to see this place get destroyed."

"You really think it's gonna happen?" I said.

"We're in the middle of fucking nowhere up here."

"We're beyond nowhere," he said. "We're way north of nowhere. But it doesn't matter. They'll come eventually. You can't keep this place a secret forever."

"I hope you're wrong," I said. "But I guess I wouldn't bet against it."

I kept driving. Jackie leaned his head back and closed his eyes.

"Speaking of betting," I said. "You're not going to make me play cards with that jackass again, are you?"

"No," he said. "I don't imagine he'll be inviting us back."

We were past everything by then. There were only the trees, the shoreline, waves gently breaking, the dark water going out forever.

Chapter Five

I went to the Glasgow Inn for lunch the next day. I wanted to see how Jackie was doing. I wanted to show him, too, that I wasn't going to go right back into my hermit routine.

When I opened the door, he wasn't there. I couldn't remember the last time that had happened. When you go into the Glasgow, Jackie is there. That's just the way it is. Instead his son was behind the bar. Jonathan Junior, usually just Jonathan, or when he's in trouble, just Junior—he was a little squirt like his father, with the same salt-and-pepper color hair, just a little more of it. Behind his glasses, Jonathan's eyes were as blue as his mother's, a woman who I had seen exactly once in my life, the day her son graduated from Michigan Tech over in Houghton. He went down to work for a computer company in North Carolina, meaning to leave the Upper Peninsula winters long behind him. He was back in two years.

"Where's your father?" I said, sitting on a stool.

"He's upstairs in bed now. Finally. He was up all night."

"I don't get it," I said. "I dropped him off here a little after one."

"I know, I heard him come in," he said. "When I came down here this morning, though, he was sitting over there. He had a fire going in the fireplace all night, and I guess he was just sitting there looking at it."

"Did he tell you what happened over at Vargas's house?"

"He gave me the quick version," he said. "It sure put him in a weird mood, which I can understand, I guess. Still . . ."

"What is it?"

"He actually hugged me this morning, and told me he loved me and he was proud of me."

I couldn't help smiling. "If I had a son," I said, "after last night I would have done the same damned thing."

"All right," he said. "Whatever you say. If you think him sleeping at noon is okay, then I won't worry about it."

"He'll be himself by tomorrow," I said. "God help us."

I had my lunch, and caught up with Jackie's son. The man himself never came downstairs. When I got back to my cabin, the message light was blinking on my answering machine. I pressed the play button.

"Alex McKnight," the voice said, as warm and soothing as a belt sander. "This is Roy Maven. I'd appreciate it if you could stop by today."

That was it. I wasn't surprised. I knew he'd find me eventually. With a full stomach and not a hell of a lot to do that day, I figured why not, might as well get it over with. I fired up the truck and headed to the Soo.

I didn't feel like taking Lakeshore Drive again, didn't feel like seeing the machines working on the golf course, or the old railroad car that had put such strange thoughts in my head. I took the main roads, M-123 to M-28, a straight line east through Raco and Strongs and then north on I-75 to the Soo. The City-County building is on the east side of town, just past the locks and not that far from Vargas's house on the river. I didn't feel like seeing that house again, certainly not the very next day.

I parked behind the City-County building, back by the entrance to the jail and the little twelve-foot-square cage that serves as the outdoor grounds. There's one picnic table in there, and on this day two men were sitting on top of it, one lighting a cigarette off the end of the other's.

I told the receptionist at the desk that I was there to see Chief Maven. She led me to the little waiting area outside his office. It's a place I knew well enough, having spent some time there on a couple of memorable occasions. Chief Maven and I had taken an instant chemical dislike to each other, and it had gone downhill ever since. I remembered reading about Prometheus, and how the gods punished him for giving fire to mortals by chaining him to a rock where a raven would come every day for eternity to pluck out his liver. For me, this would be my ultimate punishment, to sit outside Chief Roy Maven's office every day, waiting to go inside to see the man himself.

Today, he didn't keep me waiting. No sooner had I sat down when the door opened and he stuck his head out. "Alex," he said. "Come in."

I followed him into the office and sat down in front of his desk, trying to remember if he had ever called me by my first name before. His office hadn't changed. It was still four walls of concrete. Maven hadn't changed, either. He had the drill sergeant haircut, the weather-beaten face. He was yet another tough old bird, like Jackie, like Bennett O'Dell. It was a sort of natural selection at work. Men in their sixties who lived up here year-round had to be as hard as granite. If they weren't, they either died of heart attacks shoveling snow, or just gave up and moved to Florida.

"I appreciate you stopping by," he said. He looked down at the police report in his lap. "I understand from my men that it was a pretty tense situation you were in last night. I'm glad nobody was harmed."

"Okay," I said. "Me too."

"The owner of the residence, Winston Vargas, he invited you to play poker? Are you a friend of his?"

"I had never even met him before. He really didn't invite me, but Jackie is one of the regular players, and they needed a sixth."

"Three men broke in around eleven o'clock, it says here. All with handguns. Glocks, according to you. One of them took Mr. Vargas upstairs, the other two stayed downstairs with the other five players. It looks like you got as much of a description of those two as would be possible under the circumstances. It's fortunate you were there, Alex. Your training as a police officer came in pretty handy."

"Anything to help, Chief. You know me."

He let that one go without even blinking. "Breaking and entering, armed robbery, vandalism. It sounds like they were pretty cool about it. Like it was all business."

"I'd say so. You have any suspects in mind?"

"Not at this point. We sent a copy of this over the bridge today, based on your judgment that one of the perps sounded Canadian."

"What was the grand total, anyway?"

"Grand total?"

"You know," I said. "What they stole, what they destroyed."

"Mr. Vargas says he had just under five thousand dollars in the safe. Says he likes to pick up hundred-dollar bills at work. I guess he's got an appliance store down in Petoskey. Custom kitchens, that sort of thing. When he sees a hundred in the drawer, he says he puts a hundred of his own money in, takes the bill, puts it in the safe. He's got a five-year anniversary with his wife coming up, his second marriage, I presume. Says he was going to give her five thousand dollars in hundreds, tell her to go buy whatever she wanted."

"Five thousand dollars," I said. "That's not big a score, for all the effort they put into it."

"Good point," he said. "The vandalism hurt him

a lot more. All that stuff he was collecting. And the telescope. Just about all of it they threw into the river. It doesn't make any sense. What do you make of it, Alex? Do you have any theories?"

"Do I have any theories? Chief, if you're setting me up for something, I'd appreciate it if you could cut to the chase."

"I'm not setting you up for anything. Why would I be setting you up?"

"It's either that or you've been taken over by aliens," I said. "If I go to your house, I'll find pods in your basement, right?"

"Alex . . ."

"In fact, that's why you weren't there last night. Your detective said you were out of town. Little did he know."

"You want to know where I was last night, Alex? I'll tell you. I was on my way back from a retreat down on Mackinac Island. My wife and I went together. You want to know why?"

"This is even scarier than the alien thing," I said. "It's starting to sound like you're talking to me like one human being to another. But go ahead."

"It's really a couple of different things that all happened at the same time," he said. "First thing was, my doctor told me I was killing myself. I mean, literally killing myself. High cholesterol, high stress, no exercise. I was a coronary waiting to happen. Second thing was my wife tells me one day, she says, Roy, we've been married almost forty years now, and I've never had the nerve to tell you this until now. You're bringing your job home with you every night, and I'm sick of it. You either quit the job, or you talk to somebody about how to handle it better, or you find yourself a new wife. I'm not going to watch you kill yourself."

He stopped. I just sat there. I couldn't think of a single thing to say to him.

"The third thing," he said, "was my oldest daughter told me I was going to be a grandfather. She's due in . . ." He looked behind him at a calendar sitting on a credenza. "Ten weeks, Alex. I'm gonna be a grampa."

"Congratulations," I said, finally finding a word.

"So this retreat, it was just something my wife and I did. There was a lot of New Age mumbo-jumbo they were talking about. I didn't have much use for most of it. But one thing they said made sense. You want to hear it?"

"Why not?"

"They said that in life there are all sorts of things you have no control over. The only thing you *can* control is your *reaction* to those things. It's a pretty simple idea, but I don't know, it just hit me. All this stuff I get upset about every day, I can't stop it from happening, no matter how hard I try. But I *can* choose how to react to it."

"Okay . . ."

"This is a perfect example," he said. "In fact, maybe it's a little test. You know, somebody upstairs seeing how I'd do. Here I come back from vacation and I've got three men breaking into one of the most expensive houses in town. They're holding six men at gunpoint, breaking into a safe, destroying the man's valuables. I look at the list of people who were in the house, and who do I see? Alex Mc-Knight! What do you think my reaction's gonna be?"

"I don't know," I said. "But it wouldn't be pretty."

"That's how it *would* have been," he said. "That's how the old Chief Maven would have reacted. But not now, Alex. Not now. In fact, it's a good thing you *were* there. Look at this report! You're the only one who gave us any kind of physical description. For all I know, you were the only guy there who kept his cool and showed everyone else how to get through it. If you weren't there, it might have all turned out pretty badly. I'm glad you were there, Alex. I really am."

"If all this is true," I said. "And I'm still not sure I can believe it. But if it's true . . ."

"Yes?"

"Then I guess I'm surprised, Chief. Surprised and even a little impressed."

He raised his hands, sat back in his chair. If he had wished me a good day right then and sent me on my way, I might have left the place fully convinced he was a new man.

But he didn't do that.

"Besides . . ." he said. He picked up a pen and twirled it in his right hand, looking down at the report again. "Even though you seem to show up every time there's a major crime in my town, look at how well it turned out this time."

"How do you mean?"

"Nobody was killed," he said. "Nobody was abducted. I'm not out looking for anybody. I'm not dragging the lake for bodies. And the best part of all . . ."

He looked up at me. He was smiling.

"The best part of all," he said, "is that you won't even be involved this time. I won't be seeing you every time I turn around. I won't be hearing your name every time I pick up the phone. Because you . . ."

He put the pen between his two palms and rubbed it back and forth, like he was a Boy Scout starting a fire.

". . . are not . . ."

He kept rubbing and smiling.

". . . a private investigator . . ."

I couldn't decide which was more annoying.

". . . anymore. Am I right?"

"Yes," I said. "You're right."

"This man Vargas," he said. "You don't work for him."

"No."

"You never will work for him."

"I'm sure I won't."

"You'll never work for *anybody* again. Not as a private investigator, anyway. Not in my town."

"Are we about done, Chief?"

"I saw your old partner last month," he said. "Leon what's-his-face. I was getting some lunch and I saw him on Ashmun Street. He actually has an office there now?"

"I wouldn't know."

"No, I guess you wouldn't. I asked about you, and he said you weren't his partner anymore. Said you never wanted to have anything to do with private investigation ever again. Said you hadn't even talked to him in quite a while. I gotta tell you, Alex, I sensed some hurt feelings there."

"I appreciate the insight," I said. "Are we done now?"

"I think we are. I think that covers it. Thank you for your help on this case. And if I'm ever out in Paradise, I'll buy you a beer."

Maybe I should have left right then. But I couldn't resist.

"You know, Chief," I said, "I'm only getting this secondhand, but I do believe that Vargas has a private investigator working for him."

He just looked at me. He stopped rubbing the pen between his hands. He stopped smiling.

"But as much as Vargas wants to find out who did this to him, I'm sure he'd never ask his man to get in your way. I'm sure he'll only be trying to help you. And if you think *I'm* helpful, wait 'til you see what this man can do."

"Who?" he said. "Not . . ."

"The only private eye in town," I said, "now that I'm gone. His last name is Prudell, by the way. Leon Prudell. You should remember that, because I think you're going to be hearing from him. A lot."

I heard the pen break just before I closed the door.

Chapter Six

It was a beautiful day in Sault Ste. Marie. For much of the year you couldn't say that with a straight face. In the dead of winter, especially, it would be nothing but gallows humor. On this day, the day after the Fourth of July, Sault Ste. Marie was a better place to be than anywhere else I could think of.

The rest of the country was hot that day. I saw it on the weather map in the paper that morning, all the nineties and hundred-pluses throughout the South, the West, the Midwest, even the Northeast. It was ninety-three degrees in New York City that day. It was ninety-two in Detroit. I've been in that kind of heat in Detroit. I've done it wearing a police officer's uniform and watching what it does to everybody else around me.

On this day in July, while the rest of the country stewed and simmered, it was eighty-one degrees in the Soo, with a constant breeze off Lake Superior. I didn't feel like getting right back in my truck. I just

couldn't do it. The City-County building sits at the
east end of Locks Park, so I took a walk along the
St. Marys River. There was one freighter heading
toward the locks, along with a few smaller boats and
a couple of jet skis. The center of town was busy. It
was a holiday week, and such a goddamned gor-
geous day, I wasn't surprised to see all the people.
I suppose I couldn't blame them for wanting to be
here. I'd take the tourists any day over a man like
Win Vargas, with his new-money dreams of condos
and golf courses. The tourists came up here for a
few days at a time, they stayed in one of the new
hotels, they watched some ships go through the
locks, bought T-shirts for their kids at the gift shops.
Maybe they had their own boats on trailers, took
them out on the lake for a few hours, caught a few
whitefish. With the casinos up here now, maybe we
had a few more tourists than we ever did before. But
I could live with them. They come, they spend some
money, they take some pictures, and then they go
home.

I walked up Water Street, past the Ojibway Hotel.
This was one of the original buildings in town, with
a formal dining room overlooking the locks. All the
new hotels, they were out on the Business Spur,
close to the highway.

Vargas had said something about one of those hotels, about his wife being there with Swanson the
lawyer. And his private investigator documenting
every move. I thought about that and laughed out
loud. Then I replayed my little meeting with Chief
Maven and laughed out loud again.

Hell, I was in town anyway. I had to see for myself. Ashmun Street, the Chief said. His office had to be right here in town, with Ashmun running perpendicular to the river, through what passes as a business district and then across the old power canal. I didn't figure it would be too hard to find. Hell, I knew it would be the only private investigator's office in this part of the state, let alone this particular street.

I started at the intersection with Portage Street, and worked my way south. There were gift shops on either side of the street, where you could buy your postcards, your imitation Indian headdresses, and of course your little iron-ore freighter replicas, with "Sault Ste. Marie, Michigan" embossed on the side of the hull. There was an ice cream shop after that on one side, a bookstore on the other, another gift shop, this one specializing in crystal jewelry and those little ceramic figurines that people collect. A restaurant, one more gift shop, and then it crossed Spruce Street. I knew I was getting warmer, because I was seeing serious business going on now. A three-story bank on one side, an accounting office on the other, then a travel agency and a place where they'd make you a sign for your business in twenty-four hours.

I almost missed Leon's door. It was set between the sign place and a car insurance office. The lettering on the door read "Prudell Investigations, Second Floor."

I opened the door and went up a narrow flight of stairs. There was a small hallway at the top, with a

couple of different offices that looked empty. I stood
in front of the last door on the left, looking through
the glass at my old partner Leon Prudell. He was
sitting at his desk, looking out his window at the
street below. He was the same man I knew, fifty
pounds on the heavy side, and that hair, so red it
was orange and pointing in every direction. He
didn't have his flannel shirt on, though, or his hunting boots. He was actually wearing a white shirt and
tie. For a moment I just stood there watching him,
remembering the night he had come out to Paradise
and waited at the Glasgow Inn for me, drinking
Jackie's whiskey and working up the courage to
fight me in the parking lot.

I had taken his job—or so he thought. He'd been
doing some work for Lane Uttley, a lawyer here in
town. Lane found out that I had been a cop once,
that I had been shot and still had a bullet in my chest.
He came to me and talked me into trying out the
private investigations business. I was dumb enough
to give it a shot, just long enough for some truly
horrible things to happen. Leon was the odd man
out. To this very day, as I stood in front of his office
door watching him sitting at his desk, he still didn't
know what a great favor I had done him.

After that, being a private eye was the last thing
in this world I wanted—or even worse, being a private eye and also Leon's partner. But he wouldn't
take no for an answer. He started *acting* like my
partner, and damned if he didn't help me out of a
couple of tight spots. He even saved my life. So I
told him, okay, I'll be your partner. Your *silent* part-

ner. Your occasional, call me if you really, really need me partner. He helped me out of another tight spot, but this time I figured it was time for me to stop getting into tight spots in the first place. I asked him to take my name off the business, and off the Web site he had made up. No more Prudell-McKnight Investigations. No more business cards with the two guns pointed at each other. I hadn't talked to him much since then. I couldn't help but feel a little guilty about it.

It doesn't take a hell of a lot to become a private investigator in the state of Michigan. All you need is either three years as a law enforcement officer, or a college degree in police administration. Leon went the college route, right here in town at Lake Superior State. He should have left, though. He should have gone south and started his business down by Detroit, or any other city downstate. Somewhere where there was enough business, somewhere where everybody didn't remember him from school, that goofy fat kid with the glasses who always sat in the back row and got in trouble for reading the private eye novels during class.

I rapped my knuckle on the glass. Leon twirled around and looked at me. He looked puzzled for just one second, and then he smiled. "Come on in, Alex," he said. "The door is open. What do you think of my office?"

I stepped in, looked around the place. It was small, maybe ten feet by twelve. There were some file cabinets, Leon's desk. Two guest chairs in front of it. He had a calendar on one wall, with the Lake

Superior State hockey team on it. "Go Lakers!" it said. There was a print on the other wall, the International Bridge shrouded in fog. And then the window, looking down at the street one story below. It looked exactly like what a private investigator's office would look like, if somebody had gotten the crazy idea of putting such an office in Sault Ste. Marie. "It's perfect," I said. "It's you."

"Thanks. It's good to see you."

"I was over seeing my old friend Chief Maven," I said, sitting down in one of the guest chairs. "He told me you had an office now. I thought I'd stop by and say hello."

"Chief Maven, huh? I bet I know what the two of you were talking about."

"Yeah, about this guy Vargas . . ."

"My client," he said. "Winston Vargas."

"Yeah, your client."

"You were present at his residence last night," he said. One of the things I've always loved about the guy is the fact that he'll say I was "present" at a "residence," instead of just being in a house.

"I was there," I said. "He happened to mention that you were working for him. Something about his wife."

"As long as he told you I was working for him, yes, I can confirm that."

I looked at the ceiling. Confirm that, he says. "Leon, what's the deal? Are you following his wife around, trying to catch her fooling around with the family lawyer? What was his name, Swanson?"

"My activities on his behalf are strictly confidential, Alex. You know that."

"Leon, for God's sake, it's me, okay? I was your partner."

"You *were* my partner, yes."

"Look, I told you—"

"It's okay, Alex. I don't hold that against you. I'm just saying, you know I can't discuss this with you."

"Leon, I don't care what—" I stopped, made myself slow down. Maven was right, it's all in how you react to things. Leon's putting on his one-man show, which always drives me nuts. So I should just stop letting it get to me. "I'm just making conversation," I said. "I wouldn't ask you to divulge any information that would jeopardize your relationship with your client."

"Fair enough," he said. "Thank you."

"But I was there last night, when you called him. He told us that you had followed them to a hotel. And then I think he was getting ready to accuse us of covering for Swanson. Or accuse Jackie and Bennett and Gill, anyway. I was just the innocent bystander. Me and Kenny."

Leon took a manila folder off his desk and opened it. "Those were the five other players at his house last night."

"Yes," I said. "Until the men with the guns joined us."

"I'll ask Chief Maven for a copy of the police report. I understand you were the only man who could help them with physical descriptions."

"I sort of figured Vargas would ask you to look into it," I said. "I told Maven to expect to hear from you."

"How did he react to that?"

"I don't know. Maven doesn't let himself react anymore. Doctor's orders."

"I'm sure we'll get along fine," Leon said. "I know you and Maven never hit it off."

"I'm not on his Christmas card list, no. But that's not what I'm worried about. I'm just wondering what Vargas is gonna ask you to do now. Is he thinking his wife and Swanson were behind this?"

Leon looked up at me.

"I know, I know," I said. "You can't share that information. I was just wondering, okay? It's just natural human curiosity."

"I understand," he said. "I do. You were there. It's natural."

"He's gonna have you running all over the place, isn't he. Trying to get to the bottom of this."

Leon just shrugged at that.

"I'll save you some time," I said. "I'm the guy you're looking for. It was all my idea."

"Come on, Alex. This isn't a joke."

"You're not doing your other job anymore? The snowmobile thing? And the outboard motors in the summer?"

"I'm a private investigator, Alex. Full-time."

"This office has to cost some money. Do you have any other clients besides Vargas? I mean, you don't have to tell me any names . . ."

"Most of my time is going to Mr. Vargas right

now," he said. "He's keeping me busy, believe me."

"Leon, I hope he's not going to ask you to do anything stupid, okay? That's all I'm saying. He seems like the kind of guy who could do that."

"You know I always play it straight, Alex. Straight down the middle." Another thing that only Leon would say.

"What does your wife think about all this?"

"She's letting me give it a shot," he said. "She wasn't so sure about it at first. But hey, she knows how much it means to me. I'm lucky to have her."

"That's true," I said. "Kids are okay?"

"The kids are good."

"Say hi to them for me."

"I'll do that."

"I'll let you get back to work."

"Fair enough," he said. "I'm glad you stopped by."

"Me too," I said, getting up. I shook his hand. "I'll see you again soon."

"Alex," he said. "You know that you'll always be my friend, right?"

I looked at him. The late afternoon sun came in right over his shoulder, casting a long shadow across his desk. "Of course," I said.

"You know my first priority has to be to my client," he said. "And my second priority has to be the official channels of law enforcement."

"Why are you telling me this?"

He let that one hang. "That's just the way it has to be," he finally said. "You know that."

"Sure," I said. "Of course. When you're done

with all this, give me a call. I'll buy you a beer."

He nodded and gave me a little smile. Then he turned and looked down at the street. I left his office, closing the door behind me. "What the hell was that about?" I said aloud as I walked down the stairs. Something was going on in Leon Prudell's head, and as usual, I couldn't even guess what it was.

I made my way back up Ashmun, cutting east behind the Coast Guard installation, back to the City-County building. I got in my truck and headed out of town.

Just for the hell of it, I stopped in at O'Dell's place. It was a big wooden two-story building at the end of Bermuda Avenue, in a neighborhood they call "The Shallows." The river narrows there, just before opening up into Whitefish Bay. I figured I'd have a quick one, and see how Bennett was doing.

I parked right in front of the place. It looked like it had been there for at least a hundred years. The cedar siding was weathered gray by the wind off the water. You'd have to pay a lot of money to get your house looking the same way. The "distressed" siding alone would kill you.

Bennett was pouring a draft behind the bar when I went in, looking just like the owner you'd expect— a big man who'd seen it all, rough around the edges, like the bar itself. He was looking up at the Tigers game on his big-screen TV. The place was pretty quiet for a late summer afternoon—I knew it would pick up around five o'clock, and stay busy until two in the morning.

"Alex McKnight!" he said when he saw me.

"What brings you here? Where's Jackie?"

"Last I heard, he was still in bed," I said. "And while you're pouring . . ."

"Coming right up," he said. "Yeah, I don't blame the guy for sleeping that one off. I was awake myself most of the night. You know what I mean? Just staring at the ceiling."

He did look a little ragged. But then he was no movie star to begin with. "Thanks," I said when he slid the draft over.

"You know what I was thinking as I was staring at the ceiling all night? That it was all my fault."

"How do you figure that?"

"Vargas, that horse's ass, when he was building that house over there, he stopped in here a few times. I got to talking to him, he asks me if there were any regular poker games going on. So I told him yeah, I got a few guys who play here a couple of times a month. You know, Jackie and Gill and a few other guys. He starts coming over on poker nights, but he's playing for bigger stakes than most guys here want to play for. So eventually we sort of break off this other game, just Vargas and that Kenny who works for him, me and Gill, and Jackie. And Swanson . . ."

He stopped and looked at me. He couldn't help smiling.

"Until he started nailing Vargas's wife, I mean. Then we needed another player, so Jackie dragged your ass along. Don't you feel lucky now?"

"I am truly blessed."

"Jackie was feeling a little bad for you, Alex. I

hope you don't mind me saying that. He said you were keeping to yourself too much. Said he hasn't seen you much lately."

"I was in a little slump," I said. "I'm okay now. Really."

"That's good to hear, Alex. Jackie's just looking out for you, you know that. He's a good man. Hell, Jackie and me, we go back almost fifty years now, can you believe that? We used to do our homework together, right over there in the corner." He pointed to the far corner of the bar, where now a dartboard hung on the wall.

"Must be a lot of memories in this place for you."

"Alex, you don't know the half of it." He looked up at the screen again. "Can you believe this new ballpark they're playing in now? Comerica Park, they call it? Is that for real?"

"I've seen it," I said. "It's not like Tiger Stadium, I tell you that much."

"Of course not," he said. He picked up a wet dish towel and threw it at his son. Ham O'Dell was even taller than his father, at least six foot six. He'd played power forward at Northern Michigan. He was what the newspapers politely called a "physical player," meaning that he couldn't do much besides get in other people's way. Ham peeled the wet towel off his face and threw it back at his father, missing the man by three feet.

"Basketball players," Bennett said. "No coordination."

That started a series of arguments about sports, and then about which generation had it harder.

Somehow it went to fishing after that, and then finally to women. That brought Mrs. O'Dell out of the kitchen. Margaret O'Dell was a truly lovely woman, and neither of the two men in the room deserved her. That's what she said anyway, and when she put me on the spot I was more than glad to agree with her.

"How's Jackie doing?" she asked me. "I haven't seen him in I don't know how long."

"He's still the same," I said. "Aside from last night, he's doing fine."

As I talked to her, I remembered something that Jackie had told me. Or had *almost* told me but not quite, about how he had loved Margaret once, years ago, and about how he had lost her to his best friend. I wondered if he had seen her face when his life was flashing before his eyes.

It was dinnertime when I got back to Paradise. I stopped in at the Glasgow again. Jackie was out of bed, God bless him, and sitting by the fireplace. He still looked a little tired, but nothing a little friendly needling wouldn't cure. I had my dinner with him, and told him about my day—my meeting with Maven, then with Leon, and finally how I stopped in to see Bennett. And Margaret.

He gave me a slow nod and a smile at the sound of her name. "You really got around today," he said. "Not bad for a hermit."

When I finally made it back to my cabin that night, the light on my answering machine was blinking again. There were two messages this time. I pressed play and heard a voice I didn't recognize at first. Then it came to me. It was Winston Vargas, inviting me to have lunch with him the next day. On his boat, of all places. The second message was from Eleanor Prudell, Leon's wife, asking me to call her back as soon as I could.

It was late, but I figured Vargas's message was one invitation I shouldn't leave hanging. He had left his number—I dialed it and waited through five rings until a woman answered.

"Is this Mrs. Vargas?" I said. "I'm sorry to call so late. Is your husband there?"

"Who is this?"

"My name's Alex McKnight. I was one of the men playing poker at your house last night."

"Let me guess, you had so much fun you're calling to set up the next game."

"No, actually, your husband invited me to lunch tomorrow. On his boat. I was calling to decline. I hope I didn't wake you, ma'am. I wasn't thinking."

"He's not here right now," she said. "He's out having some kind of meeting with his hired goon."

"With Leon Prudell? It's almost midnight."

"I don't know his name. He's the big guy with the orange hair, the one who's been following me around for the last few weeks."

I wasn't going to touch that one. "Well, can you give your husband the message, ma'am? That I won't be having lunch with him?"

"I'll do that," she said. "I hope it doesn't break his heart."

"Thank you, ma'am. And good night."

"Alex, was it? Sleep tight, Alex."

I was going to save Eleanor Prudell's call for the next morning, but this business with Vargas was getting stranger by the minute. The way Leon had been acting, and that line about his first priority being his client, his second priority being the police. I was thinking that was just Leon being Leon, but now I wasn't so sure. I figured it was worth returning his wife's phone call, even this late at night. She answered on the first ring.

"Eleanor," I said. "This is Alex. I take it you weren't sleeping."

I'd gotten to know Eleanor Prudell, enough to like her and to admire the way she put up with her husband's private eye dreams. When Leon broke both his ankles, I watched her carry him around the house like he was a basket of laundry. If I ever needed back-up in a bar fight, Eleanor would be my first choice.

"It's good to hear your voice," she said. "It's been so long, Alex."

"Is everything all right? You sounded a little upset in your message."

"I'm just wondering what Leon's got himself mixed up with this time," she said. "This crazy Vargas character called him seven times today. They're out at some bar right now, having some kind of 'pow-wow,' he said."

"A 'pow-wow?' "

"That's what he called it. He's been acting real

weird, Alex. I mean, even on the Leon scale. I was hoping you'd know something."

"I really don't," I said, feeling a small stab of guilt. "I haven't been spending any time with him lately."

"I wish you would," she said. "You know how to bring him back to earth sometimes."

"Eleanor, I'm sorry . . ."

"You don't have to apologize, Alex. I know you're not really his partner anymore. I was just hoping you could find out what he's up to."

"Maybe I can," I said, rubbing my eyes. I couldn't believe what I was about to do. "Vargas wants to have lunch with me tomorrow. Maybe I can find out what's going on with Leon."

"God, Alex, would you? I feel better already."

I said I would, she thanked me a few times, promised she'd hug her kids for me, thanked me again, and then said good night.

I called Vargas's number, apologized to his wife again, and told her I'd be making the lunch date after all.

"I'm so glad to hear that," she said. "I was just sitting here crying about it. Now I can sleep."

I let her have that one, wished her a good night, and hoped to God that I'd never have to meet her in person.

Before I went to sleep myself that night, I lay there in the dark, listening to the wind coming in off the lake. I wondered what the hell was going on, what Leon was up to, and why Vargas would want to have lunch with me.

Go to sleep, I told myself. You'll find out tomorrow.

Lunch on a boat. How bad could it be?

Chapter Seven

The Kemp Marina is on the St. Marys River, not far from the Coast Guard station, east of the Soo Locks. There's an old freighter docked on one side of the marina—you can walk through it and see how the seamen lived on it for months at a time. Then there's the marina itself, where you'll see just about every kind of private boat money can buy, from small sailboats to sport fishing boats, all the way up to the hundred-foot yachts. I stood at the front gate, asking myself two questions. First of all, why was I here? It had seemed to make some sense the night before. Now in the light of day I wasn't so sure.

The second question was, how the hell would I find his boat? I walked down a couple of the docks. Some of the boats had a little sign with the owner's name on it. Most didn't. I finally went back to the shed by the front gate, hoping to find the harbormaster, or the dockmaster, or whatever you'd call the guy.

There was a woman in the shed, trying to type with two fingers on a manual typewriter and having a rough time of it. "Be with ya in a second, hon," she said, as she hunted for the next key. "Two hundred dollars," she finally said. "That's how much it costs to fix a computer. Two hundred dollars. You'd think he'd spring for that, wouldn't you?"

I listened to her say a few more things about the man who wouldn't call the computer repairman. I hoped it was her husband, because some of the things she was saying you shouldn't say about somebody you're not married to. "Sorry about that, hon," she said, finally looking up at me. "What can I do for ya?"

"I'm looking for Winston Vargas's boat," I said.

She rolled her eyes. "Vargas, there's a piece of work."

"Do you know if he's here right now? He told me to meet him at noon. I'm a little late."

"I'm sorry, I shouldn't talk about him like that," she said. "You must be a friend of his."

"No, I wouldn't say that."

"Okay, then. Never mind. Anyway, let's see. You go back out there, go to the last dock. He's in the second-to-last slip on the right."

"Thank you, ma'am. I appreciate it. I hope you get your computer fixed."

"I'm not holding my breath," she said, and then she went back to her typing.

I walked down to the last dock and then all the way down to the end. The sun was high in the sky and gleaming off the shiny metal trim on the boats.

One man was sitting on a lawn chair on his deck, reading the paper. He looked up at me and nodded. The boat next to his was probably the biggest yacht in the marina. It looked like it probably slept twelve people quite comfortably. I couldn't imagine what it cost.

Vargas's boat wouldn't be quite as big as this one, I thought, but I was betting on something pretty obscene. When I got to the second-to-last slip on the right, I was a little surprised at first. The boat couldn't have been more than forty feet long. There was a cabin, but it probably slept three, maybe four people. Compared to some of the other boats here, it was downright modest. But then on second thought, it made sense. Those mega-yachts were probably slower than hell. Vargas's boat had a long hull, and probably had twin diesel engines from the looks of the stern. This thing was built to go fast.

I didn't see anybody on deck, but I didn't want to just jump aboard. I remember somebody telling me once that a man's boat was just as inviolate as his house, maybe more so. You don't go on board without being asked.

"Ahoy!" I shouted. "Anybody home?"

The door to the cabin opened, and Vargas looked out. He looked even more bald in the light of day, if that's possible. "Alex," he said. "Come on aboard."

It was a long step from the dock to the side of the boat. I felt a little zing in my groin muscles as I stretched for it, just another daily reminder that I was getting old. As soon as I stepped foot on the deck, the dog came running out of the cabin, barking at me like I was Satan himself.

"Miata, take it easy! It's just Alex! You remember Alex!"

The dog danced around me like a bantamweight, moving side to side and looking for an opening. Vargas picked him up with one hand. "Sorry, Alex. He's still a little high-strung since the other night."

"That's all right," I said. Since the other night, my ass. That dog was born high-strung.

"Frankly, Alex, I'm a little surprised you came. I don't imagine you had a very good experience at my poker party."

"You didn't have such a great time yourself," I said. "I know it wasn't your idea to get robbed."

"No," he said, rubbing the dog's head. "That wasn't the plan."

"I guess I'm wondering why you invited me, though. I know I'm not your first choice for a lunch date."

"There may be a thing or two I'd like to ask you about," he said. "Just to get your opinion. But why don't we head out first? It's such a nice day for it. Do you fish much?"

"Once in a while," I said. "Not as much as I'd like."

"Perfect then," he said. "We'll catch a couple of whitefish."

He put the dog back down on the deck, which set off another round of barking and carrying on. "Don't make me put you inside, Miata. Just go lay down over there."

The dog barked a few more times, but then finally backed away and sat down next to Vargas's captain's chair. He watched me as I sat down, ready to leap at my throat if I made any false moves.

"I had to bring the dog today," he said. "My wife is out. Again." He hung on the last word, shaking his head. I didn't feel like asking him about it, or hearing anything about what was going on between his wife and the family lawyer. Or telling him what his wife had told me the night before, that she knew he had hired Leon to follow her. The whole scene was already uncomfortable enough, and I was beginning to regret it.

Vargas fired up the boat. I could feel the deck vibrating, the twin engines throbbing with so much power it was like sitting on a rocket. He stepped past me to untie a couple of lines, the dog barking again just on general principle. Then he sat back down in his captain's chair and pulled the throttle back a notch. There was a furious churn behind the boat as he backed it and quartered, then he kicked it forward and we were on our way.

"You ever been through the locks before?" he said as we cruised down the St. Marys.

"No, that I haven't done."

"Sometimes you have to radio ahead," he said, "but it looks like there are already a couple of boats lined up. It gets interesting when you've got a freighter in the lock at the same time. You feel like a very small fish in a tank with a whale."

There were three pleasure boats waiting for the southern-most lock to open. Vargas fell in behind them. Almost immediately, the gates to the lock opened. Two giant steel doors, each one at least fifty feet across, swung open. The three boats ahead of us proceeded into the lock, and then Vargas joined them. I could see the viewing platform above us. With the water level down, it felt like we were at the bottom of a well.

A bell rang as the gates closed behind us. Slowly the boat began to rise, as the water from the other side was fed in from below. The gates on the far side were holding back the crushing weight of Lake Superior, which seemed at that moment like a ridiculous idea. A thin stream of water was leaking through the line where the two gates joined, like they would break open at any second. But of course they didn't. Ten minutes later, the boats had risen the twenty-one feet, and the gates began to open. The people on the viewing platform were at eye level now. A few of them waved to us. The dog barked back at them.

Once we cleared the locks, we still had a couple of miles of river to negotiate, under the International Bridge. We went around the bend where the river narrowed, past the Shallows, O'Dell's place prominent on the shoreline.

I could be in there right now, I thought, having a cold beer and watching a baseball game. Instead I'm on a boat with Vargas and his dog.

When we passed the last bend, we finally hit the open water of Whitefish Bay. The sun came out from behind a cloud and lit up the water, turning it a thousand shades of green and blue. Vargas pushed the throttle up and we were off, the bow rising as we gained speed, the cold spray lashing at our faces. He tried to say something to me, but his words were lost in the noise of the engines. The lake was as calm as it ever gets, but even so we started bouncing around on the deck. I grabbed onto the gunwale. The little dog was getting thrown around like a beanbag, until Vargas caught him in midair.

He really opened it up, pushing the boat to the limit and sending us screaming out into the heart of the bay. Any boats that were puttering around behind us were long gone. I imagine he was trying to impress me. I just held on and waited for him to slow down.

Finally he did, kicking it down to an idle and letting us drift. We were miles from shore now, so far out I could see only the barest outline of land on the horizon.

"Tell me the truth, Alex," he said, wiping off his face. "Is this a boat or what?"

"You've got a boat here," I said. "I'll give you that one."

"I've got some poles here, if you feel like catching some whitefish. Of course you can't depend on catching your lunch, so I brought some sandwiches. And some cold beer."

"I'll pass on the fishing for now," I said. "I was hoping you'd tell me what's on your mind."

"Fair enough," he said. "But not on an empty stomach." He pulled out a big cooler and opened it, set me up with a pastrami and Swiss on rye bread, and a cold Molson's. It was American Molson's, but it went down well enough as I sat there in the glare of the midday sun. It was all starting to feel a little surreal, with the bright light and the gentle rolling of the boat on the lake. I felt like I was being lulled to sleep.

Finally, Vargas broke the spell. "You have some problems with me, don't you," he said. "I picked up on that the other night, before everything else happened."

"I'm sitting on your boat, eating your food and drinking your beer," I said. "I'm not sure this is the right time to criticize you."

"But I know you'll give me an honest answer," he said. "You're a straight shooter."

"Let's just say I don't agree with you on some things."

"Like what?"

"We don't have to go through them," I said. "I know I'm not going to change your mind about anything."

"Who says you won't? Try me."

"Look, the other night you were telling me how much you love it up here, right?"

"Yes."

"Okay, but it doesn't seem to mean much to you if you can't *own* it—if you can't buy it just for yourself and maybe a few of your friends, rope it off and put a 'No Trespassing' sign at the gate."

"Like Bay Harbor," he said.

"Like Bay Harbor."

He took a bite of his sandwich, and looked out at

the lake. The dog watched him, waiting for some food to come his way.

"Even that stuff you collect," I said, "up in that room of yours. Those things from the shipwrecks. The Indian artifacts. It's not enough to just appreciate what they mean. You have to own them and put them in a glass case. In your own little room where nobody else can see them."

"You seem to have a strong opinion about that."

"Not strong enough to break into your house and destroy the whole room," I said. "But yeah, it does bother me."

"Like I said, I knew you were a straight shooter. I respect that. I happen to think you've got it all wrong. I don't think you understand me at all. But that's all right. That's not why I brought you out here."

"Are you gonna finally tell me why you did?"

"It's simple," he said. "I wanted to ask your opinion."

"On what?"

"On what happened the other night. And who might be responsible."

"I don't see why you're asking me," I said. "And to go to all this trouble . . . Hell, I know it wasn't fun getting robbed, Vargas, but if you only had five thousand dollars in the safe . . ."

"That's the figure I gave the police."

"Okay, so it was more. A lot more?"

He didn't say anything. He just looked at me.

"Why would you want to keep a lot of money in your safe?" I said. "A guy like you, I figure you'd invest it in something. This way, you don't even get any interest . . ."

"Yeah, no interest," he said. "I also don't have to give a big chunk of it to the IRS. Or to my first wife, for that matter. But let's not talk about why I had money in my safe, or how much, or how it got there. I just want it back. I thought you might be able to help me."

"You already have a man working for you."

"Yes," he said. "Your ex-partner, it turns out. Wasn't that an interesting development."

I didn't say anything.

"But you're the one with the experience," he said. "You're the one who wore a badge, down in Detroit. You're the one with the bullet in your chest." He looked down my chest, like everybody does when they happen to be talking about it. Someday I'll get used to it.

"Look, Vargas . . ."

"Let me lay it out for you, Alex. Then you tell me what you think. That's all I want. Then we'll go back, I promise."

"Lay it out."

"Besides myself," he said, "there were only five people in this world who knew about that safe. Not even my wife knew about it."

"Come on, how could she not know?"

"I had the builder put that in. She hardly saw the place until it was done. Anyway, I'm at a poker game a couple of months ago. At O'Dell's place, in the back room. Bennett was there, Jackie, Gill, Kenny, and Swanson. That was before I had any idea about Swanson and my wife, mind you. That was back when I still thought I was happily married. I had a few drinks that night. Too many, I suppose. I was losing a lot of money, and I said something stupid like maybe I had to go into my safe, to get some more cash."

"That was it? That's all you said?"

"All right, I may have said a little more. You know, I may have bragged about it a little. All the cash I had in my wall safe, and how my wife didn't know about it. How she'd spend it all. Or something. Hell, I don't even remember half of what I said."

"So based on that . . ."

"Based on that, my first reaction to the other night is that it had to be Swanson. He knew it was poker night. He knew I'd be there to open the safe. It makes sense, doesn't it? Isn't that what you'd be thinking?"

"I only met Swanson once," I said. "At Jackie's place. We didn't say more than ten words to each other. So I don't know what to tell you."

"But just based on the list of suspects, Alex, isn't Swanson the name you'd come up with?"

"I know you can rule out Jackie," I said. "And Bennett and Gill. I don't know Kenny . . ."

"Assume it's not Kenny," he said. "Kenny's got no reason to do this. No reason at all."

"Okay, then that leaves Swanson. Assuming that nobody else knows about the safe."

"Exactly," he said. "That's exactly what I was thinking."

"That's it? That's the opinion you wanted from me? Just to agree with you on that?"

"That's what I was thinking at first," he said, "but now . . . Let's say that certain things have caused me to see it another way."

"Certain things. Like what?"

"Let's talk about you for a minute," he said.

"Why do you want to talk about me?"

"Leon had some interesting things to say about you. So did Roy."

"By Roy, I take it you mean Chief Maven? What are you, best buddies or something?"

"Not at all. He's just a good police chief trying to solve a crime. Naturally we talked about the other men who were at my house that night. He seemed quite . . . agitated when your name came up."

"Why am I not surprised . . ."

"Leon paints a very positive picture of you," he said. "Maven, maybe not so positive. But I put both pictures together and I see something very intriguing. A failed baseball player, a failed cop. A failure as a private investigator even, although naturally Leon didn't come out and say that. He did say that he hasn't spoken to you in a while, and that you seem to have changed. I'm thinking, with everything you've been through, all the hard knocks you've taken, what do you have to show for it? You've always done the right thing, stayed on the straight path, for what?"

"I don't have a few million dollars like you do," I said. "Is that what you're getting at? Would it occur to you that I don't care about that?"

"You've never committed a crime in your entire life," he said, "but now maybe you're in a state of mind where you'd be . . . a little more receptive to the idea of trying something."

"I can't believe this. You really think I did it."

"No," he said. "Not at all. I know you didn't set this whole thing up. But maybe, just maybe, if some person . . . or persons . . . were to approach you with this idea of playing a key role in a takedown."

"A takedown," I said. "My God, you are completely insane."

"You were the inside man, weren't you? You've been around criminals, and around guns. You knew how something like this works, what bases had to be covered. You knew how to make sure it went smoothly. With you right there on the scene, how could it not? If anything unexpected happened, you'd be there to deal with it."

"This is quite a yarn you're spinning," I said. "It's downright entertaining."

"At first, I'm thinking, why do it with all those other people there? Why not just catch me alone? Or just me and my wife? Then it hits me. This way is better. This way is actually a lot safer. If I was by myself, I might have tried something stupid. Figure what the hell, it's just me here, I'm gonna try to disarm this guy, shoot it out. And if it was me and my *wife* . . . Somebody putting a gun to my wife's head? Again, assuming that I didn't know she was screwing Swanson behind my back and I still gave a fuck what happened to her? I'd be a madman. I could do anything. Try to take them all on at once."

"I seem to recall you just about wetting your pants the other night," I said. "But go ahead. I don't want to ruin your fantasy."

"With five guests in the house, five men who I feel some responsibility for, but not so much that I'm crazy about it, you knew I'd play along. No problem at all."

"Okay, so if I was brought in as the inside man," I said, "then who asked me? Whose idea was this, Vargas?"

"You know who we're talking about."

"Who? If it's not Swanson and it's not Kenny, who are we talking about? Jackie? Gill? Bennett? Hell, didn't Bennett take a nice shot to the ribs trying to protect you?"

"That was just for effect," he said. "He was acting. I know he wouldn't have done it if it was for real."

"Do these men know that you've foiled their grand plan?"

"No," he said. "I thought I'd bring it to you first. If you can round up all the money and give it back to me, maybe I'd be willing to drop the whole thing."

"That's big of you."

"Stop playing games with me," he said. His face was red now. Hell, his whole head was red. "It's bottom-line time. I could just as easily go back to shore with one less person on board. A tragic accident, and you on the bottom of the lake." He stood up from his chair. The dog stood below him, right between his legs. Two against one.

"I assume you've got a gun," I said.

"I don't need a gun," he said. "You know why?"

"Because you're a total fucking moron?"

"You ever hear of Moo Duk Kwan?"

"Sure, with rice and an eggroll. . . . It's delicious."

"It's a Korean martial art," he said. "I picked it up when I was stationed there."

"Does it work on boats?"

"You're about to find out," he said. "Stand up." He went into his pose, left hand down, right hand in a fist. He lifted his left leg slightly off the ground, no doubt ready to kick the living shit out of me. The dog stayed on all fours.

I didn't get up. I figured that's the last thing I wanted to do, get on my feet, put my dukes up, then get cut in half. If I keep sitting here, I thought, he's not going to do anything yet. I didn't think they taught him how to attack someone sitting in a deck chair.

"Stand up," he said. "What's the matter with you?"

"I'm trying very hard not to laugh," I said. Stay calm. Act like it's all a big joke. Keep him off balance. I picked up my bottle of beer, took a hit off it. As I put it back in the little bottle holder on the gunwale, I glanced down at the little shelf that ran along the deck. Life jackets. A seat cushion. A fire extinguisher.

"McKnight, if you're a man you'll stand the hell up." The dog picked up on the hostility in his master's voice, started dancing around again and barking.

"You know what your problem is, Vargas?" I said. "Your problem is . . . *Look out for the dog!*"

He looked down. It was all I needed. I came out of the chair at him, and as he lashed out at me with a side kick, I dropped to the deck and swept his back ankle. Before he could get up, I grabbed the fire extinguisher and hit him in the head with it. I stood over him, ready to hit him again if I had to. The dog went absolutely rabid on me, jumping at me with fire in its little bug eyes, trying to tear my kneecaps off.

"You're gonna be bait in about two seconds, dog. Get the hell out of my way."

I grabbed some rope and tied Vargas's hands behind his back. There was a big welt already rising on his forehead. For a sick moment I wondered if I had hit him too hard, but then he started to come to. I sat him up against the door to the cabin and took the captain's chair, threw the throttle forward and nearly flipped the whole damned boat over. That got the dog going again. I had to kick him away a few times while I throttled it back to a reasonable speed and headed back to shore.

"What the fuck . . ." Vargas said, shaking his head. That welt was going to look terrible, I could tell. Not a good thing on a bald man.

"Hold on, Vargas," I said. "We're going home."

"Goddamn it, I should have known you'd be a cheap-shot artist."

"Vargas, you're the one who brought me out here and threatened to leave me on the bottom of the lake. I figure that gives me the right to fight dirty."

"You're going to be very sorry about this," he said.

I gave the steering wheel a quick turn, sending Vargas ass over tea-kettle.

"Sorry about that," I said. "I've never driven a boat like this. Maybe you better just keep your mouth shut so you don't distract me anymore."

He worked himself back up and just sat there the rest of the way, staring at me like he was memorizing every detail. When I got back to the mouth of the St. Marys River, it occurred to me that I had no desire to take the boat all the way back to the marina, figuring out how to get into the locks, sitting there for ten minutes while all the people on the deck watched us, no doubt wondering why one of the men in the boat was tied up. As we rounded the bend, I saw the Shallows, and O'Dell's place. It was a welcome sight.

There were a couple of docks right on the river. I picked the one closest to O'Dell's and killed the engine, letting the boat drift into range. I threw one of the ropes over the post, and climbed out of the boat. The dog took one more shot at me, hanging on my shoelaces for a few seconds before I shook him free.

"You can't just leave me here," Vargas said.

"I didn't tie your hands very tight," I said. "You'll work your way free. If you don't, have your dog chew the ropes off, just like in the movies."

"I gave you a chance, Alex. Just remember that. We could have settled this the right way. Everything that happens is on your head now."

"Vargas, I don't know where you came up with this idea, but—"

"I've got you nailed," he said. He rocked himself forward, onto his knees. "All of you. And you, my friend, are about to find out what's going to happen. In a big way."

"So long, Vargas." I left him there to work on his ropes. As I walked over to O'Dell's place, his words rung in my head. He's got us nailed, he says. What the hell could he be talking about?

Something started to come together in my head. A connection. I waved it off. I couldn't imagine he really had something.

In my wildest dreams, I couldn't imagine.

Chapter Eight

It was dark and cool in O'Dell's bar. It felt good just to walk into the place. Bennett was sitting at one of the tables, having a late lunch. His son was mixing drinks for two men sitting at the end of the bar. His wife was washing glasses.

"Alex!" Bennett said. "You're becoming a regular customer! What's the matter, Jackie kick you out of his place?"

"You're not going to believe this," I said. "I need a ride over to the marina. My truck is there."

"What'd you do? Swim over?"

"It's kind of a long story," I said. Which meant I had to tell it. With Bennett getting up from his lunch and getting me a beer, of course I had to tell him the whole thing.

"He thinks I was involved in the robbery," I said, getting to the punch line. "He thinks you were involved, too."

"What is he, nuts?"

"You know that shot to the ribs you took for him? He thinks it was staged."

"Yeah, it was staged all right," he said, rubbing his left side. "That's why it's been keeping me up all night. All I gotta do is roll over the wrong way and *ka-pow*! It's like somebody sticking me with a cattle prod."

"You need to go to the hospital," Margaret said from the sink. "It might be broken!"

"Go on," Bennett said, waving his hand at her. "What are they gonna do? They don't even tape up broken ribs anymore. They just give you pain killers and send you home."

"So you get pain killers," she said. "What's wrong with that?"

"I don't need pain killers," he said, giving me a little wink. "I've been married for forty years. I've built up a natural immunity to pain."

"I'll show you pain," she said. Which got them started again. But it was all good-natured, and I just sat there with my cold beer watching them. It was a hell of a lot better than being out on that damned boat.

A couple of beers later, Bennett finally took me across town to the marina. "What is this, a Ford Explorer?" I said, looking around the inside of it. "It's nice."

"Yeah, it's got four-wheel-drive," he said. "Runs like a tank in the winter. You still got that old truck, I see."

"Why not?" I said. "It still runs."

"Yeah, just like me," he said. "Hey listen, take

care of yourself, eh? I'm sorry you got involved with this in the first place. Hell, it's all because Jackie hates playing poker with only five guys."

"It's all right, Bennett."

"What do you figure Vargas is gonna do now? It sounds like you made an enemy today."

"He's all noise," I said. "Don't worry about me." I thanked him and let him go. I took a quick look over the fence at the last dock. I couldn't see Vargas's slip with all the yachts in the way, but I didn't think his boat was back yet.

I got in my truck and headed west, back to Paradise. I felt a little tired and sore. "God, what a horse's ass," I said out loud. "Moo Duk Kwan, I'm gonna have to look that one up."

When I got home, I checked on the other five cabins. Everybody was out somewhere, enjoying the day. I went back to my own cabin, cleaned up a little bit, sat down, and tried to read something. But I couldn't concentrate. I kept seeing Vargas's foot coming at me, missing me by maybe an inch. And the great red welt I had put on his bald head. And the teeth on that dog.

You're gonna have nightmares about that dog, I said to myself. You're gonna have nightmares about a three-pound Chihuahua.

A few hours later, I made my way down to the Glasgow Inn. Jackie was there behind the bar. He still looked a little tired, and every few minutes he'd stare off into nowhere, like he was watching something going on a million miles away. I figured he still wasn't over it yet.

I didn't tell him about my little lunch date with Vargas. That one I'd save for another day.

As I had dinner there, I caught up with the local paper, the *Soo Evening News*, "serving the Eastern U.P. daily since 1903." I always start with the police beat on the second page. The man who writes up the crimes is a real character, and he always puts his own unique spin on everything he reports. My all-time favorite was still the item titled "Unlicensed Operator." Somebody had gone into a store and left a dog in the car, who proceeded to knock the stick into first gear. The car rolled into the street, causing damage that was estimated at over five thousand dollars. The police beat reporter summed up the entry with a simple statement: "The dog was not cited."

The crimes on the blotter are usually just drunk driving and the occasional vandalism, the petty thefts and the possession of drugs in small quantities—the "forbidden weed," as the reporter once called it. It's not often that he gets to take the lead story on page one, and write about something big, like what happened at Vargas's house. The day before, he only had time for the bare details—break-in at local residence, armed intruders, nobody harmed, Soo police pursuing the case. In today's paper, with more time to develop the story, the good readers of the *Soo Evening News* got the full treatment, complete with a trio of "costumed assailants," who methodically ransacked one room of the house while five guests lay facedown on the floor. Mercifully, they didn't list the names of the guests.

Anyone with information pertaining to the case was asked to contact Chief Roy Maven immediately.

"Quite a write-up, huh?" Jackie's son said.

"I think some people will be locking their doors in Sault Ste. Marie tonight," I said. "And keeping their shotguns loaded."

Jackie just listened to us talk about it. He didn't say anything himself.

"Jackie, are you gonna tell me what's bothering you?" I said. "Or are you just gonna keep moping around the place?"

He looked at me without smiling. "I'm sorry," he said. "I didn't mean to ruin your evening."

"Relax," I said. "If you're still working on what happened, I understand."

"Good," he said. "I'm glad you understand. I gotta go change the tap."

I looked at his son. He just shrugged his shoulders.

Two minutes later, Jackie was back. "I'm sorry, Alex," he said. "I shouldn't take it out on you."

"Don't apologize," I said. "If you want to talk about it . . ."

"I will," he said. "In a few days. Okay? Give me a few days."

"Whatever you say, Jackie. I'll be here."

He smiled for the first time since I had walked into the place. "Yeah, I don't think I'll have any trouble finding you."

I left a couple of hours later, after finishing the paper and another cold Canadian or two. Instead of

turning onto my road, I kept going north, all the way
to the top of Whitefish Point. I got out and walked
past the Shipwreck Museum, out onto the beach.
There was real sand here, unlike most of the rocky
shoreline on this lake. I walked west, picking up
driftwood as I went. The surf broke against the sand.
The sun went down and put on its show for me. It
was the right way to end the day.

When I got back to my cabin, I stood just inside
the door, trying to figure out what was wrong. Nothing was missing. Nothing was out of place. And yet,
somehow, I knew someone else had been there.

I looked at the door. There was no sign of forced
entry. I looked at the windows, found two of them
open and unlocked. I always left them open in the
summertime, and never thought about intruders way
the hell out here in the woods.

I walked around the place, trying to figure it out.
If nothing was stolen, and I had nothing worth stealing in the first place . . . If nothing was destroyed or
even moved . . . Then somebody was looking for
something. And apparently didn't find it. Assuming
it happened at all. Assuming I wasn't just acting par-
anoid after the strange day I had just lived
through . . .

Vargas. Could he have sent somebody to search
my cabin while I was out on the lake with him? I
wouldn't put it past him.

"Oh, Leon," I said out loud. "You didn't do this,
did you?"

I called his number. I owed his wife a call back,
anyway. When she answered, I realized I didn't have

much to tell her about my meeting with Vargas—we never did get around to talking about Leon.

"Is he home?" I said.

"No, he isn't," she said. "I don't know where he is."

"Was he gone all day?"

"Ever since this morning, yes. He left the house with a real black cloud over his head, Alex. I've never seen him like this. I thought he was supposed to be loving this private investigator thing."

"Tell him to call me," I said. "As soon as he gets in, no matter how late."

She promised she would, and wished me a good night.

Leon never called.

The next morning, I worked out on the hard floor of my cabin, doing push-ups, sit-ups, whatever else I could think of. Then I went outside and ran down my road, all the way to the end and back. I was glad it was a deserted old logging road, with nobody around to see me walk the last quarter mile. I went inside and hit the shower. Then I went down to Jackie's place.

As soon as I reached the main road, I saw the police cars. As I got closer, I saw more and more of them. They were all parked in Jackie's lot. Maybe ten of them, maybe twelve. I couldn't count at that point. I could barely think.

I pulled off to the side of the road, just before his lot began. I got out of the truck and walked to the front door of the place. I saw Soo police cars on one side, Michigan state police on the other. I was about ten feet from the door when a state trooper stepped right in front of me. He put his hands up like he was going to have to catch me.

"This building is closed, sir. You're going to have to step back."

"What happened?" I said.

"Please, sir. Nobody's allowed on these premises. You're going to have to leave."

"Tell me what's going on," I said. "Where's Jackie?" My imagination ran through all of the possibilities, none of them good. My stomach felt like it had been turned inside-out.

"Sir, I'm going to have to ask you again . . ."

"The owner is my friend," I said. "Just tell me what happened."

The trooper looked to the sky. He was just a kid, no more than twenty years old. "Your friend has not been harmed," he said. "I hope that puts your mind at ease, sir. Now, please . . ."

The front door opened, and out stepped Roy Maven.

"Maven, what the hell's going on here?" I said.

"Take it easy, McKnight. Unless you'd rather spend the rest of the day sitting in the back of a squad car . . ."

"Where's Jackie?"

"He's inside," he said, stepping up next to the kid. "I'll take care of this gentleman, Trooper. Thanks for the help."

"I want to see him," I said.

"You can't do that. He's under arrest."

"Under arrest? For what?"

"Receiving stolen goods, for one," he said. "Conspiracy to commit armed robbery. We'll see what else comes up."

I stood there and looked at him, the hot sun bouncing off the police cars. I waited for it to make sense. It didn't happen.

"Maven, this is insane. This is something Vargas did, right? Is that what this is about? Because I gotta tell ya—"

"The only thing Vargas did was get himself robbed at gunpoint," he said. "We served a search warrant to your friend Mr. Connery a couple of hours ago. We've already found one of the stolen items hidden in his bedroom."

"What? What did you find?"

"At this very moment, we're also executing search warrants against Bennett O'Dell and Gill LaMarche. All three of them will be taken down to the station and charged within the hour. As a material witness I should advise you that you'll be contacted soon for more questioning. I think that's about all I need to say right now."

It took a little while to absorb that. All three of them, arrested. "Why are you here?" I finally said. "The other two are in your town. Why are you out here in Paradise? To rub my face in it?"

"This is a Soo case, McKnight. You know that. I came out to this one because I knew you'd show up eventually. You'd want to know what the hell was going on and nobody would tell you. Which means you'd get all tangled up with some poor trooper and you'd end up getting arrested yourself. With me here, I can at least tell you what you need to know, and save you some embarrassment. That's why I'm here, McKnight, not because I'm getting any enjoyment out of telling you this."

"Yeah," I said. "I'm sure this is breaking your heart."

"Hey, I'm trying to give you something here. I know this must be frustrating, seeing your best friend arrested."

"If you've got a warrant," I said, "you had to have something to give you probable cause. What is it? What did Vargas come up with?"

"I told you, this isn't Mr. Vargas's doing. Beyond that, you know I can't discuss the details of this case."

"Tell me," I said.

He let out a long breath, took his hat off, and wiped his forehead with his sleeve. "Well," he said, "I suppose you're gonna find out pretty soon anyway."

"Find out what?"

"We've got a videotape, McKnight. We've got the whole thing, in living color."

"What are you talking about? How in the world did you—"

I stopped. Somehow, I knew what he was going to say, before he said it.

"We got the videotape from your ex-partner," he said. "Good old Leon Prudell."

Chapter Nine

I wanted to do something, get in the way, demand to talk to somebody, tell them they were making a mistake. But I knew I'd be about as effective as Vargas's little dog, barking and nipping at their heels, without changing a damned thing. So I just sat there waiting in my truck, the windows down so I didn't suffocate in the heat, watching the cops go in and out of Jackie's place. At one point, Jackie was led out the front door. He was blinking in the sudden glare of the sun, his hands in cuffs. I got out of the truck and stood there watching as they took him to one of the Soo police cars. What could I do?

They opened the back door for him. He looked up just before he got in, caught my eye, and gave me a look that I couldn't quite figure out. I've seen a lot of people taken away in a squad car. First-timers look completely stunned and defeated, the way an animal looks when a lion has it by the throat. Career criminals, on the other hand, try to look cool about it, like it's no more than a taxi ride. Jackie didn't look like either one of those. Hell, he almost looked like he was amused by it all. He gave me a little smile and a nod before he bent his head down and slid into the car.

I resisted the urge to follow them all the way to the police station. I knew it would take a while to process him, and even longer if they tried to question him. The best thing I could do at that moment was stick around and try to find his son, make sure he was okay, and ask him if Jackie had a good lawyer.

The cops were there about another hour. The state troopers left first, then the Soo police. The last man out apparently had the key to the place. He locked the door and tested it to make sure it was shut tight, and then he and his partner got in their vehicle and kicked up some gravel on their way out of the parking lot. With everybody gone, the place had an eerie calm to it. The only sounds came from the bees buzzing in the wildflowers on the edge of the parking lot, and the waves breaking on the rocks a hundred yards away.

I got out and went to the front door. There was a handmade sign stuck on the inside. It read "Closed for the day." I looked in. It was dark. I knocked on the door.

Nothing.

I went around behind the building, to Jackie's private entrance. I knocked. I knew that Jonathan was keeping a room just above that door. He'd be sure to hear me if he was there.

Nothing. Where the hell was he?

As I walked back to my truck, a car pulled into the parking lot. A man got out, somebody I'd seen at the bar a few times but had never talked to. "What's going on?" he asked me. "Is Jackie open?"

"Jackie is closed," I said. "Come back tomorrow."

"Why is he closed?"

"Come back tomorrow."

The man huffed at me and got back in his car. On his way out, he kicked up even more gravel than the cops.

As I drove into the Soo, I called Leon's office. He wasn't there. I left a message for him to call me as soon as he could. I called his home number next—no Leon, no Eleanor. I left the same message.

Then I called Jackie's number and left a message for his son. I'll be at the station, I said. Come on down when you can.

When I got to the City-County building, Jonathan was already there.

"Alex!" he said when he saw me. "I've been calling you!"

"How'd you get here?" I said. "I didn't see you at the Glasgow."

"At first they told me I should stick around," he said. "Then later they told me to leave. They said to call the station later to find out his status. But hell, where was I gonna go? I'd be going crazy. So I just came down here."

"I must have missed you," I said. "Tell me everything that happened."

"Let's see," he said. He took a long breath and ran his fingers back through his hair. "They came this morning. I don't know, maybe nine o'clock, nine-thirty. There were half a dozen Soo policeman, and half a dozen state troopers. Chief Maven was with them. He said they had a warrant to search the entire building. There were a couple of guys there having breakfast—Maven chased them out, told them we were closing down for the rest of the day. They had my father sit down at one of the tables with a Soo man watching him the whole time. Then, God, they went through everything, Alex. They started in the bar and just worked their way through the whole house. My room. My father's room. Maven came down—that's when he told me to leave. I think the official arrest happened as soon as I was gone."

"What did they find?" I said. "Do you have any idea?"

"No, Alex. I can't even imagine."

"Have they told you anything about what's happening to him right now?"

"They said he'd be here a while. I don't know if they're questioning him now or what."

"If they are, I hope he has the sense to keep his mouth shut."

"He didn't do anything, Alex."

"I know that," I said. "Even so, he should keep his mouth shut for now. What about a lawyer? Does he have a lawyer, do you know?"

"There's a man in Brimley," he said. "He's done work for my father before. You know, a will, stuff like that. I gave him a call but he wasn't in, so I left him a message to get down here."

"Okay, good," I said. "If all goes well, they'll set bail by the end of the day."

"We're gonna bail him out, right? We don't want him spending the night in jail."

"We'll bail him out," I said. "Don't worry. We've got to get a bondsman down here. Problem is, I think Leon is still the only bondsman in town."

"So we get him."

"No, we can't do that," I said. "I'll explain later. I'm trying to remember—when Leon got into that business, he told me that the next closest bondsman was all the way down in Mackinaw City. There's a phone book over there—go look up 'Bail Bonds' in the yellow pages and see if you can find him. I want to go talk to Maven again."

"Okay, if you think that's a good idea . . ." He didn't look like he thought it was. I wasn't so sure myself, but I didn't know what else to do.

There was a receptionist sitting there at the front desk. I waited for her to get off the phone and then I asked her if I could see Chief Maven. She told me that Chief Maven was extremely busy at the moment, and asked me if I wanted to leave a message. I asked her to please call him and tell him that Alex McKnight wished to speak to him immediately regarding today's arrests. She thought about that for a second, then picked up the phone and called him. "He'll see you now," she said. "Do you know where his office is?"

"I'm afraid I do."

He was waiting at his door when I got there. I went in and sat down in my usual chair.

"I assume you wish to add something to your original statement?" he said. "The one you gave to the officers on the night in question? I've got some paper here if you want to write it down."

"Am I a suspect now?"

"Not at this time, no. But if you do know anything else about this matter, and you wish to make a statement now . . ."

"I don't know anything else."

"Even though your best friend and two of his friends all appear to be involved in this, you have no further information yourself?"

"They were not involved," I said. "The only other information I have for you is that you've made a big mistake."

He leaned back in his chair. "A big mistake. So I should be letting them go right now. Is that what you're saying?"

"I want to ask you a couple of questions," I said.

"McKnight, I got a lot of work to do here."

"First of all, when can I see Jackie?"

"When he makes bail," he said. "Assuming he does. It hasn't been set yet."

"Did he ask for a lawyer?"

"I don't know," he said. "I haven't talked to him yet."

"What's on this videotape you've got?"

"I can't discuss that."

"You said Prudell made the tape," I said. "I don't see how that was possible. He called Vargas that night. He was apparently following his wife around. According to Vargas, she was at a hotel with Swanson. If he was tailing her, how could he have taped anything at Vargas's house?"

"Same answer," he said. "I've got nothing to say about that right now."

"He wasn't there," I said. "It's as simple as that. Even if he supposedly came over to the house, I tell you, *he wasn't there.* What could he have taped?"

Maven looked at his watch.

"Those three men were lying on the floor," I said. "At gunpoint. What the hell can be on a videotape that would implicate them? This doesn't make any sense."

"I can see why you're puzzled, McKnight. I'll say that much."

"Vargas did this," I said. "You've got to realize, Maven, this is all Vargas. I had a run-in with him yesterday. He *warned* me he was going to do something."

"I'd advise you to stay away from Vargas. In fact, I'll do more than just advise you . . ."

"What did you find in Jackie's bedroom?" I said. "Money from Vargas's safe? Is that what it was? Is that what you found at Bennett's and Gill's?"

Maven just looked at me.

"You said receiving stolen goods? Does that mean the money? There were no other 'goods' stolen. They just trashed the place and left."

"McKnight . . ."

"Whatever it was, you don't think it could have been planted there?"

"I'll keep that theory in mind," he said. "Are we about done here?"

"That's my friend in there," I said. "This is a man who once turned around and drove a hundred miles back to a restaurant, just because he realized he hadn't left enough money on the table. If you think he had any part in this, you're wrong. And I'm sure that goes for Bennett and Gill, too. Something is very wrong here, Chief, and I'm gonna find out what it is."

"I figured you'd get to that one, McKnight. Only this time, you're not a private eye anymore, remember? This time, you're a material witness who happens to be about one inch away from being detained yourself. What you *will* do is remain in the general area in case I need you. What you *won't* do is get in the way of this investigation. I realize that's a tricky concept for you. So I'll make it simple. Go home to Paradise. Stay there until I tell you otherwise. That's it. Think you can do that?"

I stood up. "Just out of curiosity," I said before I went to the door, "what happened to the 'new Chief Maven' I was talking to a couple of days ago?"

"He's still here," he said. "For you, I figured I'd bring out the original model. Just for old times' sake."

When I got back out to the lobby, business had picked up. Ham O'Dell was there now, towering over everybody and looking like he wanted to break something. I saw a pair of men from the Sault tribe, as well.

"Alex, what the hell is going on?" Ham said. "Nobody will talk to me. I came in this morning and the place was closed down. There were cops all over the place. They said my dad had already been arrested."

"We're all gonna work on this together," I said. "Jonathan, did you get hold of the bondsman?"

"He's on his way," he said. "I figured Ham could use him, too."

"You'll need ten percent of whatever the bail is," I said. "Can you both do that? If not, I can help out."

"Whatever it is," Jonathan said, "I'll get it."

"Same for me," Ham said.

"You might want to ask those gentlemen over there about Gill," I said. "But I don't imagine they'll need a bondsman. The tribe will probably bail him out."

"God knows they have enough casino money," Ham said.

I let that one go.

"Did you reach Jackie's lawyer?"

"I did," Jonathan said. "He's on his way, too."

"Okay, then both of you guys better just sit tight here. I don't know how long they'll be in there, but it'll be a while before the bail is set."

"What are you gonna do?" Jonathan said.

"I'm gonna find an old friend," I said. "And talk to him about a videotape."

Chapter Ten

I drove the few blocks from the City-County building to Leon's office on Ashmun Street, parked the truck on the street, and climbed the narrow set of stairs to his office. Through the window I could see he wasn't there. There was no sign on his door indicating when he might be back.

I went back down to the street, got in the truck, and thought about what to do next. Leon's probably with Vargas, I thought. I wasn't sure I was ready to knock on Vargas's door and ask for him. The hell with it, I thought. If that's what it takes, I'll do it.

I drove over to the east side of town, to Vargas's house on the river. There was a blue Miata in the driveway, a Saab in the open garage. Leon's little piece of crap red car was nowhere to be seen.

Okay, so I don't have to go knock on Vargas's door, I thought. Not yet, anyway.

Instead I went back through the middle of town and caught I-75 going south. A few miles later, I got off at the Rosedale exit, made my way over to Leon's house, near the Chippewa County Airport.

As soon as I was on his street, I saw him come out the front door of his house. He put a briefcase into his car, and then got in himself. He started to back down his driveway. I pulled the truck in behind him, blocking his way.

I got out of the truck. He didn't move. He stayed in the car, staring straight ahead. His windows were already down, so I didn't have to rap my knuckles on them to get his attention. He was not only wearing a tie today—the man actually owned a suit.

"Leon," I said. "We have to talk."

"I have to go meet my client."

"You can do that. Right after we talk."

"There's nothing to talk about, Alex."

"Oh yes," I said. I leaned my forearms on the hood of his car, my face not more than twelve inches from his. "Yes, there is."

"What are you going to do?" he said. "Are you going to assault me now?"

"Why would I do that?"

"Because you're upset. That's what you do when you're upset."

"Leon, I don't assault my friends."

He looked up at me for the first time. "I'm sorry it worked out this way," he said. "The other day, when you came to see me, I had been sitting in that chair for two hours straight. I was trying to figure out the right thing to do."

"And you decided what?"

"That I had to give the tape to my client. I expected him to take it right to the police. It looks like he waited a day to do it, but eventually he did."

"What else have you done for your client? Did you search my cabin, for instance?"

"No," he said. "Of course not."

"Somebody did."

"I wouldn't do that, Alex. Even if he asked me."

"Does he have anybody else working for him?"

"Not that I know of."

"Okay, never mind," I said. "It's not important. So what's on the tape?"

"I can't tell you."

"You don't have to tell me," I said. "You can show me."

"I gave the original to Vargas," he said. "I don't have it."

"Show me the copy."

"Who says there's a copy?"

"You just did," I said. "You wouldn't have said 'original' if there wasn't a copy."

He shook his head. "I can't show it to you, Alex."

"Okay, I guess I'll have to assault you then."

He looked up at me again.

"I'm kidding," I said. "That's not why you're going to show it to me."

"Why am I?"

I let out a long breath. Two squirrels chased each other up the tree in Leon's front yard. "Jackie's in jail," I said. "He's down there right now, waiting for Maven to get through with him, then he'll be arraigned, and bail will be set. Assuming this isn't all just a nightmare, there'll be a trial. Whatever's on that tape will come out then. I'll be in that courtroom, watching it along with everybody else . . ."

I let that one hang. After a moment, Leon cleared his throat and said, "And?"

"And nothing. None of that's going to happen. You don't want it to happen, for one thing. Because you know it's not right. To hell with Vargas and Maven and anybody else. You know they couldn't have done this."

"That's not up to me," he said.

"Yes, it is. It is up to you. You have the tape. You're gonna show it to me right now. Not because I'll beat you up if you don't. Not because you're my friend, or because you used to be my partner. None of that matters. The reason you're going to show me that tape is because *it's the right thing to do*. I can't help those men unless you help me first, Leon. You don't have to make me a copy of it. You don't have to tell anybody about it. You just show me the tape once and then I'll leave."

"You make it sound so simple," he said. "It's the right thing to do. Like that's all there is to it. Never mind my responsibility to my paying client. Or the oath I had to sign about cooperating with the police and the courts. None of that counts, huh?"

"Right this second it doesn't," I said. "And you know it."

He thought about that one. "Alex, get out of the way," he finally said.

"I'm not leaving."

"Get out of the way of the door," he said. "So I can get out."

I let him out of the car. I followed him into his house. He brought his briefcase with him.

"Where's Eleanor and the kids?" I said.

"They're at a birthday party. I would have gone, but things are a little crazy right now."

"Tell me about it. She's worried about you, you know."

"I know."

He led me into the family room, where his television sat in the middle of a wall unit, one of those huge, particle board things with the imitation wood grain. There was one VCR on top of the television, a second one on the floor.

"I just finished making one more copy," he said. "I was on my way over to Vargas to deliver it. I had given him the original—it was actually a compact VHS tape—about this big." He showed me about three inches between his thumb and forefinger. "You ever see one?"

"No."

"You put it in an adapter box to play it on a regular VHS machine. Vargas tried to make his own copy of it, but he couldn't figure out how to do it. You see, you need to play the tape on one VCR, and then feed it into the second . . ."

"Okay," I said. "Skip that part. If I ever need to do it myself, I'll call you."

"Yeah, well, this is actually a copy of the original," he said, holding up a regular VHS tape. "So I had to make him a copy of a copy. I don't know how good the quality is going to be. I suppose I should give him the good copy. Anyway, here it is . . ." He turned the television on, put the tape into one of the VCRs, then hit the play button.

After a few seconds of snow, an image came onto the screen. It was jumpy and hard to focus on. It was tilting, too, from one side to the other, enough to make you seasick if you watched it too long. It was a hallway of some sort. There were many doors.

"It's a hotel?"

"Yeah, sorry about all the movement here. I'm walking while I take this. I'm gonna just fast-forward through this . . ."

"No," I said. "Let me see the whole thing."

"There's no reason to," he said. "Let me just—"

"I want to see the whole thing, Leon. Just let it go."

He rubbed his forehead. "Oh God. All right."

"What's happening now?"

"This is the Best Western," he said. "Down on the loop. I followed Vargas's wife there. Swanson's car was already in the parking lot. I've seen it a lot lately, so I certainly recognized it."

A face appeared on the screen, taking up every inch of it. I didn't recognize Leon at first—probably because I've never seen him with curly black hair and a long mustache.

"Leon, what the hell are you wearing?"

"I'm in disguise."

Before I could say anything else, Leon's urgent whisper began on the tape. "This is Leon Prudell at the Best Western Hotel in Sault Ste. Marie, Michigan. I've observed Mrs. Cynthia Vargas checking in at the front desk, and then coming here to room one-seventeen." The camera swung back to the hallway, the doors passing by as Leon made his way to the room in question.

"What are you doing, a newscast?"

"I'm just establishing time and place," he said. "It's important if it ever becomes evidence."

"You're really walking down the hallway with a video camera?"

"No, not really," he said. "It was hidden in my wristwatch."

"Your wristwatch? Are you kidding me?"

"There's a wire running up my sleeve," he said. "It connects to the recording unit, which is hidden under my jacket."

"I don't believe this," I said. "Why does he need a video? If you've already caught her sneaking off with Swanson . . ."

"Mr. Vargas is sure his wife will be filing for divorce soon. With Swanson as her lawyer, no doubt."

"You told me yourself once that Michigan is a strong common-property state. Fooling around on your husband isn't going to change much when they split up the assets, is it?"

"I told Mr. Vargas that," he said. "He didn't seem to mind. I think he wanted the tape for other reasons."

"Such as?"

"Such as embarrassing the hell out of both of them at the divorce proceedings."

On the TV, the camera swung to Leon's face again. "I am standing in front of room one-seventeen. I will attempt to document the presence of both Douglas Swanson and Cynthia Vargas in this room."

"What are you wearing there?" I said.

He cleared his throat. "I'm dressed as a room service waiter. I'm bringing them a complimentary bottle of champagne."

"Oh my God . . ."

"Here we go," he said, pointing at the screen. "Here's where things sort of go haywire."

The hotel room door opened. Counselor Swanson appeared, wearing a white bathrobe. He did not look happy to be interrupted. "What is it?"

"Champagne, sir. With our compliments." The voices all sounded distant.

"We didn't order any champagne."

"With our compliments, sir. It's on the house."

"For what? Why do we get free champagne?"

There was a voice in the background. You could barely hear it. It sounded female, and just from context you assumed she was asking who was at the door.

"It's a man with champagne!" Swanson turned to look back into the room. As he did, he pulled the door slightly more open. There was a flash of white in the background, another bathrobe. Then something obscured the image, taking up the whole screen. There was the sound of impact, then of someone yelling. The camera swung around wildly, then seemed to settle on the ceiling. After a couple of seconds, the screen went black.

"What happened?" I said.

"I tried to get a good shot of Mrs. Vargas," he said. "I turned the camera in my watch and dumped the tray right on Swanson's head."

"Leon, on another day, this would be the funniest tape I've ever seen."

"I'm so glad it has entertainment value," he said. "Unfortunately, I didn't get a solid shot of Mrs. Vargas. All it does is make me look like an idiot."

"So what happens next here?"

After a few more seconds of blackness, another image came onto the screen. It was nighttime, but with all the lights he had on, there was no mistaking whose house we were looking at. Leon hit the pause button and froze the image.

"Let me tell you what's going on here," he said. "Before you see this."

"That's Vargas's house," I said. "This is the night that—"

"Yes. This is still the same night. After my little mishap, I figured I'd check in with Mr. Vargas, see what he wanted me to do next. I called him on the cell phone again. It rang a couple of times, but then the signal went out. I knew he was *dying* to hear how I made out, so I tried again. But I didn't get through. The battery on my phone was just about dead—damned thing never did hold a charge—so I figured I'd just call him from a pay phone, although I didn't want to go back into the hotel to do it. Anyway, I'm trying to think where the nearest pay phone would be. Then I figured what the hell, I was ten minutes away from his house."

"So you drove up."

"I parked in the driveway. Right behind this Ford Explorer you see here."

"That's O'Dell's. He gave me a ride in it yesterday, in fact."

"It's O'Dell's vehicle, yes. Anyway, just before I got to the front door, I heard a loud noise, like a window breaking. Instead of knocking, I went around to the side of the house. I saw a telescope flying out one of the back windows."

"You were there," I said, "when it was all going down. Did you call the police?"

"Well, I didn't have my phone right there with me, assuming it would even work. The first thing I did was, I snuck around to the back porch, and tried to get a look inside. I saw a man come right up to the window. It looked like he was wearing a surgical mask. And he had a gun."

"Yes. The two men who stayed downstairs— while they were waiting, one went and looked out the back window."

"I ducked down so he wouldn't see me. Then I made my way back to the car. The first thing I did was back out of the driveway and down the street a little bit. I turned the lights out. Then I tried the phone again. It didn't work, Alex. It just didn't work. You know that stupid little cord that plugs into your cigarette lighter? The one that recharges your batteries?"

"Yeah, I've got one."

"I've got a two thousand dollar miniature video camera hidden in my wristwatch, but I don't have the cord that recharges my cell phone."

"So what did you do?"

"I knew I had to get to a phone. But I had this idea. I took my watch off, and I put it on the dashboard, so it was pointed at the house. There was another house just down the road—I figured I could get out and run down there . . ."

"And your magic little watch would record whatever happened at Vargas's house. At least on the outside . . ."

"Exactly. So I take the watch off, and put it on the dash, get it pointed just right . . . And then they come out. Just as I'm getting ready to open the door."

"The three men?"

"Three of them, yes. So now I have a choice to make. Do I wait for them to leave, and then go call the police? Or do I follow them?"

"Oh Leon, you're not serious . . ."

"It was a gut call at that point," he said. "I knew you'd be calling the cops yourselves, once they were gone. I thought the best thing I could do for everybody was to follow them."

"Okay, so this has to be their getaway car here, right?" I pointed to the car on the left side of the driveway, right behind Jackie's Lincoln.

"No, I believe that's Gill LaMarche's car," he said.

"Okay, that makes sense. He got there after we did. But if that's not their car, where is it?"

He hit the pause button again and set the whole thing in motion. What I was about to see would make my head spin.

At a distance of thirty or forty yards, with less than ideal lighting, it was hard to make out exactly what was happening. But not so hard that you couldn't get the general idea. Three men leaving the house—maybe they still had the masks on, maybe they didn't. It didn't matter, because you wouldn't see their faces anyway. All three of them got into the Ford Explorer, the lights came on, the vehicle backed out of the driveway, and took off down the street.

"That's O'Dell's car," I said. "What are they doing?"

"They're driving away, Alex. Of course, I didn't know at the time that it was O'Dell's car. I was just glad that my car wasn't parked right behind them anymore."

"This doesn't make any sense. Did they steal it?"

"Did he happen to mention that his car was stolen?"

"No, he didn't. And like I said, he had it yesterday, when he drove me over to the marina."

On the videotape, Leon's car was in motion now. O'Dell's Explorer was about a hundred yards ahead. You could see the arc of the headlights, the glowing red taillights, the lighted rear license plate.

"Wait a minute," I said, watching the screen. "Who says that's O'Dell's car, anyway? You know what? Come to think of it, I don't even remember seeing his car in the driveway when we got there." I thought about it. I put myself back in Jackie's car, pulling into the driveway, wondering why I was coming to this stranger's house to play poker. I open the passenger's side door and step out . . .

"No, I'm almost positive," I said. "O'Dell was already there when we got there. But I don't think his car was there. That's not his car they're driving, Leon."

"Keep watching," he said.

The image on the screen moved from one pool of light to the next. As the car ahead passed under each street lamp, it confirmed that Leon was following the same car, and doing a good job of it.

"Where are they going?" I said.

"You'll see," he said. "Soon."

I looked over at him. He was sitting very still, watching the tape with no expression on his face.

"Here it is," he finally said, as the brake lights on the Explorer glowed bright red. The vehicle was pulling into a parking lot.

"Where is this?"

"Look closely," he said. "Do you recognize it?"

I looked. It was a two-story building. There were beer signs glowing in the windows. "That's O'Dell's place."

"Yes it is. And here's where I had to make another decision. Watch what happens."

Two men got out, opening up both passenger's side doors. I still couldn't see their faces, although it looked like they had taken the masks off. The two men got into a car parked right next to the Explorer. Before they could even start it, the white reverse lights on the Explorer came on, and it started to back up.

"Our men are separating here," Leon said. "So who do I follow?"

"The Explorer," I said.

"That's what I figured. It's still the 'object' vehicle. I did make sure to get the plate number on the other car, though."

"You gave that to the police, too."

"Yes," he said. "It was an Ontario plate, by the way."

"I thought one of the men might be Canadian. So I'm not surprised. Did they trace the number yet?"

"I'm sure they have," he said. "Why don't you ask Maven about it?"

"I'll do that. I'll bring it up the next time we go out drinking together."

"In any case, we lose both those men here. They probably just went over the bridge. I continue following the original driver. And here's where I'll start fast-forwarding a little bit. It's just more of me following him." He pushed the button and everything started flying past.

"You taped every second of you following him?"

"I didn't want a break in the tape," he said. "It's a stronger document that way, in case it becomes evidence."

I gave him a look. I had become absorbed in watching the tape, and had forgotten about the implications. Hearing the word 'evidence' brought it all back.

"Okay, here's stop number two," he said. "Recognize where we are?"

A huge building came into view, with a lot of

lights and the distinctive triangular design on the roofline. "That's the Kewadin Casino," I said.

"Yes. We're going to go to a private residence here, just a couple of blocks away."

There was a street lined with houses, the Explorer turning into a driveway.

"I'm gonna pull up a few houses down, like I'm parking on the street. As you can see, the driver's getting out to do something, but it won't take long."

It happened just as Leon said. The door opened, the driver got out, went to the side of the house, then returned to the vehicle and backed it out the driveway.

"You never got a good look at his face?" I said.

"Never did."

"I don't suppose I have to ask you whose house that was."

"Gill LaMarche," he said.

"I've got a bad feeling about what's going to happen next."

"I'll fast-forward again," he said. "This is a long haul, all the way out of town."

"Just tell me, Leon. His next stop is Jackie's?"

"That's where he went next, yes. Do you want to see it?"

"Yes," I said. "Keep going."

We watched the whole trip in fast motion, out M-28 to M-123, all the way up to Paradise. He put it back to normal speed just as the Explorer hit town.

"What time was it at this point?" I said.

"Maybe midnight, or a little after."

"So we're still at Vargas's house, talking to the police."

The Explorer came to a stop in Jackie's parking lot, over by the side where Jackie parks his own car. As the driver got out, he paused for a moment and looked around the place.

"You can almost see his face here," I said. "Damn it, if there was only more light."

"I think he's getting a little spooked at this point," Leon said. "It's not easy to follow somebody all over Chippewa County."

The man disappeared from view for a short time, maybe fifteen seconds. Then he was back in the vehicle and on his way.

"What did he just do there?" I said.

"It looks like he's just dropping something off," Leon said. "But that's just what we're assuming. We don't actually see it happen."

"If he did drop something off, he must have just left it on Jackie's doorstep. He didn't have time to go into the house." Which didn't seem to help Jackie too much, not if whatever was dropped off was found underneath his bed.

"I'm trying to be careful here," he said, as both vehicles left Paradise and went back on the lonely stretch of road. "I don't want to give myself away, so I'm staying back a little bit."

"Where does Santa Claus go next?" I said.

"Well, a couple of things happen here. First of all, the tape runs out. Those little compact VHS tapes only hold so much. So we're not going to see much of anything else here. In fact, right about now . . ."

The screen went blank.

"But you kept following him?"

"Yes, I did. But like I said, I gave him some more distance this time. A couple of other cars got between us. I lost him for a while, so I figured I'd go right back to O'Dell's. When I got there, the Explorer was parked in the lot. But there was no sign of the driver."

"The place was still open?"

"Yeah, I think it was around one-thirty."

"Did you go inside and look around?"

"I did, yes. There might have been, I don't know, ten or twelve men in there. But I had no idea who I was looking for."

"Who was behind the bar? O'Dell's wife? His son?"

"Both of them were. I knew it wasn't either of them driving the car. It was definitely a man, for one thing. And O'Dell's son is what, six foot six?"

"Thereabouts."

"It wasn't him."

"So you gave this tape to Vargas when? Two days ago?"

"Yes. I told you—"

"It's all right, Leon. You don't have to give me the speech again. I understand, you did what you thought you had to do. You gave Vargas the tape, and I understand he asked you some questions about me."

"You were on the list, Alex. You were there that night."

"He thinks I was in on this," I said. "He thinks I

was the inside man. Did you know that?"

"That's news to me," he said. "I'll have to persuade him otherwise."

"While you're persuading him, why don't you persuade him that this whole thing was a setup? I'll have to talk to Bennett about his vehicle, but I'm sure something's not adding up there. And as for Jackie and Gill, hell, that guy could have just been planting evidence. Even if Jackie did take it into his house, so what? It's an honest mistake. I still don't even know what it was they found. That'll be the first thing I ask him when I see him."

"Who'd want to set them up like that?"

"Off the top of my head, how about Swanson? He knew about the safe, he knew Vargas would be there all night—hell, he's already got his wife in a hotel room, why not make the evening complete? And because he's not a complete fool, he makes it look like Bennett, Jackie, and Gill were behind it."

"That seems a little far-fetched."

"It's less far-fetched than those three guys really doing it. What do you say we go talk to Swanson, and see how he reacts when we lay that on him? If he passes the test, we can try Kenny."

"How are 'we' going to be doing anything, Alex?"

"I thought you might want to be my partner again," I said. "Help me find out what really happened."

"You mean, help undo the mess I've already made for your friends?"

I looked at him. "This isn't about you, Leon. This

is about Vargas. And about the police having the wrong guys in that jail."

"Vargas is still my client, Alex."

"Your client is probably a little pissed off that the police didn't pick me up, too. I'm fighting back, Leon. Whose side are you gonna be on?"

"I want to get to the bottom of this, too," he said. "I'm not on anybody's side."

"Meaning I'm on my own."

"Hey, I showed you the tape, didn't I?"

"Do one more thing," I said. "Write down all the information you've got on Swanson and Kenny, will you? For God's sake, what's Kenny's last name, anyway?"

"It's Heiden."

"I'm sure you've got their phone numbers. They're on the master list of suspects, after all. Right under McKnight."

"If you really want to talk to them, I can't stop you."

"And when you see your client today, give him a message for me, okay?"

"What's that?"

"Tell him that whoever really ripped him off is laughing at all of us."

Chapter Eleven

From Leon's house, it was a twenty minute trip back to the City-County building in the Soo. I thought about him the whole way, what he had said, and not said. I had cost him his job once. Now that he had finally set himself up as a private investigator again, here I was asking him to dump his only paying customer. I suppose I couldn't blame him for refusing to throw away his lifelong dream, even though I did feel like wringing his neck.

When I got back to the police station, I saw Bennett and his son coming out the door. Bennett was blinking in the sunlight, like he had been working in a coal mine all morning.

I caught up to them before they got into Ham's car. "Bennett, are you all right? Where's Jackie?"

"Jackie and Gill already left," he said. "I think I got the extra-special treatment today."

"They made bail already?"

"The judge was already here," he said. He looked

at the residue of fingerprint ink on his fingers, and then wiped his hands on his pants. "He arraigned them and set ten-thousand-dollar bonds. Mine was twenty."

"Did you have a lawyer here?"

"Why would I need a lawyer?"

"Because you got arrested, Bennett. That's why you need a lawyer."

He kept looking at his hands and then wiping them on his pants again. It wasn't doing much good. "I don't need a lawyer to tell them they're full of shit. I can do that all by myself. Alex, I could really use a beer about now. How about you?"

"Let me just ask you a couple of questions," I said.

Bennett looked over at his son. "More questions," he said. "Just what I need."

"It's important," I said. "I'm just trying to help out here."

"I know, Alex. Go ahead."

"What did the police ask you about?"

"I seem to recall my Explorer coming up in conversation," he said. "Like about seven hundred times."

"Did they tell you why they were so interested in it?"

"They gave me the general idea. It sounds like my car had just as much fun as I had that night. It's impounded, by the way."

"What about your house? Did they find anything there?"

"No," he said. "They just took the car."

"When Jackie and I got to the game, your car wasn't there. Am I right?"

"That's right."

"How did you get there?"

"Usually, Gill comes and picks me up. But that night, he called me and told me he might be a little late. So I said, no problem, I'll have my wife drop me off, she was coming over this way anyway. Gill was still planning on giving me a ride home afterwards."

"You never drive to poker games yourself?"

"No, Alex, not if I can help it. My night vision isn't so hot these days. And if I happen to have a drink or two while I'm playing, well . . . Let's just say as a bar owner I've seen enough people with no business getting behind the wheel."

"All right, that makes sense," I said. "It explains a lot. Now, is it possible that somebody else was driving your car that night?"

He looked at his son again. "Yeah, this is what I tried to get across to those guys in there," he said. "I'm not sure if they bought it or not. You see, my wife and I have this bad habit of leaving the keys underneath the driver's seat. We used to have two sets of keys, but we lost one of them. Which was a pain because we'd both be busy doing stuff around the bar, and one of us would have to run out and get something, you know, so we just started leaving the keys in the car."

"You go to the hardware store," Ham said. "They make you a copy. It takes ten minutes."

"Thank you, Mr. Smart Guy," he said. "I didn't

know that. They can actually copy keys, huh?"

"I'm just saying."

"I know I should have gotten a new key, okay? I just never got around to it."

"All right, all right," I said. "Did anybody else know that you and your wife were doing this?"

"Hell, I don't know. I suppose I've mentioned it to people before, you know, friends in the bar."

"How about the poker gang?"

He thought about that one. "Yes," he said. "As a matter of fact, I did. I remember, because somebody told me that was a great way to get the car stolen, and I said something like, fine with me, I wouldn't have to make the payments anymore."

"Okay," I said. "That could be important."

"Are you thinking . . ." he said. "Wait a minute, are you thinking that somebody else from the poker gang used my car that night? Or else they got *somebody else* to use my car that night? 'Cause obviously they couldn't have used it themselves, not if they were there. Except for Swanson, I mean."

"What about Swanson?" I said.

"Swanson? Are you kidding?"

"I'm just asking. You tell me. Could he have done this?"

Bennett put his hands on the hood of Ham's car, staring at his reflection in the finish. "Swanson?"

"Watch the car," Ham said. "You're gonna get that ink all over it."

Bennett took one look at his son and then tuned him out. "Swanson set us up?" he said.

"*Somebody* set you up, Bennett. You and Jackie

and Gill. I'd like to find out who did it."

He looked up at me. "How are you gonna do that?"

"I have no idea," I said. "But that never stopped me before."

"I really need that beer, Alex. Come on over to my place, we'll talk about this."

"I'm gonna take a pass right now," I said. "I'll catch up with you later."

"Okay, Alex, you do that. But make sure you stop by later, you hear me?"

"I will, Bennett. You guys go on home."

He looked up at the building. "You heard the man," he said to his son. "Let's get away from this place."

I sat in the truck and watched them leave. I stayed there a while, thinking everything through. It seemed like a high-risk move to add to the whole equation, "borrowing" Bennett's car for the getaway.

Or was it? They knew Bennett would be at the poker game. They knew his wife would be covering at the bar. They knew that the keys would be in the car, or at least they knew it was a good bet. With Bennett's car, not only do they maximize the setup, there's nothing to trace back to them, no danger of their own car getting stranded at the scene if something goes wrong. Hell, Leon had almost done that himself. Imagine coming out and seeing your getaway car blocked in the driveway?

But damn, the whole thing still sounds so professional, like somebody who really knows what he's doing, covering all the bases.

No kidding, Alex. Think about the way they acted in the house. The coordination, the disguises—they did have a master plan, and they executed it perfectly.

Now all you've gotta do is figure out who made it all happen.

I took out the piece of paper Leon had given me, with the phone numbers for Douglas Swanson and Kenny Heiden. I tried Swanson's office number first, got his secretary and found out he'd be in court most of the day. I told her I'd call back later. When she asked me for my name, I hung up.

Then I tried Kenny. There was no answer at his home number—no surprise at this time of day. I told him I wanted to ask him a couple of questions, and to please call me when he got in.

Finally, I called Gill, and left the same message.

It actually occurred to me to call Chief Maven, ask him about that Canadian license plate. That's when I knew I was going overboard. Just take it easy, I told myself. If you get impatient, you're gonna drive yourself crazy. You've done what you can so far. Let the rest come to you.

One more call, I thought. Thank God for cell phones, even if you only use them once every two months. Even though I knew I'd be seeing him soon, I called Jackie's number. Jonathan answered.

"How's he doing?" I said. "Is he there?"

"He left, Alex. He said he was gonna go walk on the beach."

"Walk on the beach? Since when does Jackie

walk on the beach? Since when does he walk any-where?"

"Hey, that's what he said. I figured he had a tough enough day, he can do whatever he wants."

"Did he say anything about it? What happened at the station?"

"Not a word."

"Did he happen to mention what they found in the house?"

"No, Alex. He's not talking about it."

"We'll see about that," I said. "When he comes back, tell him I'll be there in a little while. Don't let him go anywhere else."

"If I tell him that, he'll go back out again. Just on general principle."

"Sit him down and make him a drink," I said. "I'm sure he can use one. I'm on my way."

I hung up the phone and threw it on the passen-ger's seat. Just as I was pulling out of the parking lot, it rang. I picked it up.

"Alex, this is Gill."

"I'm glad you called me back," I said. "How did it go?"

"Pretty routine," he said. "These felony arrests are getting monotonous."

"I'm glad you can joke about it. Any chance of me asking you a couple of questions?"

"I don't see why not."

"You know, I'm still in town here. I was gonna go back to Paradise, but why don't I swing by your place first?"

"Do you know where it is?"

I thought about the videotape. "Yeah," I said. "I know the way."

"You've never been here before, have you?"

"No, never," I said. "But I've seen the movie."

You can see the Kewadin Casino from halfway across town. It's easily the biggest building in the Soo, and it sits over on the east side, on land that was carved out of the city and given to the Sault tribe. As I drove past it, I couldn't help noticing how many cars were parked in the several acres of asphalt surrounding the place. There was one special parking lot on the side, just for RVs—there had to be a couple hundred of them. All the summer people who came through here, almost all of them ended up at the casino at least once.

There was a health clinic right across the street, then the Big Bear Arena, all fruits of the casino money. The whole scene looked a lot better in the bright sunlight, as opposed to the grainy dark video I had watched in Leon's living room. I followed the route I remembered seeing, turning after the casino into a new neighborhood they had built in its shadow. I knew a lot of the people who worked at the casino lived in these new houses, including Gill.

Gill was sitting outside on his front porch when I got there. He had a big glass jug filled with lemonade sitting on the table waiting for me. I sat in the empty chair, looked out at the street with him for a few minutes, and at the casino a half-mile away. We sat in the shade, drinking lemonade as a soft breeze came down the street to us. It would have been a perfect afternoon if not for the fact that Gill was sitting here only because he had made bail. I almost didn't want to mention it. But that's why I was there.

"What did the police ask you?" I finally said.

"They didn't get the chance to ask me much of anything," he said. Looking down at the remains of the ink on his hands, he wiped his pants with them, just as Bennett had done. "My lawyer was there practically before I was. They did most of the talking to him."

"What did they say to him?"

"They wanted to know who did the actual breaking and entering," he said. "They wanted the men with the guns. They made it clear to my lawyer that any cooperation on my part would be very much appreciated."

"What did your lawyer say to that?"

"He said that I would love to cooperate in any way possible, but that I had nothing to give them."

"What did they find in your house?"

He looked at me for a moment. "They found some artifacts," he said. "Apparently, they came from Vargas's house."

"That's all they found? No money?"

"Just the artifacts, Alex. They were on my porch when I got home that night—the night everything happened."

"What did you do with them?"

He looked back out at the street. "Well, you've got to understand a couple of things. First of all, I wasn't thinking clearly. I had been held hostage, lying on the floor, at gunpoint. . . . Well, you know what I'm talking about, of course. You went through the same thing. By the time the police got done with us, it was what, after one in the morning? When I finally got home, there was this box next to my side door. To tell you the truth, and this is what my lawyer told the police chief today, I honestly had no idea where it had come from. Remember, Alex, all of this had just happened. And here's this box by my door when I got home. I assumed someone had left it there that day, and I just hadn't seen it. I don't go out that side door too often. Or else they had left it that evening, when I was out. I certainly wasn't thinking that it was stolen from Vargas's house. It felt like I had just been there five minutes before. How would it even get to my house so quickly?"

"So you open the box . . ."

"Yes."

"You didn't recognize the artifacts? I mean, you'd seen them before, right? That night, when he gave me the tour, you said you had already done it."

He let out a small laugh. "He gave me the tour, maybe three months ago, the last time we played at his house. Now that I've had time to think about it, yes, I suppose I should have recognized that stuff. It just didn't stand out in my mind."

"I would have thought him having that stuff would have really bothered you."

He laughed again. "Alex, let me tell you something. All that Ojibwa stuff he had up there? It was essentially worthless. A couple of pieces were interesting, although they weren't in very good shape. I suppose the museum at the community college would take them, but I'm sure they wouldn't exhibit them. They were too damaged."

"You're kidding me."

"You know the best part? You remember that oar he had in his case, right in the middle?"

"Yeah, the one that looked really old," I said. "With the carvings."

"That oar was not old, first of all. You take a wooden oar and you drop it in fresh water, it's going to disintegrate. Salt water is a different story, but fresh water, after one year it's going to look like that oar in his display case. And those carvings? Please, Alex. It looked like somebody had been horsing around with a knife, some kid maybe, or some old guy who was sitting around on his porch all summer. Sort of like me." He smiled at that, and stopped talking long enough to take a long sip of lemonade. "Of course, I don't sit around ruining my oars with fake carvings."

"Was that oar in the package you got?"

"I would have recognized that oar," he said. "And gotten another good laugh at it. No, it was falling apart in that case, I remember. I don't imagine you could move it."

"This is good," I said. "I'm glad you're telling me this."

"You know what's *really* good," he said. "Imagining that Vargas paid somebody a ton of money for that oar, thinking it was some sort of authentic Ojibwa relic."

"I see what you mean," I said. "But what I'm

thinking is, this proves you had nothing to do with this. Because why would you? The stuff's worthless."

"Worthless in a material sense," he said. "It did belong to somebody. But yes, you're right. It would not have been worth stealing."

"And the fact that somebody would leave it at your house can only mean one thing . . ."

He looked at me with those dark, careful eyes, waiting for me to finish my thought.

"You were set up," I said. "Whoever did this thought it would look incriminating to you, to have this stuff found on your premises."

He thought about that one, slowly shaking his head. "There was someone here again," he said. "Last night."

"Do you know who it was?"

"I was at the casino," he said. "My neighbor saw somebody, right here on this porch. We all look out for each other, you understand."

"What was this person doing? Did your neighbor get a good look at him?"

"No, he didn't. He moved like a man, that's all he knows. He said he was here one moment, and then gone. He just disappeared."

"Something strange is going on here," I said. "Somebody's playing games with us. With *all* of us."

"Cat and mouse," he said. "And you want to know who the cat is, don't you . . ."

I looked him in the eye. "That's the idea."

"I know why you're doing this. Jackie is the best friend you have in this world."

"I'm doing it for all three of you."

He smiled. "It's okay, Alex. No matter why, I want you to know how much I appreciate it."

"Don't thank me until I get somewhere."

"I have no doubt you will," he said. "Jackie talks about you all the time. He says you're the most stubborn man who ever lived."

"The pot calling the kettle black, that's what that is."

"Have you seen him since this morning?"

"No, not yet. I'll go there next."

"Tell him not to worry," he said. "Tell him he has a good friend watching out for him."

"I'll do that," I said. I thanked him again, and then I left, going back out past the casino, and then west, out of town, into the woods, heading back home to Paradise.

It was cat and mouse, like Gill said. And I had one more mouse to talk to.

Chapter Twelve

I tried Swanson again on the way to Paradise. His secretary must have recognized my voice, because she told me he was still in court and suggested maybe I'd like to leave a message this time instead of hanging up on her. I thought of saying something cute like, "Tell him it's his worst nightmare," but thought better of it. "Tell him Alex McKnight called," I said. "Tell him I really need to speak to him as soon as possible."

"Do you wish to engage his services in some way?"

"I don't need his services," I said. "Just some answers. Good day."

I hung up the phone, hoping she'd give him the message exactly as I said it. If he's suddenly unavailable for the next few weeks, that'll tell me a hell of a lot.

I was about to dial Kenny's number again, then remembered he probably hadn't even heard my first message yet. I put the phone down, told myself again to take it easy. Getting too anxious wouldn't help anybody.

I kept telling myself that as I rolled into Paradise and stopped at Jackie's place. I was surprised to see that it was open for business again, with the usual six or seven cars in the parking lot. The police invasion of that morning, just a few hours ago—if I hadn't seen it myself, I wouldn't have believed it.

And Jackie himself, standing behind the bar mixing a drink, didn't seem as if anything unusual had happened that day—until he looked at the fingerprint ink on his hands and tried to wipe it off with a towel.

"Tell me something, Alex," he said when he saw me. He was already putting a Canadian on the bar for me. "This gunk they use for the fingerprinting, why is it so hard to get off?"

I sat on a stool at the bar. "Jackie, are you all right?"

"What do they make it out of, Kryptonite?"

"Jackie . . ."

"If I use rubbing alcohol, will that work?"

I felt like reaching over the bar and grabbing the front of his apron. "Jackie," I said, slowly, "please tell me how you're doing."

"I'm fine," he said, finally looking me in the eye. "Don't worry about me."

"Your son told me you went for a walk on the beach."

"Did me a world of good, too. I'm gonna have to start doing it every day."

"Tell me what happened," I said.

"Can we talk about this later?"

"No, we can't."

He threw the towel down on the bar. "What do you want me to tell you? You know what happened. They came with a search warrant, they took me in . . ."

"What did they find here?"

"Stolen goods," he said. "They found stolen goods in my bedroom."

"Are you going to tell me what it was?"

"Do I have to?"

"Actually, I think I can guess," I said. "I just saw Gill, and he told me about the Indian artifacts somebody left on his doorstep. Turns out they were pretty much worthless, which tells me one thing."

"Yeah, what's that?"

"It had to be a setup. Somebody took the money, Jackie, and they made it look like you and Bennett and Gill were behind it. In your case, I'm guessing they left some kind of thing that people would naturally associate with you. Maybe something Scottish. Am I right?"

He looked at me for a moment. "Yes."

"What was it?"

"It was a mug," he said. "An old pewter mug."

"I think I remember it," I said. "In Vargas's display case. What, did it have something engraved on it?"

"It was the Royal Navy flag," he said. "And the Scapa Flow emblem on the other side. It's an old naval base in Scotland."

"And would you have any reason to steal that kind of thing?"

"It was pretty beat up," he said. "I don't imagine it would be worth much."

"Okay, then. That makes sense."

"If you say so."

"Why did you take it inside?" I said. "Didn't you realize it came from Vargas's house?"

"I don't know what I was thinking of, Alex. Obviously, I made a big mistake."

"What were you gonna do with it?"

"I wasn't sure," he said. "I might have asked *you* at some point. I never got the chance."

"What did they ask you at the police station? I hope you didn't say anything without your lawyer being there."

"Of course he was there. I'm not stupid. They told me we were looking at felonies, but that things would go a lot easier if I gave up the men who pulled off the heist. That's the word your friend Chief Maven used, the 'heist.' He's quite a character, isn't he. . . . And he has such a fond regard for you."

"He should be looking for whoever really did this," I said. "But I don't think he's going to. Did they set a trial date yet?"

"No. My lawyer thinks they'll hold it over our heads for a few days, try to get more information out of us."

"A few days . . ."

"I won't crack," he said. "I'll never rat out my accomplices."

"This isn't a joke, Jackie. You could go to jail over this. I want to talk to a few people, starting with Mr. Swanson."

"I'm sorry I got you involved in this, Alex. Now I want you to just let it go. I don't want you to go knocking people's heads around."

"Too late," I said. "Heads have already been knocked."

"Damn it, will you leave this alone, Alex? For once in your life, will you please just stay out of it?"

I took a hit off the bottle and put it back down. "When you came to my cabin the other night," I said, "and made me come out to play cards with you—why did you do that?"

"Because I'm dumb as a turnip."

"You did it to help me, Jackie. I was in a funk and you took it upon yourself to help me get out of it, whether I wanted you to or not. Now I'm returning the favor. I'm gonna help you, like it or not. And there's nothing you can do to stop me."

Later that afternoon, I called Swanson's office again. I was sitting at the bar, using Jackie's phone, so he got to hear me having it out with Swanson's secretary. Swanson wasn't in court anymore, she told me, but he was now having a late dinner meeting. Yes, she gave him my message. No, she didn't know when he might call me back. He was a very busy man. The tone in her voice told me she knew I was obviously not too busy myself, if I had the time to be bothering her every hour. When I asked if he might possibly be available at his home number, she gave me the iciest "no" I had ever heard. And I've gotten more than my share of those before. That was the end of the conversation.

When I hung up, Jackie stood there looking at the phone. "You're really going after Swanson," he said. "Based on what?"

"If he had nothing to do with it, he's got nothing to worry about," I said. "I just want to ask him some questions."

"What, you think he'll tell you if *did* have something to do with it?"

"You know what the hardest part of police work is?"

"Getting shot?"

"Aside from that," I said. "I mean as a general rule."

"Tell me."

"I'll tell you what it isn't first," I said. "The hardest part isn't figuring out who did the crime. In fact, that's usually the easiest part. The hardest part is making the case."

"Proving it, you mean."

"Yes. I knew a few detectives in my precinct, guys who had to build cases every day, and Lord knows I saw my share of guilty men. And women. Hell, mostly men, let's be honest. If Franklin and I were out in the car, we'd usually be the first on the scene. Somebody dead on the floor, or in bad shape at least. We'd get backup in there, and an ambulance, and eventually a couple of detectives would show up. We'd hand it off to them at that point. The guys I knew, they'd come right up and ask me. First question was what happened. Second question was who did it. Because most of the time, I'd know. Inside of five minutes, it would be obvious. I'd know, Franklin would know, the detective would know as soon as he looked at the guy. All you got to do is look him in the eye and say, 'Did you have anything to do with this?' And they say, 'No way, officer.' It might as well be written on their forehead."

"So you're telling me, all you're gonna have to do is ask Swanson if he did this, and no matter what he says, you'll know the truth, just like that."

"I don't know that for sure," I said. "But I've gotta give it a try, see what my gut says when I hear it from him."

"What if your gut is wrong? Hasn't that ever happened?"

"I suppose it has, once or twice."

"Once or twice? You want me to name a few times your gut's been wrong, just the ones I've seen myself? Hell, I could make a good living betting against your gut, Alex. I could buy a new car and retire to Florida."

"You're a funny man," I said. "I'm so glad you made bail today."

"Alex, I'm begging you. Take your gut and go home, will ya? Go back to being a hermit for a while. You're gonna get us all in even bigger trouble than we are already."

"All right, take it easy, Jackie. I know you've had a tough day . . ."

"I need some Rolaids," he said, patting his apron

pockets. "Where the hell did I put my Rolaids?"

Jackie's stomach didn't get any better that night. I didn't get any less pissed off at him for being a stubborn, ungrateful jackass. Right after dinner, he did the unthinkable, going upstairs and leaving his son in charge of the place. I couldn't remember him ever doing that, not when it was still light outside.

I stuck around for a while and helped Jonathan clean up the place. "Hey, I was going to ask you," I said, "have you noticed anything unusual around here? Anybody snooping around?"

"Like who?"

"I don't know. Just anybody out of the ordinary."

"No, can't say that I have. Although . . ."

"What?"

"It's nothing."

"What? What is it?"

"It was just today, when we got back here," he said. "I went in the back door and it was like, I don't know, something didn't seem right."

"You think somebody was in the house?"

"Well, remember, we had the cops all over the place this morning, so I figured I was still just kinda weirded out, you know what I mean? But when we got back, I'm walking up the steps, and I'm thinking, what is that smell? It was like cigar smoke or something."

"Cigar smoke."

"Yeah, but it was sweeter. You know what I mean?"

"Yeah, I think so."

"The door was locked," he said. "How could somebody get in here?"

"I don't know, Jonathan. I just don't know."

"Like we don't have enough going on around here," he said.

"I hear ya."

"I know one thing," he said. "I'm taking my deer rifle to bed with me tonight."

"Do me a favor," I said. "Keep it on the floor. Don't actually put it in your bed, okay?"

He laughed at that one. I helped him finish up, said good night, and then headed out.

As I was driving back up to my cabins, the cell phone rang. I hoped it was Swanson, calling to see what the hell I was harassing him about, but instead it was Kenny.

"I just came home and heard your message," he said. "What is it you wanted to talk to me about?"

"Thanks for calling me back," I said. "I just wanted to ask you a couple of questions about the other night."

"I don't understand. We were both there. What would I know that you don't already?"

"You know Vargas a lot better than I do," I said. "I was hoping you might have some better insight."

"I still don't understand, Alex."

"Are you aware that Jackie, Bennett, and Gill were all arrested today?"

There was a long silence on the line. "I knew *something* was up," he finally said. "Win was in a pretty strange mood today."

"He was at work today? You saw him?"

"Just for a few minutes. To tell you the truth, I've been avoiding him. Ever since that night, he's been driving everybody crazy."

I wanted to keep him talking, but I knew it would be better if I could ask him my questions in person. "Is there any chance of me coming down there?" I said. "I'd really appreciate it."

"You really want to come all the way down here?"

"You're in Bay Harbor, right? It'll give me a chance to see it for myself."

"I thought you hated this place."

"I've never been inside," I said. "I should give it a chance, right?"

"I don't think you're being straight with me, Alex . . ."

"Kenny, I've got three friends who got put in a jail cell today, and I'm just trying to help them. A few minutes of your time is all I ask."

"All right, all right," he said. "I'll be here tomorrow morning. Just go to the front gate. I'll give them your name."

"You don't have to work tomorrow?"

"I told you, he's driving everybody crazy. It's about time for a day off."

"Nine o'clock okay?"

"Make it ten," he said. "I'm going back out now. It might be a late night."

I thanked him and hung up. It's not the order I wanted to do this in, I thought. I'd rather get to Swanson first, work from the top down. But there'd still be plenty of time tomorrow to take another shot at him.

I stopped the truck in front of my cabin, sat there in the darkness for a while, listening to the engine cool down. The light from a three-quarter moon was shining through a break in the clouds, outlining the cabin against the woods behind it, this cabin built of pine logs thirty years ago by a retired auto worker and his baseball-player son. On this night it looked as lonely and forgotten as that abandoned railroad car over in Brimley.

A light was on inside. That wasn't right. I did not remember leaving a light on.

I got out of the truck, went to the front door. It was unlocked. I pushed it open. The sweet smell of smoke hung in the air.

I stepped inside. I waited to hear something, anything, the sound of a foot falling, a word spoken, even a breath. There was nothing. Nobody was there. At least not at that moment.

There, in the center of the room, on my table . . . There were papers all over it. I took a step closer. I saw all of my bank statements, the stubs from my disability pension payments, my life insurance, even the deed to my land. It was all there, all of my financial records, my whole life, laid out on the table. Next to the papers was a saucer from my kitchen, with five cold cigar butts on it. They were those sickly sweet little cigars, the kind my father would take hunting to keep the bugs away. Somebody had been sitting right here in this chair, looking through these papers, smoking these cigars and using this saucer as an ashtray.

And this time, he wanted me to know it.

Chapter Thirteen

The next morning, I got up early enough to scope out Swanson's office before heading down to Bay Harbor. I had put away all the papers the night before, and thrown away the cigar butts. But even with the windows open all night, there was still a hint of the smoke in the air. It was not a good way to start the day.

Swanson's office was in the business district of the Soo, not far from Leon's office. It was an old brick building on Augusta Street. Somebody had spent a few bucks making the outside of the place look like something out of the 1920's, right down to the ornate gaslight fixtures on either side of the front door. Either business was going well, or Swanson knew how to fake it.

It was just before eight o'clock, so I didn't figure to catch Swanson, not unless he was an early bird. I looked in through the door, hoping maybe I'd see his secretary, and really make her day by being the first person she got to talk to that morning. But no luck.

I headed south, settling in for the two-hour trip to Bay Harbor. I-75 took me down to the Mackinac Bridge, and then when I crossed into the Lower Peninsula, I headed southwest on M-31, right down the Lake Michigan shoreline. When I hit Petoskey, I saw Vargas's store in the middle of town. The sign read "The Vargas Custom Home Center." I could see a big whirlpool tub in one front window, and in the other some kitchen cabinets made from dark cherry. Everything else was green plants and gold finishings and lots of mirrors. I would have stopped in to say hello, and maybe to ask him about who might have been in my cabin the night before, but I had that ten o'clock appointment and I was running late.

When I left Petoskey behind me, it was just open shoreline again, with the lake on my right and the hills of sand and grass and low trees on my left. The sky was blue, the air was clear—it was a beautiful stretch of land to build on, no doubt about it. I couldn't blame them for dropping their new town here. And at the same time, I knew the awful truth. Vargas was right. As beautiful as it was down here, it was even better on Lake Superior.

It was only a matter of time.

With that cheery thought in my head, I came around the last bend in the road and hit Bay Harbor. The yacht club was first, with the white gatehouse made to look like a lighthouse. Then the golf club. And then, God help us all, the huge Bay Harbor

Equestrian Center high on the hill, overlooking everything.

It was all new money, that was the problem. I already knew all about old money. Hell, the Fulton family had enough money to buy this whole town. They had a cabin not far from Whitefish Point, in fact, if you can call a six-thousand-square-foot building a "cabin." The thing was, you never saw it. There was an unmarked road, at least a mile long, before you even knew it was there.

I had heard of a place, out on the western side of the Upper Peninsula, called the Huron Mountain Club. The Fultons, and people like them, automotive money from Detroit, *old money*, they'd go to the club, do their hunting and fishing. You never saw them. Hell, I wasn't sure I could even find the club if my life depended on it.

That was the difference. Old money has always been around. They just know enough to be discreet about it. New money has to flaunt it. They have to put it right in your face. That's what I was thinking as I passed the equestrian center and looked for the right entrance to get to Kenny's place. Bay Harbor was new money at its worst.

When I found the entrance, I pulled in and stopped at the gatehouse. It was surrounded by flowers and was so white it looked like it had been painted that morning. A man in a uniform came walking out. It said "Bay Harbor Security" on his hat.

"Good morning," I said. "I'm here to see Kenny Heiden."

The man looked my truck over.

"A hundred and forty thousand miles," I said. "And still going strong. It's a lot more dependable than my Rolls Royce."

He gave me a look. I was really making his day. "Your name, sir?"

"Alex McKnight."

He looked on his clipboard. "Mr. Heiden is number forty-two," he said. "Take a left and go down about halfway. The house will be on your right."

I thanked the man, waited for him to press his button and raise the big white stick in front of me, and then I rolled through. As I looked back in my rearview mirror, I couldn't help wondering if he was calling in the surveillance team. Dilapidated truck heading for unit forty-two, make sure he leaves without incident.

On my way to Kenny's place, I passed a few million dollars worth of houses on either side of the street. Every house was some sort of neo-Victorian, each more elaborate than the last, with lots of windows facing the lake. I saw one man outside his house, washing a black Mercedes. He barely glanced up at me as I passed him, probably thought I was there to work on somebody's yard.

Kenny's house was as grandiose as the others on the street. He answered the door wearing blue jeans and a gray sweatshirt. He was barefoot.

"Come on in," he said. "You got through the gate okay?"

"The guy didn't look too happy about it," I said. "But yeah, no problem."

"They get kind of fussy out there," he said. "It comes with the territory."

He led me through the living room and into the kitchen. The place was an absolute knockout. The furniture was beautiful, the paintings were beautiful, the plants were beautiful, and not one thing was overdone or out of place. It all went together like something out of a magazine. When I looked out at his deck, it got even better. There were a lot more plants out there, some white wicker patio furniture, a huge green umbrella you could hold a wedding under, and a grill that looked like it could handle the reception afterwards.

"Most of this is from Vargas's store," he said. "Do you like it?"

"Yeah," I said. "You obviously know how to put a house together. That's what you do for Vargas, right?"

"I'm his lead designer, yes."

"I appreciate you taking the time to talk to me."

"Like I said, it's kinda weird down at the store this week anyway. You want to sit out on the porch? Is it too early for a beer?"

"Ten o'clock is not too early," I said.

His refrigerator was huge, and it had the same wooden finish as the rest of the kitchen. He grabbed a couple of bottles and led me out onto the deck. I had to stand at the railing for a few moments, just drinking it all in. There was a pristine beach just below us, and then the blue water of Lake Michigan sparkling in the sunlight. A stiff wind was coming in off the lake.

"Is it always this windy?" I asked. My eyes were already starting to water.

"This is nothing," he said. "You know what somebody just told me? Apparently, the Indians never used to camp on this part of the shoreline, because the constant wind would blow their tents over."

"It's gotta be tough on these houses. Were they built to stand up to it?"

He smiled as he sat down under the flapping umbrella. "Wouldn't that be funny if they weren't?"

I sat down across from him. "I won't waste your time," I said. "I want to ask you about the other night."

"Go ahead," he said. "Ask me anything. I have nothing to hide."

I looked him in the eye. "Apparently, not that many people knew about the money in Vargas's safe. Whoever put this thing together was obviously one of those people."

"So naturally you assume the queer did it," he said. "Those men were three of my rough boyfriends."

"I'm not saying anything like that," I said. "Not at all. I'm just asking if you have any ideas."

He kept looking me in the eye. "To tell you the truth," he said, "I thought it might have been you. You were the stranger there that night."

"I was the one man who *didn't* know about the safe."

"That's true," he said. "But even so . . . "

"Let me ask you this," I said. "In all the time

you've known Vargas . . . How long is that, anyway?"

"Twelve years."

"Okay, but say in the last year or so, since he built that house, have you ever heard him tell anybody else about the safe?"

"I haven't," he said. "In fact, I was surprised he said anything at all. I mean, I could see he was hammered, but still . . . Normally, he's very private about his personal finances."

"Okay, so if it had to be one of the players, who do you think it is?"

"That's not up to me to say, is it? The police arrested those three men. I assume they had a good reason."

"What about Swanson?"

"I don't know the man," he said. "Except that he's a good poker player. He can bluff like nobody you've ever seen."

I leaned back in my chair, took a long swallow of cold beer. "Why do you play cards with Vargas, anyway?" I said. "He treats you like a trained monkey."

"He treats everybody like a trained monkey."

"So don't you get enough of him at work?"

He thought about that one. "You know, when I got out of school, I was living in Manhattan, in the tiniest little apartment. I was totally broke, trying to get jobs. There were a couple of men who could have really opened some doors for me, but I wouldn't sleep with either of them. So I wasn't going anywhere. Then I heard about this Winston Vargas out in Michigan of all places, looking for a New York City interior decorator. I figured what the hell. I called him up. The first thing he asked me was, 'Are you really from New York City?' I said yes. He said, 'If you're calling me from Ohio, I swear to God I'll kick your ass all the way back home. I want somebody from New York City.' I had to give him my phone number, with the Manhattan area code, so he could call me back and make sure. He flew me out here and showed me the store, told me what he was planning on doing with it, how I would be his lead designer and we'd all make a ton of money. Well . . ."

He looked out at the water.

"All my friends, they thought I had lost my mind. Michigan! They thought the whole Midwest was just farmers and bigots and homophobes, you name it. But I said, hey, I'm tired of living in a closet. I mean, in an apartment the size of a closet. I'm going out there for a year, see what happens. Twelve years later, here I am."

I looked out in the same direction. It was hard to argue with.

"At first, when he asked me to go play poker with him, I didn't know what to think. You know what he said? He said, 'You guys play poker?' Like there was some kind of gay code, what we do and don't do. Anyway, I ended up playing. I like playing poker, and you know, why not? It gets lonely around here. What else am I gonna do? Stay at home all night, live like a hermit?"

"You wouldn't want that."

"There was another reason, too," he said. "You see, Win was hiring some other designers. They all worked for me, but if I didn't play, and one of those guys did . . . Hell, they'd kill for my job. A little after-hours time with the owner, getting to be pals, you know how it is."

"You were protecting your territory." I said.

"Something like that. Interior design is a pretty cutthroat business."

"I've heard that," I said. "Worse than the Mafia."

He looked at me, maybe deciding how offended he was supposed to be. Then he laughed.

"Sorry," I said.

"Don't worry about it." Then his smile drifted away. "I didn't steal his money, Alex. You know why?"

"Why?"

"I've already sold my soul," he said. In an instant, his voice had changed. "I've already made all the money I'll ever need. Why would I steal more?"

"All right, Kenny. I get the picture."

"Please," he said. "Call me Kendrick. That's my real name. I wish Win would call me that."

"Kendrick," I said. "Okay. I like that better, anyway. I think we got off on the wrong foot the other night . . ."

"Yeah, I wasn't exactly charming. I guess it's a defense mechanism. Win's friends tend to be the dumb jock type. It's like high school all over again."

"Believe me, I'm not one of his friends."

As I drove away a few minutes later, I knew he

had no part in the robbery. At least, that's what my gut told me.

I gave the man in the gatehouse a little wave on the way out. He had the gate up so fast I didn't even have to slow down. When I was out on the open road, I picked up the cell phone. I had left Kenny's house, make that Kendrick's house, actually liking the man, and feeling a little sorry for him, if getting rich meant he had to put up with Vargas. Now it was eleven o'clock and I hadn't even ruined anybody's morning yet. So I called Swanson's secretary.

"Good morning, ma'am," I said when she answered. "I'm wondering if Mr. Swanson is there today."

"He most certainly is not," she said. I didn't have to wonder if she had recognized my voice. "He will not be in the office at all today."

"Is he in court? That's right next to the City-County building, right? Maybe I can catch him there."

"He's not in court today, either."

"Ma'am, why do I get the impression he doesn't want to talk to me? All I want to do is ask him a couple of questions."

"I'll give him the message that you called again, sir. Now if you'll excuse me . . ."

"That's all right," I said. "I'll just catch him later."

"As I said, he will not be in the office at all today."

"Yeah, I got that one. Don't worry, I'll find him. Have a good day."

I hung up before she could say another word. I put the phone on the passenger's seat, right on top of the piece of paper Leon had given me. It just so happened to have Swanson's home address, right there in black ink. It was about time to make a house call.

I drove for a while, then picked up the phone again. After that call to Swanson's secretary, I needed to talk to somebody who would truly appreciate the sound of my voice. I dialed the Soo police station and asked for Chief Maven. I got bounced around, put on hold, had to ask for him again, put on hold again, and then finally the man himself came on the line. I was going to ask him about the Canadian license plate. Then I was going to ask him if he had any revelations yet—like maybe realizing that somebody was leading him in the wrong direction, and he was falling for it.

I didn't get the chance.

"McKnight, where the hell are you? I've been calling you all morning!"

"I'm downstate," I said. "What's going on?"

"Downstate? Where?"

"Just outside of Petoskey," I said. "Are you gonna tell me what's going on or not?"

"How soon can you be here?"

"A couple of hours," I said. "About one o'clock."

"Make it twelve-forty-five, McKnight. I'll be waiting for you at War Memorial."

It took a few seconds for that to sink in. "Chief, what the hell happened?" I said. "Why do you need me at the hospital?"

"Go downstairs to the coroner's office," he said. "You're the only man who got a good look at those guys. . . . We want to see if you recognize this one."

"One of the gunmen? He's dead?"

"No, McKnight, we just thought he'd be more comfortable waiting down here in the morgue."

"Take it easy, Chief. I'll be there as soon as I can."

I hung up and punched the accelerator. Whoever was behind this, it looked like the stakes had just gotten a lot higher.

Chapter Fourteen

War Memorial Hospital is right in the middle of the Soo's business district, a few blocks south of the river, a few blocks west of Leon's office. I got there a few minutes before one o'clock, and walked into the outpatient waiting room. Maven was sitting there, looking at a magazine. Aside from him, the chairs were empty. He didn't smile when he saw me.

"The hell took you so long?" he said, standing up. He threw the magazine back on the pile.

"I was going seventy," I said. "I don't have a siren I can flip on like you do."

"Let's go," he said. I followed him to the elevator.

"Were you waiting here the whole time?"

"Of course not. You think I have time to sit in a waiting room for two hours? I went to the office. I just got back here five minutes ago."

"Then why are you reaming me out for taking so long?"

"Who's reaming you out, McKnight?" he said. He

pushed the down button. "You've always been way too sensitive."

I just shook my head, got in the elevator with him, and rode down to the basement.

"When's the last time you were in a morgue?" he said.

"Nineteen eighty-four."

"The last year you were a cop?"

"Yes," I said.

"Long time ago."

"I don't imagine they've changed much."

The elevator stopped. The door opened. Maven led me down a long hallway. When he opened the door to the morgue, I smelled the antiseptic, felt the touch of cold air on my skin. Maven was right—it *had* been a long time. But it was all coming back to me.

The coroner was sitting at his desk when we came in. He stood up to shake my hand. He was a round little man, and his white lab coat somehow made him look more like a pastry chef than a coroner. "Mr. McKnight," he said. "I'm Dr. Pietrowski, the Chippewa County coroner. We appreciate you coming in."

I looked at Maven. "My pleasure," I said.

"He's in this room," the coroner said, showing me to the far door. "Are you prepared to look at him?"

"I'll give it my best shot."

"Are you uncomfortable with this?"

"No, I'm just not sure that I'll be able to recognize him."

He nodded. "Let's see what happens."

I followed him through the door, Maven behind me. There was a steel table in the center of the room. The body on top of the table was completely covered by a white sheet. The fluorescent lights hummed above us.

The coroner pulled on latex gloves, then drew back the sheet, folding it neatly across the dead man's shoulders. The face was so white it was almost blue. The eyes were half open. The mouth was half open. I took a step closer.

"Is this one of them?" Maven said.

I tried to replay the night in my head, looking down at the lifeless face, trying to make some kind of connection. It was impossible.

"I only really saw the two men who stayed downstairs with us," I said. "One was very fair-skinned, with blond hair and blond eyebrows. That's the one who sounded Canadian to me. This man obviously isn't him. The other man was heavier . . . How much did this man weigh?"

The coroner picked up a clipboard. "Two hundred twenty-five pounds," he said. "That's minus a few liters of blood."

I nodded. It sounded about right. "How tall is he?"

"Five eleven."

"He was wearing a mask," I said. "A surgical mask, and a cap, too."

The coroner went to his work table. "Like these?" he said, holding up a green mask and cap.

"Yes."

He looked at Maven for a moment, then stepped

over behind the dead man's head. He slipped the cap over the man's dark hair, then draped the mask over his mouth. "Does this help?"

I looked down at him. I took a deep breath, tried to put myself back on the floor at Vargas's house. The men were walking around. The dog was barking. "He does look familiar now," I said. "I think this may be the other man who was downstairs. I can't be a hundred percent certain."

"There was something in the report about the shoes," Maven said behind me. "Would you recognize the shoes?"

"If he was wearing the same shoes, yes, I might."

The coroner went back to his work table, opened up a black plastic bag and pulled out a pair of old athletic shoes. He brought them over to me. "Take a good look," he said. "But please don't touch them."

They were old, beat-up shoes, once white, now a dingy gray. Two blue stripes ran diagonally on each side. "These look like the shoes he was wearing," I said.

The coroner went back to put the shoes away. I looked down at the dead man, still wearing the cap and mask. "What happened to him?" I said.

"He was shot in the back," the coroner said. "Two slugs from a forty-five. One passed through the upper abdomen, the other was stopped by the sternum."

"How long has he been dead?"

"Approximately four days."

"Four days. That would be . . ." I thought about

it. "That would be the night of the robbery, after they drove away. Where did you find him?"

The coroner just looked at me while he pulled off his gloves. "You'll have to ask the chief about that."

"Let's go," Maven said. "We're done here."

"I did my part," I said. "Tell me what happened."

"I'm going upstairs," Maven said. "You can stay down here if you want."

The coroner just shrugged when I looked at him. I followed Maven back through the office, down the hall to the elevator. We stood there waiting for it.

"Where did you find him?" I said.

"Right on top of the blood."

"What's his name?"

"You don't need to know that."

"It's public information," I said. "It'll be in the paper tomorrow."

"Not necessarily. We might withhold it for a few days."

"What's the big secret?"

"If I were to bring Mr. Connery down here, or Mr. O'Dell or Mr. LaMarche, do you think any of them would recognize him?"

"I doubt it," I said. "I don't think anybody else got a good look at him."

"That's assuming they didn't know who he was already."

"Yeah, that's assuming."

"If his name happened to be Danny Cox, would that mean anything to you?"

"Is that his name?"

"I'm just asking, if it *was . . .*"

"I've never heard that name before," I said.

"That's your answer? Just like that? You didn't even take a minute to think about it."

"I don't have to think about it. I don't know the name."

"Most guys, they'd say, 'Hmm . . . Let me think. Danny Cox . . . Danny Cox . . . Nope, never heard of him.' "

"I'll think some more if it'll make you feel better."

"Never mind." He looked up at the numbers above the elevator. Without looking at me, he said, "What were you doing downstate, anyway?"

"I had an appointment."

"I probably don't even want to know, do I . . ."

The elevator opened. We got in.

"I know two of the thieves drove away in a car with a Canadian license plate," I said. "Have you traced it yet? I don't think American private investigators can call Canada for that information."

"First of all, how did you come to know anything about a Canadian license plate?" he said. "Second of all, you're not a PI anymore, remember?"

"I came out of retirement," I said. "You obviously need a little help, Chief. You're letting your personal bias get in the way here. You should be out looking for the person who's really behind all this."

"Let me guess," he said. "The appointment you had this morning . . ."

"Kendrick Heiden," I said. "I don't think he was involved, if you want my opinion."

"You know how much I value your opinion, McKnight. Who's next on your list?"

"Douglas Swanson."

"He wasn't there that night."

"Yeah, I know."

Maven rubbed his eyes. "I'm getting a headache."

"Tell me who owns that car," I said. "I'm going to find out anyway."

"Go right ahead. Knock yourself out."

"If it was a real lead, you wouldn't say that. It must have been a stolen car. Or a stolen plate, at least. Am I right?"

The door opened on the ground floor. Maven stepped out and walked quickly to the front door. In the sunshine I felt like I was a million miles away from the cold light of the morgue. "I got things to do," he said.

"So do I," I said.

He stopped and turned to face me. "You know what? You think you're helping out your friends? Let me tell you something. The district attorney had a deal on the table. The first one of those guys who flipped was gonna have the conspiracy charge dropped. It was gonna be a class A receiving stolen goods, probation and no jail time. But now we've got a dead body on the ground. He was shot in the back, McKnight, and left in the woods so a couple of little kids could find him this morning. You think I'm in any kind of mood to hear you tell me I need help on this case? And that you're the one who's gonna help me?"

"Maven, it's real simple. You're dead wrong. You're looking at the wrong men."

"Because you just know in your heart that they're innocent."

"Something like that."

"I'm the one with the personal bias," he said. "Think about it." Then he walked away.

Chapter Fifteen

I drove back over to August Street to check out Swanson's office again. I hadn't asked Leon what kind of car Swanson drove, so I didn't know what to look for. It didn't matter. There was only one car in his lot, so I figured it had to be his secretary's. It was a Toyota Camry, which sure didn't seem like a lawyer's car to me.

I put the truck in the public lot by the Locks Park, and thought about taking a peek in the courthouse. It occurred to me that I wasn't even sure if I'd remember what Swanson looked like. Trying to ask around in the courthouse didn't seem like the right way to go about it. So I grabbed some lunch in the Ojibway Hotel dining room, sitting right by the windows so I could watch a couple of freighters pass through the locks. It was another beautiful July day. There were lots of people out there enjoying themselves in the sun, people on vacation from their jobs and all of their troubles. Or so it seemed. Me, I was fresh out of the morgue, and I had enough troubles now to last me until Labor Day. I could have dropped every single one of them. They weren't my troubles to begin with. I could have forgotten the whole thing and gone back to being a hermit.

Somehow I didn't think I would be doing that.

I caught up with the news while I was waiting for my lunch. The *Soo Evening News* crime writer was having the time of his life following the "Masked Gunmen" story. He spent half of page one describing the morning arrests of two Soo residents and a tavern owner in Paradise. Somewhere around the second column he finally mentioned that the three men arrested were apparently not the masked gunmen themselves, but merely suspected accomplices. Chief Maven of the Soo police was still hoping that anyone with information on the case would contact him immediately.

As much fun as the writer was having with this story, I couldn't imagine what he'd do when he found out one of the gunmen was found shot in the back. I folded the paper in half, put it on the table next to mine, and didn't look at it again.

I drove back down to Swanson's office. There were no new cars in the lot. I pulled up to a meter, a half block down the street, and thought about what to do next. If I were a real PI like Leon, I thought, I'd wait here until he showed up. He had to stop in at the office *some* time today. I looked at my watch again. It was just past two. "Goddamn it all," I said out loud. "I do not feel like sitting here for the next three hours." But I didn't know what else to do.

Swanson was my main man at that point, and everything that had happened that day had made me even more determined to talk to him. Hell, who else was there?

I got out of the truck, went down the street to the little book store, and bought every magazine that looked half interesting. There were about a half-dozen true-crime paperbacks for sale—I was ashamed to admit I had already read every single one of them. I settled on an international spy thriller, and another book about a storm at sea. With a few candy bars and a bottle of water in the bag, I was ready for the rest of the afternoon.

I sat there in the truck for two hours, going out once to the bathroom because I would be damned if I'd piss in a plastic bottle. Cars came and went down the street, none of them turning into Swanson's lot. The sun moved across the sky until a long shadow from the buildings finally covered me. This is what a real private investigator does, I thought to myself more than once. I really, really hate it.

At five o'clock, the secretary came out the front door and locked it behind her. She looked too young to be so skillfully unpleasant on the telephone. She got into the Camry and drove away, leaving me sitting there alone in my truck.

"Okay," I said. "You didn't check in at the office. So now let's see if you check in at home."

After looking at my map, I drove up the hill by the Lake State campus and found the address Leon had given me. The house looked like a French Colonial, assuming I knew what the hell that was. I parked on the street and then rang the doorbell, even though I didn't see any cars in the garage. Nobody answered the door.

I moved the truck a couple of houses away, facing his driveway. Time to wait some more. Then a horrible thought came to me. Maybe Swanson was spending the afternoon with Vargas's wife somewhere. They could have been at Vargas's house even. Hell, for all I knew, he was banging her on the floor of her custom kitchen at that very moment.

I didn't have long to think about it, as a dark blue Acura pulled in the driveway. A woman got out. On the way in the front door, she opened the mailbox and took out the contents. Mrs. Swanson.

When I got out of the truck, my legs were as tight as piano wire from sitting in my truck so long. I went to the front door.

The woman who answered was about my age, maybe a few years older. She had dark hair just turning to gray, big brown eyes behind a pair of rimless glasses. She smiled and said hello, and asked if she could help me. I instantly felt sick to my stomach. This was a woman who didn't know her husband was screwing one of his clients.

"Is Dougie home yet?" I said.

"Dougie?" she said. "I haven't heard anybody call him that in years."

"We're old friends," I said, picking right up on that one. "I was in the neighborhood, thought I'd stop by. He's still in practice, right?"

"Yes, he is. He's at the office right now, but he should be home in a few minutes. Would you like to come in and wait for him? I'm sorry, I didn't catch your name."

"Alex," I said. "Alex McKnight."

I spent the next half hour sitting in her kitchen. It was a nice kitchen but nothing like a Vargas custom job. Mrs. Swanson cut me a piece of the best home-made carrot cake I'd ever tasted, and even asked me if I'd like a beer. We talked about my cabins, how my father had built them himself, and how he had worked for Ford Motors for thirty years. Her father had worked for General Motors. Every minute I spent with her, I hated her husband a little bit more. By the time he got home, I was ready to hit him right in the mouth.

I waited in the kitchen while she went out to meet him in the living room. "Douglas," I heard her say, "there's a man here waiting for you. His name is Alex McKnight."

Swanson appeared around the corner. He was vaguely familiar—mid-fifties, in good shape for a man who worked behind a desk most of the day, and of course the silver hair any good lawyer in his fifties had to have. I had seen him around town a few times, and I was pretty sure I had been introduced to him once, but I was quite sure I had never seen him as angry as he was at that moment. "What the hell are you doing in my house?" he said.

"I'm eating your wife's carrot cake," I said. "Having a nice conversation."

"You've got three seconds to get out of here before I call the police."

"Honey, what's the matter?" his wife said.

"Your husband's a real kidder," I said. "He always does this to me, every time he sees me. In fact, tell him about that time in college, Dougie."

"I'm counting," he said, picking up the phone. "One."

"Dougie was in this hotel room," I said. She looked at me with wide eyes, and then at her husband, and then back at me. "There's a knock on the door. He opens it and it's room service."

"Two," he said. "I'm dialing."

"The waiter has a big tray with a bottle of champagne on it. Dougie says, 'I didn't order any champagne.' The waiter says, 'Compliments of the house, sir.' And then the waiter loses his grip on the tray and wouldn't you know it, he dumps the whole thing right on Dougie's head."

Swanson stopped dialing. Either he forgot what comes after two, or I was getting to him.

"What do you say, Dougie? You want me to tell your wife the rest of the story?"

"What do you want?" he said. "Why did you come here?"

"We need to have a little chat." I said. "Is there someplace we can go?"

"In here," he said. He opened a pair of glass doors. There was an antique desk in the room, and enough law books to fill two entire walls.

"I want to thank you, ma'am," I said to Mrs. Swanson. "I apologize if I upset you."

She just shook her head. She didn't say a word. As soon as I stepped into his office, Swanson shut the doors tight.

I sat down on the guest chair. Swanson kept standing by the doors, his back to me, like he was deciding what to do next.

"You call my office," he said, finally turning around. "You harass my secretary. You come to my *house* and threaten me in front of my wife."

"I didn't threaten you."

"That little story about the champagne bottle, what was that?"

"Just an amusing anecdote."

"What do you want?" he said. "If you want money, you can just forget it. I will not be black-mailed."

"Who said anything about blackmail? I just want to ask you a couple of questions."

"Cut the crap, McKnight. I know who you are. I know why you're here. I'm telling you one more time. You will get nothing from me. Not one dime."

"Will you sit down for a minute? You've got the wrong idea. I'm not here for money."

He looked at me for a long moment, the way a man looks at someone he thinks may be demented. Then he slowly sat himself down in the chair behind his desk. "What is this about?" he said. "I know you're Leon Prudell's partner. And I know he's been following Mrs. Vargas around the last few weeks."

"I'm not his partner anymore," I said. "I've got nothing to do with that. . . . How did you know he's been following her around, anyway?"

"Come on, like she's not going to notice this big clown with orange hair following her everywhere? I knew he had to be a private investigator, and since there's only one PI firm in town, it wasn't hard to figure out who Vargas had hired to watch her. The listing I saw said 'Prudell-McKnight Investigations.' "

"Old listing," I said. "I'm out of that now."

"So it's just him doing this? Following her around like some sort of lowlife stalker?"

"I think you can rest easy," I said. "I don't think Leon ever got the money shot he was trying for. You know, the one of you with your pants around your ankles."

"Could this possibly be any less your business, McKnight? My relationship with my wife? Or whatever might be happening between Mrs. Vargas and myself?"

"Aside from feeling bad for your wife, I don't care. I don't even want to think about it."

"Then why the hell are you here? I swear to God, I was sure you were going to put the squeeze on me, try to work both sides against the middle. Believe me, I've heard about private investigators pulling this scam. Some people will do anything for a little easy money."

"I'm here because I was the lucky guy who took your place at the poker game," I said. "I'm here because I want some answers."

"What kind of answers could I possibly give you? I don't know anything about it."

"One of the gunmen turned up dead this morning."

I watched him carefully. He narrowed his eyes,

as if honestly confused. "One of the men who broke into Win Vargas's house?"

"Yes."

He shook his head. If he was acting, he was doing a good job of it. But then, that's what lawyers do. That's why lawyers were put on this earth. "I don't understand," he said. "What does this have to do with me?"

"Somebody set up Jackie, Bennett, and Gill," I said. "I'm trying to find out who."

"I knew they were arrested yesterday," he said. "What makes you think they were set up?"

"Are these your friends or not? Do you really think they were involved in this?"

"All three are friendly acquaintances," he said. "Men I play cards with once in a while. I've seen enough to never be surprised by what people will do, McKnight. Especially when money is involved."

"Let's talk about that money," I said. "You'll agree with me that whoever put this together had to know about the money in Vargas's safe?"

"That makes sense."

"Vargas claims he only mentioned the money in the safe once, at a poker game two months ago. Not even his wife knew about it."

"Therefore you assume," he said, "that one of the men present at that poker game must be responsible for the robbery."

"Yes."

"And that the same man must also be responsible for this frame-up you think these three innocent men are presently caught up in."

"You're doing beautifully," I said. "Keep going."

"And that if it was *not* in fact Jackie, Bennett, or Gill, it must have been either Kenny or myself. The two of us being the only other men who knew about the safe."

"I don't think it was Kenny," I said.

"It wasn't Kenny."

"Kendrick, actually."

"Kendrick. It wasn't Kendrick."

"You're almost home," I said. "One more step."

He threw his hands up. "You've got one man left," he said. "Swanson must have done it."

"Did you?"

"I'm not under oath here."

"Just tell me," I said. "Did you do it?"

"No," he said. "I didn't. Why would I?"

"You said it yourself. People will do anything for a little money."

"I said *easy* money. There's a big difference. It's only easy if you know you can get away with it."

"I didn't see you get arrested yesterday," I said. "So far, you're getting away with it just fine."

"Let me ask you something. Let's assume I set this up. You didn't see *me* there, did you? I must have hired three men to break into his house."

"Apparently, yes."

"These three men, aren't they entitled to some of the money?"

"Yes," I said. "I'm sure they are."

"How much money are we talking about? What did it say in the paper? Five thousand dollars?"

"That's what Vargas told the police. You and I both know it was more."

"Certainly. So let's say it was what, fifty thousand dollars? A hundred thousand dollars? Let's say it was a million dollars. A cool million in cash. That's a pretty good haul, wouldn't you say? I'm gonna hire three men to go in with guns to steal a million dollars, and then have them deliver it to me. Which of course they'll do, because even though they've just ripped off a million dollars, they're men of honor and they're gonna stand by their promise to me. But now what do you think their cut should be? You think they'll let me have a full share of it? Even though all I did was tell them about the safe, and then sit here in my easy chair while they committed armed robbery? Sure, let's say they cut me in for a full quarter. Now I've got a quarter-million dollars. I've risked my entire legal career, which by the way will probably gross between five and ten million more dollars before I retire. I've risked going to prison for what, twenty or thirty years? Everything I own, every person in this world I care about . . . I've risked it all for two hundred fifty thousand dollars. Is this the way you see it, Mr. McKnight? Is this what you think really happened?"

I didn't say anything. I sat there in the chair.

"Please, Mr. McKnight. I'd like an answer. If the answer is yes, I want to make sure I exclude you if you ever come up on jury duty. Because you'll obviously believe anything."

"You don't have to get cute," I said. "I'm sure it didn't happen exactly that way."

"Then how *did* it happen?"

"That's why I'm here. I'm trying to find out, and I thought you could help me."

"I'm sorry to disappoint you."

"As soon as you heard my name," I said, "you ran for the hills. Do you blame me for being suspicious?"

"If you had told my secretary why you had wanted to see me, we could have avoided all this."

"Yeah, but I wouldn't have experienced your wife's carrot cake."

"I think we're done, Mr. McKnight. The door behind you leads right outside. I suggest you use it."

"Please thank your wife again for me."

"I'll try to remember."

I left through his office door, walked across his lawn to the street. Some kids came by on their bikes. Somebody started up a lawnmower. I got in the truck and stared out at nothing for a while.

Swanson was right. It *was* a tough way to make money, and riskier than hell.

So maybe it wasn't about the money after all. Maybe it was something else.

Whatever it was, I hoped it would come to me before they measured Jackie for a prison uniform, or before my friend with the sweet cigars decided to make himself at home in my cabin again.

Or before somebody else got murdered.

It was time to go for broke. I picked up the phone and dialed Leon's number. Then I started the truck and headed straight for Vargas's house.

Chapter Sixteen

Leon picked up on the first ring.

"I'm on my way to see Mrs. Vargas," I said. "Is she going to be home now?"

"Alex, what are you talking about? You can't do that."

"I'm doing it, Leon. You're the guy who spent the last few weeks following her around, so I'm sure you know her routine. Will she be there?"

"I can't tell you that, Alex. I'd be crossing a line here."

"What about Vargas? Will he be there?"

"I can't tell you that, either."

"You're just looking out for your client," I said. "If he's there, it could get ugly. You want me to have to hit him in the head again?"

"I knew that must have been you . . . He wouldn't say so, but I *knew* it."

"Just tell me who's gonna be there."

"Vargas shouldn't be there for a couple more

hours," he said. "He should be at the store. He only
goes down three days a week now. It's such a long
drive."

"Okay, so his wife is there alone. That's good."

"I wouldn't assume she's alone, Alex. I'm afraid
that when she knows her husband isn't going to be
home . . ."

"Relax," I said. "I know Swanson isn't there right
now."

"Alex, what are you doing?"

"I'm just driving around, asking people questions.
What are *you* doing? How come you're not tailing
her anymore?"

"Vargas sort of lost interest in that. He seems to
have his mind on other things right now."

"Yeah, I bet. And you're just sitting by the phone,
waiting for him to call you?"

"I don't deserve that, Alex. I've been helping you
out here. I didn't have to do that."

"You're right," I said. "I'm sorry. It's been kind
of a long day."

"Just don't do anything stupid, okay?"

"Too late," I said. I hung up.

I came down off the hill, heading northeast to the
river. There were golfers putting on the green as I
passed, and then I saw Vargas's house. A blue Miata
was in the driveway. I parked behind it.

When I rang the doorbell, I expected to hear my
little friend start barking, but the sound never came.
Cynthia Vargas answered the door and stood there
looking at me, with no Chihuahua running around at
her feet.

"What is it?" she said, holding her cigarette out just so. She squinted a little, the kind of look a smoker gives you when she's annoyed at you and the smoke is in her eyes at the same time. She was blonde, perfectly put together, just what you'd shop for in a second wife. Vargas had already done it once, and now Swanson was apparently looking to pick up her option. It wouldn't have bothered me a bit if I hadn't just spent the only decent thirty minutes of the day in the company of Swanson's wife.

"Good afternoon, ma'am," I said. "I'm sorry to bother you."

"Uh-huh?" She took a drag off her cigarette.

"I was wondering if I could bother you with a couple of questions."

"Don't tell me," she said. She looked me up and down. "Your name is Alex McKnight."

"I think we spoke on the phone the other night."

"Yeah, and you were here for the poker game," she said. "You were one of the hostages."

"I don't know if I'd say we were hostages. They just encouraged us to stay out of their way . . ."

"Come on in," she said. "You want a beer or something?"

I very much did. But I took a pass.

She walked right through the house, out onto the back deck. I assumed I was supposed to follow her. It was my second back deck of the day, and the second time I was spending time with another man's wife. This time felt a lot different. Mrs. Vargas still looked a little flushed and untucked, like maybe she'd spent the whole afternoon with her underwear hanging from the chandelier.

She sat down on a recliner, put her cigarette out in the ashtray on the table next to it. She was facing west, where even at seven o'clock in the evening the sun still hung high over the horizon. She put her sunglasses on. "Sit down," she said.

I pulled another recliner over and sat down on the end of it. I wasn't about to recline. As I looked west, I noticed the cardboard still covering the broken window on the second floor.

"I don't see your dog anywhere," I said. "Usually he's so glad to see me."

"That's not my dog," she said. "That's Win's dog. He even takes it to work with him."

"That's funny. He told us a few times it was your dog."

"He tried to give me that dog the same day he bought me that stupid little car out there."

"Mrs. Vargas, I won't take much of your time. I just need to ask you something."

"You're friends with those three men who got arrested," she said. She looked out at the river.

"Yes, how did you know?"

"I overheard Win talking about you on the phone. You're the one they didn't get."

"They didn't 'get' anybody, ma'am. The whole thing is a mistake."

"These friends of yours, you know for a fact they had nothing to do with this."

"That's right," I said.

"So you're here to ask me if I did it."

She caught me by surprise with that one. "I'm just trying to find out the truth," I said.

"My lawyer just called me," she said. "Right before you got here. He said you dropped in on him."

"Is that what you call him? Your lawyer?"

She pushed her sunglasses down and looked over them at me. "Perhaps it was a mistake to let you come in," she said. "You seemed like a gentleman, but I was obviously mistaken."

"I apologize."

She put her glasses back up and looked out at the river again. "He told me you might drop by. He seems to think you'd be very persistent about it. That's why I thought I should just talk to you straight away, save us both some trouble."

"I appreciate that."

"Have you ever been to Bay Harbor, Alex?"

"As a matter of fact, I have."

"Let me ask you a question. If you had a really nice six-thousand-square-foot house there, would you sell it and move up here?"

"I don't think I can answer that. I wouldn't be living in Bay Harbor to begin with."

"Did he tell you about his idea of building a new development up here?"

"He did mention that."

"Of course he did. It's all he ever talks about. What do you think of his big idea?"

"I honestly hope he doesn't do it."

"He thinks people with lots of money will move up here," she said. "Can you believe that? Actually live here instead of in Bay Harbor?"

There was an uncomfortable silence. I wasn't sure what to say next. "The safe up in that room . . ." I finally said.

"Yes, I knew all about it," she said. "What kind of an idiot doesn't know about a safe in her own house?"

"Did you know the combination?"

She pushed her sunglasses down again. "No."

"Did you know what was in it?"

She raised one eyebrow at me. "Please. What do you keep in a safe?"

"It could have been a lot of things."

"With Win, it's either money or those ridiculous artifacts," she said. "He wouldn't keep the artifacts in the safe, because then he couldn't drag everybody up there to show them off."

"You don't seem to share his interests."

"Yeah, that's right," she said. "So I hired three goons to break in and trash his precious collection, steal his money while they're at it. Not so much because I'd get part of it, but just to take it away from him. All because I hate him so much, because I want to hurt him in any way I can. Is that what you're getting at, Mr. McKnight? I think I'm being pretty straight with you. I wish you'd return the favor."

"You're telling me you had nothing to do with it."

"Yes, that's what I'm telling you. And you know what? The more I think of it, the more I wish I *had* done it. I mean, what's he doing, keeping all that money up there in the safe? Now it's all gone, my husband has turned psychotic, and I can't even sleep at night because I'm waiting for those men to break in here again."

She picked up her pack of cigarettes, shook another one out.

"God, I hate this place," she said. "You don't know how much I hate this place."

I didn't get a chance to say anything to that. The next sound I heard was a small dog barking. The sound got louder and louder. Then the back door opened and Miata was all over me. I took a cushion off the recliner and tried to use it as a shield. It only worked so well—I could still feel the dog's teeth tearing through the skin on my fingers.

"Isn't this cozy?" Vargas said as he stepped through the doorway. The welt on his forehead had turned every color of the rainbow. "I thought that might be your truck outside, McKnight. Who else would drive something like that?"

"You're home early," Mrs. Vargas said. She didn't turn to look at him.

"Yes, the husband has come home unexpectedly," he said. "Oldest trick in the book. But I certainly wasn't expecting to find *him* here. You're really working your way down the social ladder, Cynthia."

She lifted one hand and showed him the back of her middle finger. Meanwhile, the dog kept dancing around me, looking for an opening. At that moment I could have drop-kicked him all the way to Canada.

"Will you please put this dog away?" I said.

"Why should I?" Vargas said. "What the hell are you doing here, anyway?"

"Put the dog away and I'll tell you."

"Miata, come here," he said.

The dog didn't want to back down. He had drawn blood and now he wanted to finish me off.

"Miata, get over here." Vargas scooped up the dog and put one finger on its nose when he kept barking at me. "Just take it easy," he said. "Let him speak. Then you'll get to watch me take him apart. He won't get away this time. When I'm done I'll let you piss on his face."

"All right, enough," I said. "I came to ask your wife a couple of questions. That's all. Whoever took you down took down my friends at the same time. I want to find out who did this. I should think *you'd* want to find out, too."

"That's what you think, huh?"

"Yeah, and you know what? The fact that you *don't* seem to want to find out is kind of interesting in itself. You should be *dying* to find out who did this, Vargas. You should be way ahead of me. Or at least have Leon working on it for you."

I was running out of ideas. It was time to try something desperate.

"Instead," I went on, "what are you doing? You've got somebody breaking into my cabin? Jackie's house? Gill's house? What's the point of that, anyway?"

"What? Breaking into where?"

"Whoever it is, you should tell him to stop smoking those stupid little cigars. I can't stand the smell of those things."

"McKnight, what in holy hell are you talking about?"

It sounded real. If I was going to keep following my gut, I'd have to guess he honestly didn't know. After running around all day long, hitting dead ends, now I was down to my last chance. I had one more card to play before folding.

"Maybe it was you," I said. "Maybe you set this up yourself."

"McKnight, you're insane," he said. "You've lost your mind."

"Now that would be interesting," his wife said. She finally sat up and turned around to look at us. "He robs himself. Now all the money is gone . . ."

"Except it's not really gone," I said. "It's just not on the table anymore, should anyone happen to call him on it. Like a divorce lawyer."

His bald head turned a shade redder.

"Just speaking hypothetically," I said.

"So why would he destroy his own room?" she said.

"Just for show," I said. "To make sure nobody thought he was behind it himself."

"The old red herring game," she said. "I can see him thinking that way."

"Of course, you realize one of those men turned up dead today. I hope your husband realizes that this whole thing is getting a little out of hand."

"Who's dead?" Vargas said. He looked genuinely surprised.

"One of the men who broke in here," I said. "Did you kill him yourself? He was shot in the back."

"That does sound like him," she said.

"That's enough out of you," he said. "Why don't you go put some more makeup on? I think you missed a spot."

"Not a chance," she said. "This is just getting interesting. Now you're on the hook for murder."

"I don't have to stand here in my own house and listen to this."

"What about your friends?" she said to me. "Why would he set them up like that?"

"Because they're the only people who knew about the safe," I said. "He had to set up *somebody* to take the blame."

"It's too risky," she said. "And it's not even necessary. *He's* the one who's telling everybody that nobody else knew about the safe. All he has to do is say, 'Oh, I just remembered. I think I might have mentioned it in a bar that one night. God knows who could have heard me.' He doesn't need to set up anybody."

"That's true," I said. "You seem to have a talent for this."

"Are you two about done?" Vargas said.

"Almost," I said. "We just need to know why you went out of your way to set up Jackie, Bennett, and Gill. It's gotta be something personal. Some kind of vendetta you've got against those three guys."

Vargas looked at both of us. He held the dog in his right arm, and slowly scratched behind its ears with a fingernail. "McKnight," he finally said, "can I ask you one question?"

"Go ahead."

"If you really think I set those guys up, here's what I want to know . . . How did I do it?"

"That's an easy one," I said.

"Then tell me," he said. "Put yourself in my place, and take it step by step. I want to set these guys up to take the fall for this break-in. How do I do it?"

I thought about it for a moment. I wanted to put it together in the right order, so he couldn't find any holes in it. I wanted it all to come out perfectly, thinking maybe then he'd get that sick look on his face, knowing that I had him nailed. He'd probably drop the dog, make a run for it. I'd chase him. Or call the police. Either way, the whole thing would be over.

He didn't give me the chance. Instead, he turned and put the dog down inside the house, and then slid the glass door closed before he could escape. "Never mind, McKnight. I think we've heard enough. Now, how about our rematch? This time you don't get to use a fire extinguisher."

"Vargas, there's no reason for this."

"Oh yes, I think there is." He came toward me, in the same pose I had seen on the boat, his hands poised more like a magician than a boxer, his left foot poised just off the ground. It would have looked pretty damned ridiculous if I wasn't standing there wondering just how good he really was.

It didn't take long to find out. He faked a left and then hit me in the body with his right hand, knocking the wind out of me. Then he spun around and caught me in the side of the head with his foot. It knocked me off my feet and made my head feel like a giant bell that wouldn't stop ringing.

I rolled away from him, got on my feet, and spent the next few seconds trying to catch my breath and avoid another one of his spinning back kicks. One more of those and I'd be laid out for good.

Meanwhile, his wife had finally found a reason to get out of her chair. She stood against the railing, watching us with a sort of rapt fascination. The dog kept barking and clawing at the inside of the glass door.

Vargas slipped a few more punches in, sending me backward against the rail. I went into my own version of Ali's rope-a-dope, ducking as many of the heavy blows as I could, and waiting for some kind of idea to come to me.

He finally got a little lazy, figuring maybe I was dead meat at that point. I popped him a couple of times, a left to the body and then a right to the chin. He shook that off, stepped back a few feet, and then launched himself into one more spinning back kick, this one being the *coup de grace* that would knock me right over the railing. I had this one timed, though, and as his foot sailed over my head I gave him a kick of my own, a good old-fashioned boot right in the jewels. It folded him in half.

He went down and made some ugly noises as he rolled around on the deck. I stood there looking at him, ready for the unlikely event of him actually standing up again. When it didn't happen, I checked out the damage to my face. My jaw was sore as hell, both eyes were already starting to go a little puffy, my lip was split and bleeding down my chin, and my right ear was still ringing. Aside from that I had never felt better.

Mrs. Vargas was still standing there, her arms folded around herself. She was watching her husband roll around on the deck. The look on her face was now a combination of shock and physical satisfaction so pure I felt like I should offer her a cigarette.

"I'll let myself out," I said.

That broke the spell. She looked at me and tried to say something. "Oh," she finally said. "Oh. Yes. My God."

"You'd better go fill the tub," I said. The way he kept rolling around, holding his groin, it almost made me feel sorry for him. "When he gets up, make sure he goes and sits in it. If he complains, just grab him right in the shorts and pull."

I was about to open the glass door, saw the dog ready to jump out of its skin at me and thought better of it. I went down the stairs instead, passing right under the broken window. There were still shards of glass on the ground, glittering in the last sunlight of the day. I went around the house to the front, got in my truck, and took a quick look at my face in the rearview mirror.

Bad idea.

I wiped the blood off my chin, thinking this was getting better by the minute. What a great day this was turning out to be.

Sometimes when you think about something too hard, you can't really see it anymore. Then you put it in the back of your mind for a few minutes, like when someone happens to be beating the living shit out of you. When you bring it back out, you see something you didn't see before. It all comes together.

Or in this case, it all falls apart. It falls apart like that old Indian oar he had up in that room of his— worthless to begin with, and so fragile, as soon as you touched it, it broke into a million pieces.

When Vargas asked me to explain how he did it, that was the first time I looked at it from his point of view—him or whoever it was who supposedly set this up. It didn't work. Son of a bitch, it didn't even *begin* to work.

Maven was right. That was the worst thing. Maven telling me that I was the one with the personal bias, that I was the one not seeing it clearly—goddamn it to hell, he was absolutely right.

My hands were still trembling as I grabbed the steering wheel. The adrenaline was still pumping through my bloodstream. I felt like killing somebody.

"Here I come," I said. "I hope you're ready for me."

Everything that had happened, it all went back to one man. I pulled out of the driveway and gunned it, heading right toward him.

Chapter Seventeen

He was standing behind the bar when I walked in. He didn't even look at me. He kept talking to the man in front of him, his voice low. There were a couple other men at the bar, a few more at the tables. The Tigers were playing on the big screen again.

"Bennett, I want to talk to you," I said.

"Be with you in a minute," he said, his eyes still not moving.

"It can't wait."

"Just a minute, Alex."

"At least pour me a beer while I'm waiting."

He finally looked up at me. If he even noticed the shape I was in, it didn't register on his face. "I'm a little busy right now," he said, his mouth tight. "I'll be with you in a minute."

"Bennett, what's going on?"

He looked down at the sink in front of him, his hands still on the bar. From the moment I had stepped into the place, he hadn't moved his hands.

An ashtray on the bar. Smoke rising. That smell, sickly sweet.

The man in front of Bennett, sitting on the bar stool—I hadn't looked at him when I came in. Now I did. His hair was so blond it was white, his skin so pale that in the summer he'd turn red as a beet as soon as he stepped outside. His eyebrows, you could barely see them.

He looked over at me, the same way he had looked at me when I was lying on Vargas's floor.

"We're having a conversation," he said. "What's all the fuss about?" The last word a very Canadian "aboot."

"There's no fuss," Bennett said. "Alex is just here to have a beer."

"It looks like Alex needs a little ice for his face, too," the man said. "He seems to have run into a cement truck."

He didn't take his eyes off me. I wiped the blood off my chin with the back of my sleeve and stared right back at him. I took a step toward him. He didn't even blink.

"Alex, don't," Bennett said. "Please don't move."

I looked away from the man, saw Bennett's hands still on the bar. It all fell into place. The man was wearing a jacket on a day that was far too warm for it. It was zipped most of the way down, and the man's right hand was inside. I didn't have to guess what he was holding.

"I'm not alone," he said. "I'd rather we didn't have to shoot our way out of here, but we will if we have to."

I looked behind him. Ham was sitting at one of the tables, looking like his head was about to explode. Another man sat next to him. He wasn't quite as blond as the man at the bar, but otherwise the family resemblance was unmistakable.

"Your brother," I said. "Was he the third man at our party?"

"You know who the third man was," he said.

"News to me."

"You were in this from the beginning."

"Again," I said, "news to me. You wanna start making some sense?"

"I told you," Bennett spoke up. "Alex had no part in this."

"There you go again," the man said. "Every time you say that, I get more upset. I do wish you'd stop."

"I'm telling you the truth," Bennett said.

"How about you, Alex?" the man said. "Are you gonna tell me the same thing?"

"I don't know what you're talking about."

"Then why are you here? Just dropping in for a beer? And some bandages?"

"Why were you in my cabin?" I said.

"Just doing a little research," he said. "Trying to recoup some business losses."

"Why don't you come by again tonight? I'll make sure I'm home this time."

"You know, I'm starting to feel unwelcome," he said. "In fact, I'd say it's gotten downright hostile in here."

"You haven't seen hostile yet. Believe me."

He smiled. "If you had any idea," he said. "My

God, you people actually think you can get away with this. It's almost funny."

"I saw one of your partners today," I said. "Two bullets in the back? That must have been you. Pretty gutless, wouldn't you say?"

His smile vanished. "You're about to end your own life, friend."

"I'm 'aboot' to end my own life? How come you Canadians talk so funny, anyway?"

"Alex," Bennett said. "For the love of God . . ."

"I'll be in touch with you again," the man said as he stood up. "Soon." He circled around me, never turning his back. His brother stood up and went out the door first. Then my new friend slowly backed his way out the door, giving me a little wink.

As soon as the door closed, I went to the window.

"Alex, what are you doing? Get away from there!"

I ignored him. I watched the men get into a black Audi. It was not the same car from Leon's videotape, and not the same license number, although the plate did come from Ontario.

I went back to the bar. "Give me a pen," I said, grabbing a napkin.

"What?"

"You can take your hands off the bar. He's gone. Give me a pen."

He finally unfroze himself, pushed himself away from the bar, and found me a pen. I wrote down the plate number on a cocktail napkin. Bennett leaned over the sink as though he was about to throw up.

When Margaret came out, carrying a plate of

food, she stopped dead in her tracks. "What's going on?" she said. "What's wrong? Alex, what happened to your face?"

Bennett shook his head. Ham kept sitting at the table, staring at the door.

"You can pour me that beer now," I said. "And then you can start talking."

He picked up a mug, pulled the tap, then set the mug down in front of me with a bang. The foam ran all over the bar.

When Ham finally got up and came to the bar, Bennett told him to take over.

"Will somebody please tell me what's going on?" Margaret said.

"I'll tell you later," Bennett said. "I need some air."

I was behind him so fast the door didn't even get a chance to shut. "Who was that man?" I said. "What's his name?"

"I don't know his name," he said.

"The hell you don't. He was one of the three men you got to take down Vargas."

He stopped in the middle of the parking lot. He turned to me. He was standing so close, and being a good five inches taller, he had to look down at me. He didn't say a word.

"Start explaining," I said.

He shook his head.

"I already look like hell, Bennett. I've got nothing else to lose. Start talking now or we go right here."

He let out a long, tired breath. "Come with me," he said.

I followed him around the lot, and back to the river. I saw the dock where I had left Vargas after our little lunch date. There was a picnic table back there. Bennett sat down, and then I did the same, directly across from him. A couple of boats passed by. The sun was setting. It was another goddamned beautiful sunset and this was how I was spending it.

"How'd you figure it out?" he said.

"I didn't. Not at first. That was the problem. I would have saved myself a lot of trouble if I had just thought about it for a while."

"I don't understand."

"I was thinking it was all a setup," I said. "I was thinking it *had* to be a setup. Using your car, planting that stuff at Gill's house, and then at Jackie's house . . ."

"How do you know about that?"

"I saw the videotape, Bennett. Leon showed it to me."

"Yeah, the police certainly liked that tape," he said. "I assume Vargas gave it to them. Of all the luck in the world, to have that son of a bitch tape the damned thing . . ."

"That's just it," I said. "Of all the luck. Who would have figured?"

"What do you mean?"

"You couldn't have guessed that would happen. Nobody could have."

"I still don't get it."

"The setup," I said. "It just doesn't work. If somebody was setting up all three of you, why use your car and then return it here? That doesn't set *you* up at all. Without that videotape, there's nothing to tie you into it. Only Jackie and Gill."

He thought about that one for a moment. "Okay," he said. "Okay, I see what you mean."

"What were you going to do? Call in an anonymous tip? Tell them Jackie and Gill had some of the stolen property on their premises?"

"What are you talking about?"

"You get the money," I said. "And Jackie and Gill take the fall."

"Alex, you got it all wrong. That's not why we did this."

"Who's 'we,' Bennett? Who was involved in this? Start by telling me who the third gunman was. It wasn't that other man in the bar?"

"No," he said. "It was my son."

"Your son is six foot fucking six," I said. "He wasn't there that night."

"I have more than one son, Alex."

That stopped me for a second. "I didn't know that. I've never seen him."

"My oldest, Sean, he lives down in Cleveland. He came up here to do it."

"And this other guy, the one who turned up dead. Danny Cox is his name?"

"Yeah, that's him. He was one of Sean's old friends from high school. They used to run around together. Danny was a real hood back then, used to get into trouble all the time, and Sean would sometimes be right there with him. He ended up spending the night in jail once, when Danny and him got loaded and went out joyriding. The cop clocked them doing a hundred and ten down I-75. They stopped to piss in the middle of the road. Otherwise, the cop might not have even caught up with them. Anyway, Sean looked up Danny and asked him if he'd be interested in a little something . . ."

"A little something."

"Yeah."

"When that guy had the gun pressed to my head," I said. "That was a little something."

"Well, Danny knew about this other guy, over in Canada, who could get some guns, and who apparently had a little experience with these types of things. I was a little apprehensive, but Danny told me it would all go down a lot better if they had a pro involved."

"You brought in a pro," I said. "This is getting better by the minute."

"This guy, as far as I know, they just call him 'Blondie.' Obviously, he's even more of a heavy hitter than Danny was aware of."

"You may have something there," I said, "what with Danny lying there in the morgue with two bullet holes in him."

Bennett looked behind him, out at the river. The sun kept going down and painting everything bright orange.

"Alex, this whole thing wasn't supposed to happen this way."

"You know, I just remembered something Vargas said. He said that kick in the ribs you took was all for show. He was right, wasn't he? That was all part of the script."

"It was supposed to be," he said, rubbing his side. "Danny got a little carried away with it."

"So Danny and Blondie were the downstairs men. Your son Sean was the guy who emptied the safe?"

"That's right."

"And it was Sean who delivered the stuff to Gill and Jackie—by himself, after he dropped the other two guys off."

"Yes."

"So tell me, how much did you get? Everybody seems to have a different number in mind."

He looked me in the eye. "Nothing, Alex. Sean got nothing."

"Did they take the money out of the safe or not?"

He held up his hands. "All right, look. I'm telling you what happened. Sean came up and did this thing with Danny and this other guy. Naturally, there has to be some money involved. You gotta pay off Danny, and of course you gotta pay off this Blondie character. The thing is, when they came back here and split up the money in the car, there was thirty thousand dollars in the bag. Fucking Vargas, I should have known. All his big talk about being connected and having all this cash in his safe. Thirty fucking thousand, that's only ten per man."

"Not exactly the score of a lifetime."

"No, and I'm sure this Blondie wasn't too happy about it. I guess what Sean did was, he told them each to take half of his share, because he knew it wasn't what they were expecting. So now they've each got fifteen. Still not a hell of a lot. But what are you gonna do?"

"Bennett . . ."

"This Blondie guy has been thinking about this for three, four days now, Alex. He's feeling like he made a big mistake working with amateurs, and he'll never do it again, right? Then he picks up the newspaper and sees me and Jackie and Gill getting hauled into jail, and he thinks, holy fuck, did I get played for a sucker. Because if all three of us were involved in this, which is certainly how it looks, I gotta admit, then it stands to reason that we were all in on the money."

"Bennett, wait . . ."

"And you, too," he said.

"Me."

"You heard what he said. He thinks you must have been the ringleader."

"Based on what?"

"Based on the fact that he's a pro, Alex. Based on the fact that he had a list of everybody who was supposed to be there that night, and you weren't on the list. He figures if you were the last minute wild card, you must have been added for a reason. So he checks up on you, finds out some things. That you were a cop, and then a private eye. And some other things, it sounds like. He didn't say exactly what. But it sounds like you're a known commodity."

"You did act surprised that night," I said, "when you saw me come in with Jackie."

"Yeah, I was. But at that point, it was too late."

"So now the pro from Canada thinks everybody has a big chunk of the money, and he's getting ripped off. And of course I'm the mastermind."

"He must have figured Sean was hiding most of it. Remember they were wearing those big plastic bags. You could hide a lot of money in there. I mean, that must be what he was thinking. So now he wants the rest of the money. All of it. Or what he *thinks* is all of it. I don't know what I'm going to do, Alex."

"Go to the police. Tell them everything that happened."

"Then what happens to my son?"

"You should have thought about that before."

"So he goes to jail. And I go to jail. And Blondie still thinks we stiffed him. What's going to happen then, Alex? What's going to happen to my wife?"

"Fuck, Bennett." All the adrenaline I was riding on suddenly ran out. I was tired and sore, and I needed very much to eat some dinner and drink some beer and then go to sleep. When I woke up, maybe this would all have been a bad dream.

"You gotta help me, Alex." He was looking down at the table.

"You think so?"

"You gotta."

"You got your son to rip him off," I said. "And you used your best friends for cover. Why should I help you now?"

"This wasn't about the money, Alex. Not for me."

"What are you talking about?"

He took a long breath and looked me in the eye. "Sean was in trouble. He had this debt, you see. These men he owed the money to, down in Cleveland . . . They owned him, Alex. I wanted to help him out. Is that so hard to believe? I wanted to help out my son."

"So you told him to come rob the house," I said. "At gunpoint. While we were all there."

"No, that was sort of his idea. I just told him, I said, I know this guy with some money in his safe. A real son of a bitch who I happen to hate—somebody who could use a good sticking up anyway. Hell, maybe it would even make him move back to Bay Harbor, forget about building up here."

"So he tells you to make sure we're all there when it happens."

"Yeah, he said it would go down better that way. If Vargas was alone, he'd think it was one of us behind it. With all of us there, it looks more like a random hit."

"Because who, after all, would be so dumb or crazy to do it *while we're in the house* . . ."

"Yeah, something like that."

I sat there and thought about it. It didn't get any more believable.

"There were no bullets in those guns," he said. "Did you know that? At least, there weren't supposed to be. Although, hell, I bet Blondie's gun was loaded."

"That's even more stupid," I said. "What if Vargas was armed? He could have drawn on your son."

"I guess that was another part of me being there, to make sure everything went down the right way."

"All right, now this business about giving Gill and Jackie that stuff . . ."

"That was part of the deal."

"What deal?"

"With my son. I told him, you take this money and get yourself out of your situation, but you gotta do one thing for me. You gotta take this stuff and give it to my friends."

"You're kidding me, right?"

"You saw those things up there, Alex. He shouldn't have them. They don't belong to him."

"So you told your son to take them."

"Yes."

"And give them to Gill and Jackie. Like Robin Hood."

"Yeah, sort of."

"Gill told me those artifacts are worthless. Did you know that?"

"No, I didn't. Hell, what can I say? They looked like they were important—you know, with all those Indian markings on them . . ."

"And that stupid cup, just because it had the Royal Navy flag on it . . ."

"That cup meant something to Jackie," he said. "That much I know. You should know it, too."

I threw my hands up.

"His father, Alex. You know about his father."

"No, I don't."

"He never told you the story?"

"No."

"I can't believe it."

"Tell me."

"Okay," he said. He took a breath and settled into the story. "Jackie's father was named Elias Connery. Eli for short. He came over here around 1939, just before the war. He was a deckhand on an ore freighter. You know how when the ships go through the locks, sometimes they'll sit in Whitefish Bay for a while, waiting for the weather to clear? Back then, there used to be all these little boats that would come out to the freighters, and take the men to shore to go to the bars. The Coast Guard would be running all over the place, trying to round them up and send them back. Anyway, young Eli, he came ashore with a bunch of other guys and ended up right here at O'Dell's. This is where he met Jackie's mother. She was a barmaid here. In fact, this is where Jackie was conceived, right down the street at her house."

"I thought he was born in Glasgow."

"He was. Eli's mother found the letter she wrote him, and made her come over. I guess she figured it was still safe, as long as she came over on an American ship, on account of them not being in the war yet. Eli had already enlisted in the Royal Navy by then. He was serving on a corvette, based out of Scapa Flow."

"That was the emblem on the cup."

"Yeah, that's why I knew he'd want it. Especially with Eli going down right here in the lake."

"What do you mean?"

"Alex, hasn't Jackie told you *anything* about this?"

"No, Bennett. He hasn't."

"They all moved back here to Michigan when Jackie was twelve years old. There were a lot of jobs here after the war, especially for experienced seamen. A lot of men from Scotland came over to be skippers on tugboats. That's what Eli did. He was a real character, Alex. He used to spend a lot of time here at the bar. I remember him saying that the lake was more dangerous than any ocean. It was just as deep in some parts, and other parts were shallow, with jagged rocks waiting to tear you apart. Anyway, that's when I met Jackie. We got in a fight the first week he was here. After that, we were buddies. Fifty years now. He was the best man at my wedding, did you know that?"

"Yeah, that much I knew."

"He was in love with my Margaret. Did he tell you that, too?"

"He might have hinted at it. But tell me about his father. You said he went down in the lake."

"Yeah, in 1965. Last they heard from him, he had his boat out by the Devil's Chair. They never found it, Alex. Not a trace."

"Wait a minute," I said. "You're not telling me you think that cup belonged to Jackie's father."

"I told you, there were a lot of Scottish men on the lake back then. It could have been anybody's. Hell, maybe it *was* his. I don't know. It doesn't matter, Alex. Either way, I wanted Jackie to have it."

"Did you ever think to *ask* Vargas for it?"

"I mentioned it once. He didn't even say a word. He just gave me that little look with the eyebrow and his big fat bald head. He didn't even bother to open his mouth and say 'No.' All the more reason to take it from him."

"Yeah, he really had it coming."

"That's right, he did. Running his mouth off all

the time, about what a big shot he is, how's he's gonna build these big houses all over the place. And all the money he's got hidden away in that safe of his. Which he didn't even have, turns out. Fuck him, Alex. That's what I say. He deserved everything that happened."

"And Jackie and Gill, they deserved to be arrested. And this old friend of your son's, he deserved to get killed."

"I told you, that wasn't supposed to happen. Hell, this whole thing went wrong, from beginning to end. I told you, Sean even gave up his whole share of the money, trying to make this Blondie guy happy. He got nothing out of this, Alex. He got completely screwed here."

"I can't listen to any more of this," I said, standing up. "I've gotta get out of here before I throw your stupid ass right in the river."

"Alex, you gotta help me."

"I *was* helping you," I said. "You let me run around like a maniac, trying to prove you were innocent."

"I'm sorry, okay? I didn't know what to do. But now I *really* need you. This guy is gonna be back, Alex. He thinks we're all in on this. You included. You heard what he said."

"You go to the police, Bennett. And then I'll help you."

"You know I can't do that."

"Then you're on your own," I said. "You made your deal with the devil. You can live with it now."

"I have to kill him, Alex. It's the only way. When

this Blondie comes back, I have to kill him."

I stood there looking at him in the dim light. A cool evening wind drifted in off the river.

"Just when I think you can't get any dumber, Bennett . . ."

"Alex, please. I'm begging you."

"Good night," I said. And then I left.

Chapter Eighteen

I was already mad when I left Bennett sitting there by the river. The more I thought about it, the madder I got. By the time I got back to Paradise, I was ready to take someone's head off. I should have known better than to stop in at the Glasgow. I should have just gone home.

That's not what I did.

"You knew where that cup came from, didn't you," I said. I had come right into the place and sat down at the bar.

"Good evening to you, too," he said. He was having a little late dinner, standing next to the register. "What the hell happened to your face?"

"You weren't straight with me," I said. "You let me run all over the place trying to find out who did this to you."

"Who beat you up, Alex? Did Bennett do this to you?"

"You knew all along. You could have stopped me."

"I seem to recall trying to do just that," he said. "It was Bennett, wasn't it . . . I know he looks kind of old now, but I've seen him finish some fights in his day, believe me."

"Just knock it off, Jackie. Why didn't you tell me Bennett did this?"

"Because I knew you'd go off the deep end, Alex. Just like always."

"And how come I've got to find out your whole family history from him, anyway? I thought we were friends."

"All you gotta do is ask me, Alex. When's the last time you actually asked me a question about myself?"

"Fifteen years, you never thought to mention that your father went down right out there in the lake?"

He put his sandwich down on the plate, then took the plate back into the kitchen. When he came back out, he took a cold Canadian out of the cooler and put it in front of me. "You've been living in your own little world for a long time," he said. "You'll go weeks at a time, never even stepping foot in this place. Then suddenly you'll drop in again and spend the whole day here. If you ever stopped for five minutes and said, 'Hey, what did your father do for a living?' Or even, 'When did your father die?' Anything like that, I would have told you the whole story. But no. If you say two words to me, it's to either ask me to make you dinner, or get you a beer, or to tell me about your latest problem—which is almost always just a matter of you losing control of yourself again and getting your ass kicked. And now that I've got my own problem to worry about, the last person in the world I want helping me is you. Because all you'll do is go out and stir up more trouble. From the looks of your face, you already have."

I wasn't sure what to say to that. It hurt me more than anything Vargas had hit me with that day.

"What did Bennett tell you?" Jackie said. "Did he tell you why he did this?"

"He said his son needed the money."

"His son Sean."

"Yes."

"That's what I figured. I knew Sean was in some kind of a jam."

"Do you have any idea what they've done to you, Jackie? They pulled you right into the middle of this."

"You know what, Alex? I think Bennett's the biggest damned fool in the world. You know what else? I love him for it. He did the stupidest thing I've ever heard of, but he did it for the right reason. He was trying to save Sean. And that old tin cup he made them give me. Goddamn it all, who else would do something that crazy?"

"No, it wasn't crazy at all," I said. "Think about it. Giving you that cup was just a way to cover himself. He knew you'd fall for it, Jackie. You've got that cup so now you're a part of it. You might even think he was doing it for you, just as much as he was doing it for his son. Good old Bennett. What a guy."

"You don't get it," he said.

"No, *you* don't get it. And that makes you as big a fool as he is."

He took the bottle off the bar. "I think you should leave now," he said.

"I think you're right."

I left.

When I got home, I couldn't sleep, so I sat up reading with a bag of ice pressed against my mouth. I tried not to think about anything except the words on the page. It didn't work.

I gave up and went outside for awhile, listening to the crickets and to the distant sound of the lake until the mosquitoes found me.

The phone was ringing when I got back inside. I picked it up and heard a woman's voice. "Alex, this is Cynthia Vargas."

"Mrs. Vargas? Is everything all right?"

"Oh, just dandy. My husband has been limping around here all night, calling you every name in the book. I think he wants to kill you, Alex. I mean really kill you."

"Tell him he'll have to come out to Paradise. I don't imagine I'll have any reason to visit your house again."

"That's a shame. Life will be pretty dull around here."

"I'm sure you'll find some way to keep it interesting."

"I'm just looking out for you, Alex. You don't have to be a wise-ass."

"I'm not trying to be," I said. "I mean, look, I've had a tough day here . . ."

"I'll let you go," she said. "Just thought I'd warn you. If you see him coming, be ready."

"I will. I appreciate it."

She said good night to me. If I had wanted to, I could have read some things into her phone call. Or into the sound of her voice even. On this night, I didn't even want to try. Instead I tried to sleep again, lying there looking up at the ceiling. You live in your head too much, Jackie said. He was right.

When I finally did sleep, it came on hard and didn't let go of me until late the next morning. The sound of the wind woke me up. Through the window I could see a sky the color of slate, and the pine trees bending and returning and then bending some more. It wasn't raining yet, but when it came it would be like something out of the Bible. God help anyone who was out on the lake.

I got up and stood in front of the mirror. My face was as ugly as the weather, with bruises all along the left side of my jaw and around both eyes. Any color of the rainbow—you name it, I was wearing it.

I stood under a hot shower for a good thirty minutes, waiting for my neck and my shoulders to loosen up. I had some coffee and some breakfast, and then spent the rest of the day doing nothing. I carried an ice bag around with me, holding it against whatever part of my head or body happened to be hurting.

I had lunch by myself. I read a little bit. I had a beer. I got more ice out of the freezer. Outside the storm passed without raining a drop. Just like that, it was gone. The sun came out. All of a sudden it was a beautiful day. I had no desire to go out and see it.

I read some more. I had dinner by myself, a cheap frozen dinner warmed up in the microwave. I had another beer. The sun went down.

Nobody bothered me. I didn't have to deal with Bennett O'Dell and the crazy mess he had brought upon himself. I didn't have to deal with Winston Vargas and his yapping little dog. Or some mobbed-up Canadian thug who actually went around letting people call him Blondie.

Or Jackie. I didn't have to deal with Jackie telling me to stay out of his business.

I looked at my face in the mirror again. It wasn't looking any better. "You're a real sight," I said. "It's a good thing you stayed inside all day."

Then it hit me. This is what Jackie saw last night, when he looked at me. He saw this face. He wanted me to stay out of it. From the beginning, he was pushing me away. Last night, that was him giving me both barrels, just to make sure.

Maybe there was a good reason. Look at me. He was trying to protect me, to keep me out of this because he knew I'd find some way to get my ass kicked. As usual. I didn't see it, because I was too busy feeling mad about it.

I stepped outside just in time to see a couple of minivans rolling by. It was the men from the last cabin, all dentists and orthodontists from downstate. When the lead driver saw me, he stopped and rolled down his window. "What happened to you?" he said.

"A little misunderstanding," I said.

"Sorry we're leaving so late," he said. "It was such a nice day, we figured we'd stay up here, then drive down overnight. Your helper said it was okay."

"My helper?"

"Yeah, we left the money with him. I hope that was okay."

"I'm sorry," I said. "Who are you talking about?"

"The big blond guy. He said he worked for you."

"When was this?"

"About two hours ago. Did we mess up here, Alex? He seemed legit."

"No, no, you're okay," I said. "You guys go ahead. I'm gonna go check on my helper."

He didn't seem convinced, but the minivans took off anyway. I went back into my cabin, rummaged through the bottom of my closet until I found the shoe box. I took the service revolver out and put bullets in it. Then I went back out and walked down the road, as quietly as I could. There was just enough light left to see where I was going.

The last cabin was a half mile down. As I got closer, I kept to the side of the road, the pine trees brushing against me. When I turned the last corner, I stood there for a moment and watched the cabin.

Everything was quiet. The last light of the day was all but gone.

You're a fool, I told myself. Thinking that you could stay inside all day, all by yourself, that it would all go away. It was right here, right inside this cabin.

I crept up to the door, step by step on a soft carpet of pine needles. The door was ajar. I pushed it open, ready to shoot anything that moved.

One small lamp was lit, on the big table in the center of the room. I flipped on the other lights as I moved through the cabin. It was empty, but I could smell the smoke from his cigar.

There on the center table, in the ashtray, a cigar butt. It was still warm to the touch. Underneath it were some pieces of torn paper. I picked up one piece, saw the "100." They were hundred dollar bills, maybe five or six of them. The men must have paid him in cash. This is what he did to the money.

The rest of the place looked untouched, but this alone was enough to get my blood boiling, just the fact that he was here. This was the last cabin my father had built before he died. These wooden beams he cut, these stones he put together with his bare hands to make this fireplace. This was his master-piece. More than anything else in the world, this cabin was what I had to remember my father.

Like that pewter mug? What did Jackie have to remember *his* father? The lake itself, and what else? Hell, I didn't know what to think anymore.

I threw the cigar out, left the torn money sitting there in the ashtray, locked the place up tight and went back to my cabin. It was dark by the time I got there. The stars were out. I fired up the truck and drove down to the Glasgow. When I walked in, I thought I could smell the cigar smoke again. Maybe I was imagining it.

Or maybe not.

"Jonathan," I said, "was somebody smoking one of those little cigars?"

"Yeah, I hate those things," he said. "They smell like a candy apple burning or something."

"What did he look like?"

"Let's see . . . Real fair-skinned guy, light colored hair. Almost white."

"When was he here?"

"Ah, I don't know. He left a couple of hours ago, I guess. You want to see what he left me for a tip?" Jonathan swept up the small pile next to the register. "Looks like a hundred dollar bill all torn up. Is that weird or what?"

"Where's Jackie?"

"He's not here."

"Where is he?"

"He told me not to tell you."

"Jonathan," I said. "He could be in big trouble. If something goes wrong, you gonna be able to live with that?"

He didn't say anything.

"He's with Bennett, isn't he."

"Yes."

"Where did they go?"

"He didn't tell me, Alex. I swear."

"When did he leave?"

"Around six o'clock, I'd say. Right after Bennett called him."

"What did Jackie say? Did he tell you why he was going to see him?"

"He said he was gonna go help him with something. That's all he said."

It was enough. I hit the road at top speed, hoping I wasn't too late.

Chapter Nineteen

I had just left Paradise when I picked up the cell phone and dialed O'Dell's. Margaret answered.

"Margaret," I said. "Is Bennett there? This is Alex."

"No!" she said. I could barely hear her over the din of a Saturday night crowd in the bar. "I'm all by myself!"

"Do you know where they went?"

"What?"

"I said, do you know where they went?"

I heard her yelling at somebody, then she came back on the line. "No, he's been gone for two hours, Alex! He took Ham with him! I've got thirty people here!"

"What about Jackie?" I said. "Or Gill? Do you know if they're with him?"

"He was talking on the phone before he left. I think it was Jackie, yeah. And then somebody else. It might have been Gill, I don't know."

"You have no idea where they went?"

She yelled at somebody to keep their pants on, and couldn't they see she was on the phone. "I've got no idea, Alex. But if you find him, tell him to get his ass back here."

"When he was on the phone, did he write anything down? Like an address or directions?"

"Uh . . . Let me see. Yeah, you know, I think he was writing something on this pad we keep next to the phone. But he must have taken that with him."

An idea came to me. "Margaret," I said, "do you have a pencil there?"

"Alex, can this wait? I've got people at the bar here."

"This will only take a second. It might be important."

"A pencil, a pencil. Yeah, I got one right here."

"Okay, take the pad of paper and just lightly run it across the paper. Like you're shading it in. You know what I mean?"

"I think so. You mean like they do on television, when they want to see what somebody wrote on the pad?"

"Yeah, that's it."

"I'll try it," she said. "You really think this will work?"

"Why not?"

"I'm getting something, Alex. It says . . . Let's see . . . It's the number eleven."

"Okay, good. What else?"

"Hold on." She yelled at somebody again, about how yes, she was playing with a pencil instead of getting him his beer, and if he didn't like it, he was free to go drink someplace else. "Sorry, Alex. Some people have no patience. Let's see, the rest of this says . . . It says, 'W' and then this looks like . . . P-I-E something. I can't read this."

"West Pier, maybe?"

"Yeah, Eleven West Pier. I think that's it! This really works!"

"Leon would be proud," I said.

"What's that?"

"Never mind," I said. "I'm gonna go find Bennett and send him home."

"I wish you would, Alex. I gotta tell you, I'm a little worried here. Bennett hasn't said a word to me about what's going on, but I just know this is more bad business."

I hung up the phone and put it on the passenger's seat, right next to my gun.

As I got closer to the Soo, I thought about the address Margaret had given me. I knew the West Pier was on the west side of town, not far from O'Dell's, in fact. They were there right now, I thought, doing God knows what, with Blondie involved somehow. No doubt about that.

I had taken the highways, figuring I'd get there faster if I really flew. I bailed off of I-75 just before the International Bridge, took Ashmun Street into town, across the power canal, right under the dark window of Leon's office. I headed west on Portage Street, and then got off onto the dirt road that ran under the bridge. As I roared past the old drive-in restaurant, they must have wondered where the hell

I was going so fast, but I wasn't about to stop and explain.

I slowed down to cross the railroad tracks. I rolled past some abandoned warehouses, and a quiet, empty old house. I didn't see any numbers. How the hell was I going to find number eleven?

There were a couple cars parked on the street. I couldn't imagine who would be down here after dark. I looked for Bennett's Explorer, then remembered it wouldn't be here. It was still impounded by the police. I looked for Jackie's Lincoln instead. I didn't see it anywhere.

I stopped just as the pavement was about to end. Beyond that was an old railroad spur, leading down a quarter mile to the pier itself. There was a time when boats would unload onto trains here, but that was all a distant memory. There was nothing now but a few brick buildings, rusted railroad tracks, tall weeds, and the damp smell of the St. Marys River. Whatever Bennett was up to, he picked a hell of a place to do it.

I took the gun out of my truck with me, and approached the nearest building. The front door had a "15" stenciled on the glass. There was a thick layer of dust on the glass, and nothing but total darkness behind it. All the door needed was a big spider web, but apparently even the spiders had given up on the place.

I moved to the next building. This door was solid wood, and there was an "13" scratched on it with white chalk. The next one down had to be 11.

It was a two-story building with a metal roof. It

had probably held a lot of cargo off the river, back when it was in business. You could have done something with it if you had enough money—maybe turn it into a bar or something. Nobody had thought of that yet. I tried the front door. It was locked.

There was a narrow alley on one side of the building, a wider alley on the other—wide enough that you could drive a vehicle around to the back. I took the wide alley, passing under a few dark windows, all made from those thick squares of glass you see in old factories and other places you're glad you never have to see the inside of. The ground was rutted and overgrown with weeds. The light of a half moon was reflected in a hundred small puddles.

When I got around to the back of the place, there was an old wooden loading dock and a semi trailer that looked like it had been sitting there for thirty years, everything glowing in the moonlight like something out of a black-and-white movie. Bennett, I'm going to kill you, I said to myself. If you're not dead already.

I went up some cement stairs to the loading dock. There were two large roll-down doors that I wasn't going to try opening. Beyond that was a regular metal door. I stood there for a moment, deciding how to play it. I could have yelled Bennett's name, but I didn't want to spook anybody if they were in the middle of something.

Okay, I thought, just go in quiet. If you see something going on, then do whatever you have to do. If you don't see anything, then start calling out some names.

The door was ajar. It made a horrible metallic screech as I pushed it open.

It was dark inside.

Okay, time to make some noise. "Bennett!"

The gun blast ripped through everything. I fell to the ground. It was all sudden noise and pain and fear as another blast hit the wall behind me, then another. Then a great weight fell onto my back, and I thought, this is it. I'm dead right here.

"It's me!" I yelled. "It's Alex!"

There was a silence, or at least no more gunshots. With the ringing in my ears, it felt like I'd never hear true silence ever again. The weight on my back pressed me to the ground.

Finally, a voice. "Alex? Is that you?"

"Yes!"

"Are you all right?"

"Get this off of me!"

I heard footsteps, and then the weight was lifted off my back, whatever the hell it was. Strong arms grabbed me by the shoulders and pulled me up to a sitting position. "Alex, my God," somebody said.

A light came on, blinding me. "Oh shit. Look at him."

"Will somebody tell me what the fuck is going on?" I said. "You almost blew my head off!"

The light kept blinding me.

"And will you get that flashlight out of my face?"

When I could see again, I saw that it was Bennett holding the flashlight. His other hand was wrapped around the long barrel of a deer rifle. Ham stood next to him, with another flashlight and another rifle.

They were flanked by Jackie and Gill, each with yet another rifle. I recognized Jackie's as an old Winchester lever action he had lying around. It hadn't been fired in years.

I tried hard to breathe. "Start talking," I said.

"The door fell on you," Bennett said.

"What are you doing here?"

"We blew it right off the hinges. Thing must weigh a hundred pounds."

"What are you doing here?"

"Ham, get him off the ground." His son tried to pick me up. I slapped him away and got up on my own.

"How'd you find us?" Bennett said.

"Easy, I followed the idiot tracks. Now are you gonna tell me what's going on?"

"We were supposed to meet Blondie here," he said. "He was supposed to be here an hour ago."

"And you were all sitting here with fucking deer rifles? Waiting to shoot him? Look at you guys."

"What else are we gonna do, Alex? He's the one who's making this happen."

"Jackie," I said, looking him in the eye. "Look at you. And you, Gill."

"You weren't supposed to be here," Jackie said. "This isn't your problem. Why did you come here?"

"Knock it off, okay? You've been pushing me away since this whole mess started. And I hope you cleaned that old gun, for God's sake. I'm surprised it didn't blow up right in your hands."

"I was going to call you," Bennett said. "Jackie made sure I didn't. He's just looking out for you."

"Why were you going to call me, Bennett? So I could come join your little posse? Did you actually think he'd fall for this? Why didn't you just tell him to go to the shooting range? Here, go stand down there, right in front of that target? How dumb do you think this guy is?"

"Alex, it was his idea."

"What are you talking about?"

"He picked this place," Bennett said. "He told me to be here at nine o'clock. Actually both of us."

"Who, you and me?"

"That's what he said. Make sure you bring the money, and Alex."

"He was just playing you," I said. "There's no way he'd walk into this. He was seeing what you'd do. Hell, he may be out there right now, watching us."

Bennett walked out the open doorway, into the night. He stood on the dock, looking out at the river. At this point it was a good two miles across. The lights of Soo, Canada burned in the distance. "You really think he's out there? On a boat or something?"

"If he is, you certainly put on quite a show for him."

"Fuck," he said. "That son of a bitch."

"Bennett, this guy's a pro. He's been playing around with you. With all of us. He wants that money."

"There is no money. I told him that."

"He doesn't believe you."

"What are we gonna do?"

"Where'd you guys park?" I said.

"There's a lot down by the bridge," he said. "Jackie picked us up at the bar. Why?"

"You should take everybody home, Jackie. Margaret's worried out of her head, not to mention being short-handed on a Saturday night. I'm gonna get back up to Paradise. I got a bad feeling all of a sudden."

"Why?" Jackie said. "What's wrong?"

"I'm just thinking, maybe he's not out on that river. Maybe he had another reason to get us out here."

"What, you mean to draw us away?"

"I hope I'm wrong," I said. "Go make sure Margaret's okay. I'll call her on the cell phone. And Jonathan, too."

We all walked back out of the alley together. The four men all jumped into the bed of my truck and I took them back up Portage Street to the parking lot. It occurred to me as I was driving, all I need now is a police car stopping us. He'd find four men in the back, all with recently-fired rifles. Three of them would even have open bail bonds. That's all we'd need to make the evening complete.

I dropped them off at Jackie's car, then headed back east to Paradise. I caught a look at myself in the rearview mirror. I was filthy with all the dust and other crap from the floor of that building, that on top of all the bruises I already had going. I was definitely not pretty.

I called Margaret, and was glad to hear her voice when she answered. I told her Bennett and Ham would be there any minute now. Then I called Jonathan.

"I'm on my way," I said. "Jackie'll be a few minutes behind me."

"What did he get mixed up in this time?" Jonathan said.

"You don't want to know. Have you seen the blond guy again? The one who left you the torn-up hundred?"

"I haven't, no."

"If you do, call me right back," I said. "I'll see you soon."

I hung up and took a deep breath. Everybody was in one piece, at least for the moment. "What are you up to, Blondie?" I said. "What the hell's your game?"

When I hit town, the Glasgow Inn was a welcome sight. I'd go in and wash my face in the bathroom, have a couple of cold Canadians. By the time Jackie got here, I'd almost be ready to forgive him for being such a jackass.

As I pulled into the parking lot, another pickup truck came roaring by, right behind me. I opened my door, stepped out, looked up the road, and then up into the night sky. I saw a great black dragon rising above the treeline, obscuring the silver clouds behind it, the stars, the moon.

Smoke.

That was one of the volunteer firemen racing by. He was headed north.

I got back into the truck and sprayed gravel. When I turned onto my service road, I was expecting to see the fire truck parking in front of my cabin. It wasn't.

"What the hell's going on?" I said. Then it hit me.

I kept driving down the road, all the way to the end, to the last cabin. As soon as I turned around the last bend, I saw the truck. Paradise Volunteer Fire. A bright flume of water hung in the sky, lit by the floodlights from the truck. There were seven or eight other vehicles all spread around the place. One of the men looked back at me as I got out. He had his rubber boots on, his fire hat, but no coat.

Flames. There were flames, orange and yellow and blue.

"Mr. McKnight," he said.

I didn't hear him. I walked past him, toward the cabin. I got so close I could feel the heat on my face.

"Mr. McKnight! Stand back from there!"

I felt myself being pulled backward. I kept staring into the flames. This was my father's masterpiece, the best thing he ever built, and the last.

It was burning up before my eyes.

Three hours passed. It was well after midnight when the firemen left. They didn't want to leave anything hot, not with all the dry brush around. "Last thing we want is a forest fire," the man said. "Do you have any idea how this happened?"

I didn't have anything to say to him. I just stood there and watched the men as they soaked the remains of the cabin with a fine spray of water, back and forth, back and forth. The water hung in the air and collected on my face, but I didn't wipe it off. I clenched my hands into fists, released them, and then clenched again, over and over.

"This thing went up fast, Mr. McKnight. Please don't touch anything until the arson investigator gets here."

"I won't," I said.

"We'll be back tomorrow to make sure nothing's smoking."

"Okay."

"We did the best we could."

"I know. Thank you."

When they were gone, it was just me and a pile of black rubble. The chimney was left standing, the chimney my father built with his hands, stone by stone. It stood alone in the clearing now, looking strangely out of place.

I don't know how long I waited there, or what I was even waiting for. I couldn't leave. I couldn't walk away.

Finally, I did. I took the truck back to my cabin, went inside, and sat down in a chair. I stared at the floor until the phone rang. I looked at the clock. It was 1:42 in the morning.

"McKnight," the voice said.

"I'm going to kill you," I said.

"Hold onto those dreams. It'll keep you young."

"I swear to you, Blondie. I'm going to kill you."

"Yeah, we covered that. Have I made my point yet? You guys gonna come through for me or what?"

"There's nothing to come through with, you stupid fuckhead. I had nothing to do with the robbery, first of all. And even if I did, there was thirty thousand in that safe, and nothing more."

"I know who Vargas is," he said. "I know what kind of scam he's got going on. That's the only reason I bought into this. What I get for working with amateurs, I guess. Never again, eh? When Seanie gave up his share, that was like the first clue, you know what I mean? He gave it up because he knew there was a lot more. Hell, he might have had it stashed right on his person, underneath that big bag he was wearing. Would've taken more balls than I thought he had, but hell, why not? Maybe he did. As soon as your other three friends ended up arrested, it all sort of came together, didn't it. When I found out who *you* were, this mystery guest who wasn't even supposed to be there in the first place, it all made sense. I know all about you, McKnight. I thought you acted pretty cool when I had that gun on your head. Now I know why. You knew what the score was that night. You were in on this from the beginning."

"You got it all wrong, Blondie. Everything you said is totally wrong."

"Right now, what I really need you to do is understand something, McKnight. You gotta know what you're dealing with here, eh?"

"I know what you are, Blondie. Believe me, I've seen 'em a lot better. Torching a cabin, that's really chickenshit stuff, you know that? Why don't you come here and talk to me face to face?"

"Oh, we'll do that one, McKnight. We'll most definitely do that one, eh?"

"How about tonight? How about right now?"

"Patience, eh? You Americans, I swear. What you need to do is round up all the money and go to O'Dell's place. I'll call you there tomorrow morning at eight o'clock."

"There is no money, Blondie. Simple as that. When are you gonna get that?"

"I'm thinking Vargas had at least a half million in that safe, McKnight. It might have been more. If it was, I'll just have to trust you to come through with the rest of it. I know you're an honorable man. You're the one with the cool head, too, so I'd appreciate it if you did all the talking tomorrow. We're gonna do this one out in the open. I mean real open, eh? I suggest you have a boat ready. I'll be giving you some GPS coordinates for a position out on the lake. That's where we'll meet you."

"I'm not going to be there, Blondie. It ain't happening."

"I think you will be, McKnight. I know you're a lonely old man, with no family, nobody you really care about. Except maybe one person."

"What are you talking about?"

"I got somebody here you should talk to."

There was a brief silence on the line, and in that one horrible moment I knew who it would be, before he even spoke. He dropped the men off, then he came back by himself. If he had made it home, he would have called me by now. I was too far out of my head to notice that he hadn't.

"Alex, it's me."

"Jackie. My God. Jackie . . ."

"I'm sorry, Alex. I'm sorry."

Chapter Twenty

I picked up Jonathan on my way to O'Dell's place. He came down the back stairs rubbing his eyes. As soon as he saw me, he knew something was wrong. While he got dressed, I went back out to the parking lot and looked at Jackie's car. The driver's side door was still open, the dome light still on. A dozen moths were flying around inside. The night had turned cold.

I told him what I knew as I drove. He listened to me and didn't say a word. Finally, when I was done, he said, "What are we gonna do?"

"We're gonna get him back," I said.

"How?"

"I'm not sure yet."

When we got to O'Dell's place, Gill was already there. He was sitting at a table with Bennett and Ham. Margaret was pouring him a cup of coffee. Together they looked like the most tired, most miserable four people in the world. It was almost three in the morning.

When we were all sitting down together, Margaret included, I repeated once again everything Blondie had told me on the phone.

"He wants us to meet him out on the open water?" Bennett said. "How crazy is this guy?"

"How did Jackie sound when you talked to him?" Gill said.

"As good as can be expected," I said. "Although he didn't say more than a few words."

"Why aren't we calling the police?" Jonathan said.

"We can't call the police," Bennett said.

"Why not?"

"They'll kill him if we do," Bennett said. "This is between him and us."

"Fuck that," Jonathan said. "I'm calling them right now."

Ham and Bennett both stood up to stop him.

"All right, knock it off," I said. "Jonathan, sit down. We'll keep that as a possibility. Although I'm not even sure who we'd call at this point. We don't know where this is gonna happen, whether it's Canadian water or American."

"Hell, the police will just fall all over themselves," Bennett said. "And probably get Jackie killed. Look what they've done so far."

"Everybody just relax," I said. "Drink some more coffee. We've gotta think of something."

"I can get some money together," Bennett said. "But not that much on such short notice. We're gonna have to tell him we don't have it yet."

"He's not gonna buy that," I said. "He thinks we have it already, remember?"

"I can get some money," Gill said. "I can talk to some tribal members."

"We shouldn't be paying anybody anything," Ham said. "We've got them outnumbered. All we need is a good plan."

"Like what?" Jonathan said. "Let's hear your plan."

"I don't have one yet," Ham said. "I'm just saying . . ."

"I don't think it matters if we have the money or not," I said. "Either way, I don't think they're planning on doing this in the middle of the lake and then letting us leave."

We all sat there for a while thinking about that one. It didn't do much for the mood.

"Where's your other son, anyway?" I finally said to Bennett. "Shouldn't he be here?"

"Why should he be here?"

"He's the one who put this thing together, isn't he?"

"Yeah," Bennett said, looking a little sick. "He was. The thing is . . ."

"What?"

"The thing is, I've been trying to get hold of him. He hasn't been answering his phone."

"You think somebody got to him?"

"I hope not," he said. "I mean, I don't think so. After a couple of days, I called some of his friends down there. I didn't like what they were telling me."

"What did they say?"

"He had money, Alex. All of a sudden, Sean's walking around like he's loaded. Sounds like he paid off some debts, celebrated a little. And then left."

"Where'd he go?"

"Nobody knows. He quit his job, moved out of his apartment. He just disappeared."

"So what are you telling me?"

"That maybe there *was* more money in that safe. That maybe he *did* hold out on his partners."

"Oh, this is beautiful," I said. "This is just great."

"Either way, it doesn't change anything. We're in the same spot."

"Only this way, it's your son's fault," I said.

"He's gone, Alex. Okay? He's gone. There's nothing I can do."

Jonathan stood up like he was about to go over the table at him.

"Jonathan, take it easy," I said. "Let's take care of Jackie first. You can take this up with him later." Jonathan may have been twenty years younger, but he was giving up six inches and fifty pounds, so I hoped he never did.

"I've got one good son," Bennett said, putting his hand on Ham's shoulder, "just like Jackie does. I should have stopped there, okay? I'm sorry for what Sean did. What else can I say? I'm sorry."

"All right," I said. "Just keep thinking."

We sat there some more. We were getting nowhere fast. I got up and made the one phone call I had to make.

A half hour later, the door opened. It was bad

enough I woke up Leon Prudell and asked him to come over here in the middle of the night—the reception when he arrived was downright hostile.

"What's he doing here?" Bennett said. "Alex, you didn't really call him, did you?"

"Good evening, everybody," Leon said.

"Leon always has ideas," I said. "I figured we could use some about now."

"Come on, Alex," Bennett said. "What can he do for us?"

"He got you guys arrested, didn't he? He's a man of many talents."

"He works for Vargas," Bennett said. "He can't help us."

"I got fired," Leon said. "I'm a free agent."

"Why'd you get fired?" Bennett said.

"He wanted Alex's head on a platter. I refused to help him."

That shut Bennett up, but he still didn't look happy. Leon pulled up a chair, had a cup of coffee, and listened to me as I went over it one more time.

"This Blondie is a pro?" he said.

"Yes," I said.

"He'd kill Jackie if he had to? And anybody else?"

"In a second."

"Doing this on the open water. That's a total sucker bet, you realize. He can dump anybody he wants to, right in the lake."

"Yeah, I sort of figured that was his plan."

"He's holding all the cards here," Leon said. "Somehow, we have to outmaneuver him." He

sounded like the Leon of old, and for once, on a
night that was too cold for July, with Jackie tied up
somewhere on the other side of the bridge, his voice
was exactly what I needed to hear.

"So how do we do that?" I said.

"Do you have some paper? We've got to draw
some diagrams."

Ham got him some paper and a pen. Bennett still
didn't look happy, but he watched carefully as Leon
started drawing.

"Okay, we know there's two of them, right?" He
drew two circles at the top of the page. "Any chance
there's more?"

"Could be," I said. "But I'd bet on just the two."

"Okay, so they have Jackie." He drew a square
under the two circles. "And there's how many of
us?" He counted out the five men in the room, giving
Margaret a little smile as he skipped over her.

"I'm a part of this," she said.

"You're the home base," he said.

"Like hell."

"He's right," I said. "We'll need somebody here."

"If anything happens to that man . . ."

"We're gonna get him back," I said. "I promise."

"Okay, five men," Leon said. He drew five
squares in the middle of the page. "And me." He
drew another square below the five. "And Margaret."
He drew another square below that. "We've got
them outnumbered, seven to two."

"They're not gonna let all of us come out to give
them the money," I said. "I'm sure they'll only want
one or two of us."

"The rest of us can hide in the boat," Ham said. "We can surprise them."

"That puts Jackie at risk," Leon said. "You know they'll have a gun to his head."

Margaret covered her face with her hands. Bennett tried to touch her shoulder, but she shrugged him away.

"We need another way to bring our number advantage into play," Leon said. "We need a second boat."

"We'll be on open water," I said. "They'll start shooting as soon as they see it."

"That's the problem. There's no place to hide it."

"What if we don't even try?" I said.

"How do you mean?"

"What if we don't try to hide the second boat?" Something was coming to me. On a normal night I wouldn't have even said it. But this was not a normal night. "What was that thing you tried once? Where you made those hockey goons think they were surrounded?"

"The illusion of overwhelming force."

"Yeah, that was it."

"The illusion of what?" Bennett said.

"Overwhelming force," Leon said.

"You mean like in Desert Storm?"

"No," Leon said. "That wasn't an illusion."

"How does it work?"

"You have a boat, right?" Leon said.

"A friend down the road has a good boat," Bennett said. "I'm sure he'll let me use it."

"Okay, so now we need one more. It has to be big and it has to be fast."

"Where are we gonna get a boat like that?" Bennett said.

"I know the perfect boat," I said. "What do you think, Leon?"

"What's he gonna do?" Leon said. "He can't fire me twice."

Bennett went off to wake up his neighbor, to ask him if he could use his boat. Leon and I drove across town to the Kemp Marina. At four in the morning, the streets were deserted.

"You think the marina's open?" he said.

"It's gotta be. Some people live on their boats, right? You can't just lock 'em in."

"There has to be *some* sort of security."

"We'll think of something, right? You've got your lock picks with you?"

He patted his jacket pocket. "Don't leave home without 'em."

"You think you'll be able to get his boat started?"

"We'll find out."

"Good enough."

A minute passed, then he cleared his throat. "You think everybody's up for this?" he said.

"I don't know. They're all a little trigger-happy. I got to see that firsthand."

"There's only a couple of ways this is going to end up, Alex. Whether it's us or them, somebody won't make it out alive."

"You've got little kids, Leon. You helped us with the idea. You don't need to be there on the water when it happens."

"You need me to be there," he said. "Jackie needs me. I'm the only man those guys wouldn't recognize, right?"

I thought about it. "Yeah, you're right. Blondie saw all four of us at Vargas's house, and he saw Ham when he came to O'Dell's bar."

"Besides, I'm your partner."

"Not anymore," I said. "I'm the one who walked away from that."

"Yeah, but I didn't."

I looked over at him. My partner, Leon, sitting there in the dim light of the dashboard. "You're really showing me something," I said. "Once again."

"Let's do this," he said. "Here's the marina."

We turned into the parking lot. There were maybe a dozen cars. We pulled up next to the fence. The whole place was well lit, which made sense when you consider how much money was floating here.

"I don't see anybody at the front gate," he said.

"Let's hope it's open."

We got out and approached the gate. When I pushed it, it swung right open.

"Piece of cake," Leon said.

Then a voice behind us. "Gentlemen." A man came out of the little dockmaster's shack and caught up to us. "Can I help you?"

"We're meeting Win Vargas at his boat," I said. "We're going fishing with him."

"Any unaccompanied visitor between the hours of

nine P.M. and seven A.M. needs to be on the list," he said. "I don't see anybody for Vargas."

"Oh, he did it again," I said. "Win is such an idiot. Can you believe that?"

"He's such an idiot," Leon said.

The man wasn't buying it. He had a tight-ass ex-military air about him, the kind of man who did things by the book. "You are not on the list," he said. "You're gonna have to wait here until Mr. Vargas arrives to meet you. What time did he say he'd be here?"

I remembered something. When I was here before, to meet Vargas on his boat, I had spoken to a woman, who had some colorful things to say about her computer, and about the man who wouldn't pay to have it fixed. I hoped this was that man.

"Oh, any minute now," I said. "Hey, by the way, I spoke to your wife a few days ago. She mentioned you were having some trouble with your computer."

"Yes? What about it?"

"My friend and I would be more than happy to take a look at it. You know how expensive repairs can be." I wasn't sure what we'd actually do with his computer—maybe Leon could monkey around with it. It was the only way I could think of to make some points with him.

"Too late, already had it fixed," he said. "I appreciate it, though."

"Next time," I said. "You just give us a call."

"I'll do that," he said. "Here, you can come wait inside until Vargas gets here."

"That's okay," I said. "We'll wait in the truck.

Give us a chance to get our gear together."

"I got some coffee in there, help wake you up. You especially, sir," he said, eyeing my face, "you look like you could use a little something."

"No, thanks anyway," I said. "We'll wait out here."

"Suit yourself," he said. "Don't blame me if you fall right asleep."

We went back out to the truck and got in.

"Now what?" I said.

"There's razor wire on top of this fence," he said. "We're not climbing it."

"We could grease him," I said. "What did you used to call it? Slipping him a Franklin?"

"I don't think he'll take it. He's too straight."

"We need that boat, Leon. What are we gonna do?"

"Let's go try the Franklin," he said. "If that doesn't work, we'll have to find a canoe or something. Come in from the river."

We got out, went back to the front gate. "You got a hundred dollar bill, don't you?" I said.

"No, I assumed you had one."

"Ah, hell." I took my wallet out and started counting twenties.

"Alex . . ."

"Sixty, eighty. I only have eighty."

"Alex . . ."

"What?"

"Be quiet," he whispered.

I looked up to see him standing next to the shack. He gestured to the small window. When I took a peek inside, I saw our man with his head down on the table.

"He was the one telling *me* I needed coffee," I said.

"Shh, come on. Show me where the boat is."

We tiptoed away from the shack, then made our way down to Vargas's row. "Next to last on the end," I said.

When we got to it, Leon stood there for a moment, admiring the boat. "This looks faster than hell," he said. "It's perfect."

"Come on, let's see if you can start it."

We climbed aboard. I figured we should both keep low, so I sat on the deck while he did his work. First he pulled out a small flashlight. "Here," he said. "Hold this." I held it in place while he put the tension bar into the ignition with one hand, and then started working the pick with his other hand.

Five minutes passed. He changed to another pick.

Five more minutes. He stopped for a moment, shook his hands out.

"I don't want to rush you," I said. "But Sleeping Beauty's gonna wake up and wonder why we never came back with Vargas."

"I know. Let me try again."

He worked the lock for another five minutes. "Damn it," he said. "Damn it all to hell."

"What about the cabin door? Maybe Vargas keeps a spare key in there."

"All right, let me try that," he said, shaking his head. "Damn it."

He moved to the double doors on the cabin and

did his thing in the lock. Tension bar, pick, one rake. The handle turned. "Sure, this one I can do," he said.

We pushed one of the doors in and stepped down. The first room was a little galley, with lots of shelves and compartments. "You look in here," I said. "I'll see what's in this other room."

There was another set of double doors. When I opened them, I expected to see the sleeping quarters through the next door. That's not what I found. All I saw were boxes. From floor to ceiling, nothing but cardboard boxes.

"Leon, come here," I said.

"Hold on, I'm just getting started here."

"Come here," I said.

He stopped what he was doing and poked his head into the room. "What is all this stuff?"

"Appliances," I said. "Stereos, microwaves. Those big boxes underneath are either refrigerators or stoves."

"What's he doing? Running them to Canada, you think?"

"He gave me this big speech at the poker game," I said, "about how his Canadian customers get killed with the duty crossing the border. I'm guessing that for a certain amount of cash consideration, Vargas will do a little backdoor delivery service with their very expensive American appliances. Blondie said he knew who Vargas was, and what his scam was. I think we just walked right in on it."

"Of course," Leon said. "If he went into a Canadian port, he'd have to put up the yellow quarantine flag, let the customs guys come out and check out what he's bringing in. But it's a hell of a big lake. He could dock this thing just about anywhere."

"That explains the double doors. He probably had them custom-made, just so he could haul this stuff in here."

"He must drive the boat down to Petoskey, load up down there. But why would he leave all this sitting here overnight? Seems risky."

"The weather," I said. "Remember yesterday morning? It looked like a storm was coming in. I bet he had to cancel his run."

"Yeah, that makes sense."

"Let's go get the keys. We're running out of time."

"What, you mean—"

"We've got some leverage now," I said. "Let's go wake up your former client."

Chapter Twenty-one

We rolled into Vargas's driveway around 5 A.M. The sky was just starting to brighten on the eastern horizon. With no sleep, with the sight of the cabin still burning in my head, and the sound of Jackie's voice on the phone, I was running on pure adrenaline. There'd be plenty of time to deal with it after this was done. If I lived through it.

I knocked on Vargas's front door. As we stood there waiting, I remembered the night Jackie and I had stood on this very spot, waiting for Vargas to let us in to play poker. Somewhere inside, we heard the familiar barking of the world's toughest Chihuahua.

Mrs. Vargas answered the door wearing a bathrobe, sticking her head out and blocking the dog with her leg. "Alex," she said, "what's going on?"

"We need your husband."

"Nice face you got going there, Alex. And this must be Mr. Prudell. Didn't he fire you yesterday?"

"Where is he?"

"I'm right here," Vargas said, appearing behind her. He was wearing purple silk pajamas. He had the dog in one arm. "What the hell's going on? Why are you here?"

I pushed the door open. "We came to ask you a little favor."

"What are you doing? You can't come in here."

"Call the police," I said. "Tell them we'll all meet down at your boat. Have them bring somebody from Customs, too."

"What are you talking about?"

"We don't have time for games, Vargas. We need to use your boat."

"Ha, that's good."

"Leon, you got your cell phone handy? Call the police, tell them to go to the marina."

"All right, just hold on," Vargas said. "Let's talk about this. Why do you need my boat?"

"I'll give you the quick version," I said. "One of the men who broke into your house has Jackie. He wants us to meet him out in the middle of the lake. We've got one boat, and we need one more. Something fast. You let us use your boat, we bring it back today, we forget everything we know about your little side business, you never see us again. That's the deal. Now give us the keys."

"You're telling me one of the men who broke into *this house* and put a gun to *my head* is gonna meet you out on the lake?"

"He wasn't the guy who took you upstairs," I

said. "He was one of the men who stayed down here with the rest of us."

"Good enough," he said. "Give me five minutes to get dressed."

"Vargas, you're not coming with us."

"The hell I'm not. You want the boat, you get me, too."

"No way," I said. "Absolutely not."

"You can't take the boat out of the marina without me," he said. "Mr. Shadmore will never let you out."

"That would be the dockmaster, I take it? Yeah, he's a sharp one, all right."

"You don't even know how to get through the locks," he said. "Who do you call? What channel are they on?"

I gave Leon a look. "Go on and get dressed," I told Vargas. "Make it fast. And so help me God, if you think you're taking that dog with you . . ."

"The dog goes where I go," he said.

"Vargas, I've got a gun in the truck. If you bring that dog, I swear, I'll shoot him right between the eyes."

Somehow the dog picked up on that one and started barking again. Vargas was still trying to calm him down as he went up the stairs to his room.

"You shouldn't threaten that dog," Mrs. Vargas said. "That's the only thing in this world he loves. Besides money."

"Thanks for the tip," I said.

"You're so welcome," she said. "Where are you taking the boat?"

"Mrs. Vargas, I'm sorry. We don't have time to talk about this right now."

"Okay, fine," she said. "We won't talk about it. You know, the two of you look like you could use some coffee about now."

"If you happen to have some."

"No," she said, as she left the room. "I don't."

We stood there for five more minutes, until Vargas came back down the stairs, dressed in black nylon from head to toe. Add the mask and he would have been a ninja. My heart stopped when I saw the black Baretta in his hand. I was waiting for him to point it at me. Instead, he checked the safety, unzipped his jacket, and slipped it into a shoulder holster. "I'm ready," he said.

"I hope you know how to use that gun," I said.

"We'll go to the shooting range someday, McKnight. I'll show you."

We drove to the marina in my truck. It felt a little cozy, the three of us crammed into the front seat, with Leon in the middle, but it was a short trip. When we got there, Leon took the truck and went off to pick up some supplies. "Thank God for the twenty-four-hour Super Kmart," he said. "I'll meet you back at O'Dell's place."

That left Vargas and me on the boat. The dockmaster gave us the fish-eye when we checked in. "Where's the other one?" he said. "I thought there were two of you waiting."

"He had to go home," I said. "He was too sleepy."

When we got to the boat, Vargas jumped aboard and fired it up. I jumped in behind him. "I did quite a job on your face," he said as he backed the boat out. "You been putting ice on it?"

"I hear you've been walking a little funny," I said.

He didn't say anything. He just pushed the throttle forward, heading down the river toward the locks.

"So the deal went sour," he finally said. "Your little team fell apart?"

"What team are you talking about?"

"You said one of the robbers has Jackie. You must have had a disagreement on how to split up the money."

"When this is all over," I said, "I promise you, I'll make sure you know everything there is to know. For right now, I'll tell you two things. Jackie had no part in this, and neither did I. That's the God's honest truth, Vargas. I've got no reason to lie to you."

"Okay, whatever you say."

A light fog covered the river. The sun began to rise behind us.

"So how much did they really take?" I said.

"If you were in on it, you wouldn't have to ask."

"Yeah, no kidding."

He thought about it. "They got just over seven hundred thousand."

"That's a lot of refrigerators."

"I guess you could say that."

"Was this all from payoffs to avoid the duty? Or was there more to it? Maybe a few stoves that fell off the back of a truck? That would be a hundred-percent profit, wouldn't it? Or maybe there's something else you're moving, as long as you're going around Customs?"

"You're not giving me your whole story," he said. "Why should I give you mine?"

"Fair enough."

I could see the locks appearing in the fog.

"Who's this man you're gonna meet?" he said. "The one who has Jackie . . ."

"They call him Blondie."

"I've heard that name. Blondie. Canadian guy, right?"

"What do you know about him?"

"I'm trying to think. Blondie. He was one of the men in my house?"

"Yes."

"Son of a bitch. Blondie."

"Anything you can tell me about him would help us."

"I've never met him. I've just heard his name somewhere. From some of the, um . . . well, from some of the people I deal with."

"Keep thinking," I said.

"That guy they found, Cox, he was in the house, right? I assume Blondie killed him?"

"Apparently."

"Blondie was in my house. He broke into my house with a gun."

"Yes."

"I want him, Alex."

"I want him, too," I said. "Believe me."

The locks were getting closer.

"Who was the third man?" he said.

I hesitated. "Somebody from out of town," I said. "You don't know him." It was half a lie. I didn't want to get Vargas going on the O'Dell family yet. There'd be time for that later. "Like I said, I'll make sure you know everything when we're done."

He picked up the radio handset and called the locksmaster. When we were in the lock, he cut the throttle down to an idle. We waited for the water to lift us twenty-one feet.

"I thought I was being pretty smart keeping that money in the safe," he finally said. "No IRS, no first wife, no soon-to-be-second wife. I should have known something like that would happen. You can't hide that much money for long. Some people can just smell it. You know what I mean?"

"Let me ask you one thing," I said. "You remember that pewter mug you had in your collection? The one from the Royal Navy?"

"Yeah, what about it?"

"I assume the police will give it back to you someday. You can put it back in that glass case of yours. If anybody ever asks you if they can have it, do me a favor, will ya?"

"What's that?"

"Give it to him."

It was just after six o'clock when we docked behind O'Dell's place. There was another boat already there, a twenty-five-foot cruiser. It wasn't half the boat Vargas had, but it looked like enough.

Bennett and Ham were both looking out separate windows when we walked in. Gill was sitting by himself in the corner. Margaret was nowhere to be seen, and apparently Leon was still out picking up supplies.

Bennett's eyes got big when he saw Vargas walk in behind me. "What the hell's he doing here?"

"He's letting us borrow his boat," I said. "He's got a gun, and I bet he knows how to use it. We need all the help we can get."

"He's not going out there with us."

"Bennett, whatever your problem is, just keep it in your pocket, all right? We're gonna get Jackie, and then the two of you are gonna sit down and have a nice long talk. I'm sure you'll have some interesting things to tell him."

He swallowed hard, but didn't say another word.

I pulled a chair out for Vargas. "Have a seat," I said. "We all better eat something. We're gonna need the energy."

Bennett kept one uneasy eye on Vargas for the next couple of hours. "What the hell did you have to bring him here for?" he said when he finally had me alone in the corner. "And what's this about me having a long talk with him?"

"I figured you'd want to tell him the truth about what happened," I said. "One piece of advice, though. If you guys end up going at it, you better fight dirty."

"That I know how to do, don't worry."

"Do you have a bag we can use? To hold the money in?"

"You mean what we're gonna pass off as the money."

"Unless you think your son will show up with it."

"Alex, we've been through this, okay? What else do you want me to say?"

"Show me the bag," I said.

He picked up a blue gym bag. "I put all the money I could dig up on the top," he said, opening it. "There's about two thousand dollars on top. The rest is torn-up newspaper."

"That'll have to do."

"It's Sunday morning, Alex. The banks are closed. This is all the money from the till, every dollar I could get my hands on."

"Relax, Bennett. It's not gonna matter. Blondie's probably planning on shooting you as soon as he sees you. This will be your little joke on him."

"Then what the hell are we doing, Alex? How's this going to work?"

"Wait 'til Leon gets here. Then we'll talk about it."

Leon came in around seven o'clock, with Kmart bags in both arms. We had one hour to go until Blondie's phone call. We spent that time wrapping all of the hunting rifles in black electrical tape. Leon took a black bicycle grip out of the bag and taped it to the bottom of one of the rifle barrels. "From a distance, what do you see?" he said, picking up the gun.

"An assault rifle," Bennett said.

"A *big* assault rifle," Ham said. "The kind that'll blow your fucking head off."

"Whoever goes in Vargas's boat, they put on one of these windbreakers." He pulled them out of another bag. They were all black. "One of the black baseball hats. These sunglasses. Alex says this guy has seen all of you at least once, right? So I'll be up front."

"What," Bennett said, "you mean he's supposed to think we've got the feds coming to the rescue or something?"

"That was what I was thinking originally," Leon said. "Now I think I've got something better. Or for Blondie, anyway, it's worse."

"What's worse than the feds?"

Leon looked over at Vargas. Vargas was sitting quietly in his chair, a few feet from the table, watching us.

"Mr. Vargas," Leon said. "We need a name."

He didn't say anything.

"Somebody in Canada," Leon said. "We need the one name that'll make Blondie wet his pants."

He thought about it. "If we use this man's name," he finally said, "you forget you ever heard it. When we're done here, the name gets erased from your mind."

"Understood."

"The name is Isabella."

Nobody said anything for a moment.

"I can see why he'd be scared," Bennett finally said. "That's the most terrifying name I've ever heard. For a ballerina, anyway."

"It's Mr. Isabella," Vargas said.

"Yeah?" Bennett said. "Is he some mobbed-up wiseguy over in Soo, Canada?"

Vargas stared at him. It was the same look I got

just before he did his Moo Duk Kwan act all over my body.

"Blondie and Isabella," Bennett said. "Not exactly Bugsy and Scarface, are they. Dumb Canucks can't even get their names right."

"Take it easy," I said. "You heard what he said. We use the name and then we forget it."

"Is that the plan?" Jonathan said. "The second boat comes in like this Mr. Isabella is breaking up the party?"

"That's the idea," Leon said. "It only has to work long enough to catch them off guard. We want them to think that giving up Jackie is in their best interests."

"And then what?"

"We see what happens," Leon said. "We react accordingly."

Jonathan didn't look happy. But he didn't say anything else.

It was almost eight o'clock at that point, almost time for Blondie's call. We all sat there with our own thoughts, waiting for the phone to ring. Eight o'clock came and went. Five more minutes passed. Then ten.

When the phone finally rang, everybody jumped.

"Let me answer it," I said. I went behind the bar and picked it up.

"Good morning," he said. "Is this Alex?"

"Yes."

"Good man. Are you ready to come get your friend?"

"Let me talk to him."

"He's tied up at the moment, Alex. You remember that gun I had stuck to your head at your little poker party? Your friend is getting the same treatment right now."

"I swear to God, if anything happens to him . . ."

"If anything happens to him, it'll be your fault, Alex. It'll mean that something didn't happen exactly as it was supposed to. Are we clear on that?"

"Tell us what to do."

"That's more like it. I want you and Bennett to meet us at a certain location on the lake. I'm going to give you the GPS coordinates. Are you ready?"

"Go ahead."

He gave me the latitude and longitude in digital format. I wrote them down and showed them to Bennett.

"Bennett drives, and you carry the money, Alex. Nobody else is in the boat. We see anybody else, Jackie's dead. We see a gun, we see somebody's hand on a radio, we see a fucking seagull that looks suspicious, Jackie takes one in the temple. Are we clear on that one, too?"

Bennett held up a map of the lake and pointed to the general area. It was well past Whitefish Bay, into the heart of the lake.

"This position is almost a hundred and fifty miles away," I said. "You know we can't take a small craft out there. The weather can change in a second."

"The weather is the least of your problems, my friend. We'll see you there at noon."

"At noon," I said.

Bennett threw up his hands.

"We need more time," I said. "I don't think this boat can go that fast."

"Let me put it to you this way, Alex. We'll be there at noon. If you're not there, Jackie's going for a little swim."

He hung up.

"Let's go," I said. "We've got a little less than four hours."

We all piled out the back door. I told Margaret I'd call her on my cell phone as soon as we got back into range. "If you don't hear from us by four o'clock," I said, "call the police."

Bennett and I got into the boat he had borrowed. Vargas drove the other boat, with Leon, Ham, Jonathan, and Gill aboard. The idea was they'd hang back about three or four miles behind us, and then catch up after we'd made contact.

"Wait, you need this," Leon said, as he set a television monitor on the chair next to Bennett's captain's chair. He plugged it into the cigarette lighter.

"What's this?" Bennett said.

"My wristwatch video camera," he said. "Alex is going to put it on and keep it pointed at them. They'll get to see themselves on the screen."

"I don't get it. What's that going to do?"

"Just wait 'til Alex tells them Mr. Isabella is watching them on a live feed. That should put the fear of God in them."

Bennett watched me put the watch on. "There's an actual camera in there?"

"Come on," I said. "Let's get going."

Leon went back to the other boat, and then we all

headed down the river and into the bay. Bennett
pushed the throttle all the way forward. We were
doing about thirty-five knots. The sun was finally
starting to burn off the morning fog.

"Do you have enough gas?" I said. I had to yell
over the din of the motor.

"I hope so!"

I thought about asking him why he hadn't thought
of that before. I let it go.

"This is all my fault!" he yelled.

"Don't worry about it now!"

"I thought that money could do some good for
my son! Like money could ever be good for anybody!"

I nodded my head.

"Money is bad, Alex! It's that simple!"

"Okay, Bennett!"

"I hate it!"

"Just drive the boat!"

He frowned and shook his head. I looked behind
us. Even with the heavy cargo, Vargas's boat was
having no problem keeping up with us.

Oh hell, the cargo, I thought. You should have
had him take all that stuff out of the cabin, get a
little extra speed. You gotta think, Alex. You gotta
keep your head on straight. Jackie needs you.

It took us a good two hours to clear Whitefish
Point. The sun came out and warmed our backs as
we rode the waves. A freighter went by us, heading
the opposite way, toward the locks. The sound of the
motor, the constant rise and fall of the deck, the
spray in our faces—it all became mind-numbing, al-

Shave — Now? — camping to cellar

Mattresses to lower

Wearing aid → ME

PB — Bread — Drinks x2 —

Tue.
Costco 11am

Wed
Hospital 11¹⁵

most hypnotic. I looked at the GPS read-out on the console. We were approaching 47 degrees north, and 85 degrees west. The coordinates were still more than an hour away.

This was the biggest lake in the world, over thirty thousand square miles of open water, bigger than a few states. It all made terrible sense, why Blondie would bring us out here. Nobody would see us. There was no law out here, no consequences. And the lake was deep enough to hide a dead man. Or two dead men. Or three. You just dump them overboard and they disappear forever.

As we passed the 47th parallel, Vargas started to hang back further and further behind us. Soon his boat was no more than a speck on the horizon.

"We're almost there!" Bennett said, looking at the GPS.

I picked up the binoculars and looked ahead of us.

There. I saw the boat. It was too far away to see any details, but it was there. Time to get ready.

I took my revolver out and put it on the shelf behind the gunwale. It would be easier to get to that way. I looked in the binoculars again. It was a big boat, about the same size as Vargas's. It looked like it was pointed away from us. I could make out one man standing at the back rail, and it looked like he was holding a serious weapon—some sort of assault weapon, no doubt. A real one.

I untied the anchor from its rope and tied it onto the handle of the money bag.

"What are you doing?" Bennett yelled.

"They're gonna shoot us as soon as we're in range!" I said. "Unless I give them a reason not to!"

We got closer. Bennett throttled down to half speed. The man at the back rail was watching us through his own pair of binoculars. It was Blondie's brother. I couldn't see Blondie yet. Or Jackie.

"Show time!" I said. I put Leon's video watch on my left wrist, then turned it on. An image appeared on the monitor—first the sky, then the side of the boat. I grabbed the bag and the anchor.

My hands were shaking.

Chapter Twenty-two

I held the bag out over the rail, with the anchor on the outside. I wanted them to see it. I wanted them to know one simple fact right away—if they shot me, the money would end up taking a bath, in about five hundred feet of water.

I saw Blondie's brother holding the gun in one hand now, and waving at me with the other. It looked like he was yelling something, but I couldn't hear it over the sound of the motor.

"Bring it in easy," I said to Bennett, without turning to look at him.

"Where's Jackie?" he said. "I don't see Jackie!"

"He's gotta be there," I said, mostly to myself. "Come on, Jackie. Where the hell are you?"

As we came closer, I could hear what Blondie's brother was saying. "Get back from the rail! Move back or I'll shoot!"

"Go right ahead!" I yelled back. "You shoot and this money goes right to the bottom of the lake!"

He looked over his right shoulder. There, in the shade of the awning, I could make out two men. As we came even closer, I could see Jackie standing in front of Blondie. Jackie had silver duct tape over his mouth, and his hands were behind his back.

"Get about twenty feet away," I said to Bennett. "And move that monitor out here a little more."

He moved the throttle down to just above an idle. Then with his foot he pushed the chair out into the middle of the deck.

"What is that thing?" Blondie said. I could see his pistol now, pointed at Jackie's head. "Do you want to see your friend die *right now*?"

"I wouldn't do that," I said. Blondie's brother had his rifle pointed at my chest. I tried hard to ignore him. It wasn't working.

"Take that anchor off the bag," Blondie said. "You've got three seconds."

I snuck a look behind me. As I looked at the monitor, I turned my left arm, the one holding the bag, just so. Their boat appeared on the monitor, but the rolling of the waves made it hard to maintain a steady shot.

"McKnight, did you hear me? Take the anchor off!"

I swallowed hard. It was time to do something truly stupid. Across the water, I looked at Jackie, into his eyes.

"You better smile, Blondie," I said. I had to keep my voice natural, like there was nothing to it, like I wasn't scared out of my skull. "You want to make a good impression on Mr. Isabella, don't you?"

That one got to him. He couldn't hide it. His brother looked up from the rifle barrel.

"McKnight, what are you talking about?"

"You're on a live feed right now," I said. "Look at this monitor, Blondie. Mr. Isabella is watching everything you do."

It was hard for him to see from twenty feet away, but he looked at the monitor with wide eyes, like it was something out of his worst nightmare. "What the fuck . . ."

"You made a mistake, Blondie. You took the wrong guy. You didn't realize how tight these two men are. Jackie and Mr. Isabella, they're like brothers. Isn't that right, Jackie?"

Come on, Jackie, I thought. Play along.

Jackie nodded. Blondie wrapped his arm around Jackie's neck and pressed the gun right against his temple.

"I'm not buying any of this, McKnight. Now throw that bag over. Right now."

A sound. In the distance, a motor.

"Who is that?" Blondie yelled. His face was bright red now. "I told you, anybody else shows up, your friend dies!"

"It's just a few of Mr. Isabella's men," I said. "They'd like to have a word with you."

Blondie and his brother looked at each other. For an instant I was tempted to go for my gun.

No, not yet, Alex. Not yet.

"I know you're not an idiot," I said. "You know what's gonna happen when Isabella's men get here. No matter what you do to us, these guys are gonna

kill you. Give us Jackie and we'll give you the
money. You've got a head start, you can be long
gone by the time they get here."

Blondie's brother was pointing the rifle at my
chest again.

"Take the money," I said. I was about to put my
free hand into the bag, to grab some bills and show
them to him.

Bad idea, Alex. They'll think you're going for a
gun.

Blondie squeezed his arm hard around Jackie's
neck. He kept looking out at the open water.

"Don't be a fool!" Bennett said. "Take the goddamned money!"

No, Bennett, no. This we do not need right now.

"Those guys are gonna cut you into a million
pieces!"

Shut up, Bennett. Shut up shut up shut up.

"It's seven hundred thousand dollars, you stupid
fuckheads! Take the money and run! While you still
can!"

"Throw the bag over," Blondie said.

"Give us Jackie first," I said.

"Throw the bag over!"

"Jackie first."

The boat was coming closer. I didn't dare look.
But I was sure they had all four men standing at the
rails—Leon, Jonathan, Ham, and Gill, with Vargas
at the wheel. I could only imagine what it looked
like, four men in black, with huge black guns. I
hoped it was enough.

"Holy fuck," Blondie said.

His brother didn't look up. He kept his rifle leveled at my chest. "We're not running," he said.

"Look at them," Blondie said.

"We're not running," the brother said. "I think it's a trick."

I hung the bag a little further out over the water. The weight of the anchor was making my forearm muscles burn. But I knew if I pulled it in for a second, a bullet would rip right through me.

Then, a voice from behind me. "Put the guns down!" It sounded like Leon, yelling into a megaphone.

The brother didn't even blink. "You're gonna die, McKnight."

Blondie pushed Jackie out from under the awning. "Stay back!" he yelled. "I'll put a bullet in his head if you get any closer!"

"Put the guns down *now!*"

I knew Vargas's boat couldn't come too close, or they'd see right through everything. The tape on the guns, the cheap windbreakers. It would all fall apart.

"You're blowing your chance," I said. "If you give us Jackie right now, you still might make it out of this alive."

"I'll kill him, McKnight. I swear to God."

I looked at Jackie. His eyes were closed.

"You're dead!" Bennett said. "Give him up now or you're dead!"

"Shut up," I said. "Bennett, just shut up."

"Those are Isabella's men and you are fucking dead!"

"Those aren't his men," Blondie's brother said,

without even looking up at them. "There's no way."

"No matter what," I said, "you're still outnumbered. That you can see. You'll never get out of this alive."

"So be it," Blondie said. "I guess that's the way it goes down."

Everything froze. Seconds ticked by. This is it, I thought. I waited for the first blast.

Instead, a voice.

"Hey, Marcus! Derrick!" I turned and saw Vargas standing at the rail of his boat. He was holding up the transmitter from his radio. "It's Mr. Isabella. He wants to talk to both of you."

That broke the spell. At the sound of his name, Blondie's brother turned and fired his rifle, knocking Vargas right off his feet. As I dove to the deck, I caught a flash of Blondie's gun coming away from Jackie's head, and pointing right at me. I heard glass exploding behind me, Bennett crying out and then going down hard on the deck. There were more gunshots, from Blondie's boat, from Vargas's boat. And in the middle of all of it, a splash in the water.

I grabbed my revolver from the gunwale shelf and came back up with both hands wrapped around it. I didn't see Jackie. Where the fuck was Jackie? Blondie's brother came out from under the railing, firing at Vargas's boat. I put him in my sights and pulled the trigger. There was an explosion right next to my ear, sending a spray of wood into my face. I went down again. I saw Bennett lying on the deck. He was bleeding from the forehead, but his eyes were open. "Stay down," I said.

"Jackie's in the water," he said. "I saw him dive in."

I heard two more shots, and then the sound of a boat's propeller churning the water. Somebody was moving.

I looked over the gunwale. Blondie was at the wheel. The boat was moving away from us, and moving fast. Vargas's boat kicked up, and came our way.

"Look out for Jackie!" I yelled. "Where is he?"

I scanned the water. I couldn't see him.

"Where are you, Jackie? Where the fuck are you?"

There!

I dove in, felt the sudden icy shock of the water. I swam to where I had seen him, struggling against the waves and the brutal cold. When I finally got to him, he was fighting hard to keep his head above the water. With his hands tied behind his back, and his mouth taped shut, it was a losing battle.

"I got you, Jackie! I got you!"

I grabbed onto him, tilted his head back, and tried to do the lifeguard's crawl. My body was already numb. Even in the middle of July, the lake is so damned cold. You've got a few minutes and then you're done.

Vargas's boat got to us first. Ham came down the side ladder, one leg in the water, and grabbed Jackie. He lifted him like a rag doll, and passed him over the side. Then he came back for me, put one of those long arms around me, and pulled me out of the water.

I landed on the deck, pulled myself up to my hands and knees. I tried to breathe. When I looked up, Jonathan and Gill had already pulled the tape off of Jackie's mouth. They were busy untying his hands.

Vargas lay on the deck behind them.

Oh God no. It came back to me. Blondie's brother hitting him point-blank, knocking him right over.

Vargas picked his head up. He looked at me and then put his head back down.

"Vargas!" I crawled over to him.

"Don't touch me, McKnight. Just let me catch my breath."

"What happened? I saw you go down."

"He got me right in the chest," he said. "Son of a bitch."

"What? How are you—"

"You think I'd come out here with you clowns without my vest? What do you think I am, crazy?"

I looked down at his body. The big black vest was so obvious, but I hadn't even noticed it. "You're wearing Kevlar?"

"You think Kevlar would have stopped that bullet? From an assault weapon? This is ceramic." He winced as he reached up to give it a little tap. "I had it in the cabin. But I only had one. Sorry, I was selfish."

"What were you doing on the radio?" I said. "You said their names."

"Marcus and Derrick. The Forsythe brothers. I called Isabella and found out their real names."

"You really called him?"

"Things didn't look good," he said. "I figured I had no choice." He pushed himself up to a sitting position. "Oh God, that hurts. I'm gonna have a hell of a bruise tomorrow."

"Alex."

I turned and saw Jackie's face. He looked like a drowned rat. It was a beautiful sight.

"Are you okay?" I said.

"I need a drink."

"You're shivering," I said. "We got to get you warmed up."

"I don't see my father," Ham said. "Where the fuck is my father?"

"Oh God," I said. "He's still on the boat." I stood up on shaky legs and looked out over the rail. The boat was fifty feet away, but I couldn't see Bennett. "Let's get over there."

"I'm on it," Vargas said, slowly sitting himself down into his captain's chair. He turned the boat.

Bennett was still lying on the deck, his forehead bleeding. The blood had run into his eyes, and down his nose. Ham jumped over the rail and landed with a great thud on the other boat's deck. Leon's monitor fell off the chair.

"Be careful, goddamn it!" Bennett said. "You're gonna kill yourself!"

"You're bleeding," Ham said. "Did you get hit?"

"Of course I got hit. By about fifty pieces of flying glass."

"We've got to stop this bleeding."

"Never mind that," Bennett said. "Where's Jackie? Is he all right?"

"He's fine," Ham said. "Everybody's fine."

Bennett closed his eyes. "How the fuck did we get away with that?"

"Come on," Vargas said. "We have to catch that boat."

"Why?" I said.

"Do I even have to tell you? If he gets away, you know he's gonna come back for us."

"I think I killed his brother," I said. "I'm not sure."

"All the more reason," Vargas said. "Come on, he's gonna lose us."

I tried to think of a good reason to argue with him. It didn't come.

"Gill, you better go in the other boat. One of you will have to drive, while the other takes care of Bennett. Vargas, you've got a first aid kit?"

"In the cabin," he said. "Right on the wall."

Gill went in and grabbed it, and then climbed over the side ladder to Bennett's boat.

"You guys go right back home," I said. "We'll meet you back there."

"Be careful," Gill said.

"Jonathan, you better take Jackie down below, see if you can warm him up."

"I've got some blankets," Vargas said. "Lower cabinets on the left."

As soon as Gill was in the other boat, Vargas kicked the throttle all the way forward and headed after Blondie. I sat in the chair next to him, and Leon sat right behind us. The cold air was rushing over me, making me shiver just as hard as Jackie was.

"You better get a blanket, too!" Leon said. "You're all wet!"

I went into the cabin. Jackie was taking off his wet clothes while Jonathan stood by with the blankets.

"Let me have one of those," I said.

Jackie grabbed my arm and looked me in the eye.

"You're a damned fool," he said.

"I know."

He kept looking at me. Finally, he smiled. "Good thing."

I went back out with the blanket wrapped around me and sat next to Vargas.

"You're bleeding a little bit," he said.

I touched my cheek and felt the blood.

"Splinters," I said. "The bullet just missed me."

Vargas kept the throttle open. Some clouds had rolled in. The wind was whipping the waves up to three feet. We were bouncing hard.

"Why didn't you call Isabella from the beginning?" I said.

He looked at me.

"I'm not complaining," I said. "I'm just wondering. Wouldn't it have made things a lot easier?"

"You don't just call Isabella on the phone. You certainly don't ask him questions about other people in the business."

"I understand," I said. "Of course, calling him up on the radio . . . What did you do, call his boat?"

"Yeah, I called his boat."

"On the open airwaves."

"Yeah. He actually sounded real friendly on the

radio, like I was his best buddy and he was happy to hear from me. That's not a good sign. Like I said, things weren't looking too good here. Otherwise I wouldn't have done it."

I looked out at the water. There was no sign of Blondie's boat.

"How do you know which way he went?"

"Nearest dock for him is Batchawana Bay. I figure that's where he's headed."

"How far is it?"

"From here, maybe an hour, hour and a half," he said. "Of course, that's where Isabella's boat is, too. This could get interesting."

We rode the waves for another half hour before we finally saw him. Even with the cargo, Vargas's boat was a lot faster.

"We got him," he said. "We'll run him down in about five minutes. Do you want the honors?"

I didn't know what to say. I looked at Leon. I had shot Blondie's brother in the heat of the moment. Now, to kill Blondie in cold blood . . .

I thought about Jackie, his hands tied behind his back, his mouth taped, the gun pressed to his head.

I thought about my father's cabin, reduced to ashes.

Could I do it?

"Where's he going?" Vargas said. "He's turning."

We watched the boat turn north. Then we saw why.

"Holy fuck," Vargas said. "It's Isabella."

It was hard to tell from a distance, but the boat coming at us had a long hull, and it was kicking up water like a high-performance racing boat.

"We gotta get out of here," he said. He turned the boat hard, sending everything on the deck sliding from one side to the other. As we sped away, I went to the back rail and watched the big boat turn to intercept Blondie. Even over the sound of the motor, over two miles of open water, we could hear the shooting. Any doubts I may have had about killing Blondie in cold blood were about to be made a moot point.

"I hope Blondie puts up a good fight," Vargas said. "It might slow them down a little bit."

"Will they come after us?" I said.

"I wouldn't bet against it right now."

"Is he your contact in Canada?" Leon said. "The one you deliver the appliances to?"

Vargas looked at each of us, then back at the water. "Not him directly. But he has a hand in it. I missed the drop yesterday because of the weather, and today I came out to shoot up the Forsythe brothers. It's not exactly the way he likes his business partners to act."

Vargas kept pushing the boat at top speed. The waves were up to four feet now. Jonathan poked his head out of the cabin, asked if we could ease up on the bouncing a little bit. The look on my face sent him back into the cabin without another word.

Isabella's boat was getting closer. It wasn't going to catch us soon, but it was going to catch us. Vargas didn't look behind him. He kept the boat going straight. I checked the GPS—we were still two hours from home.

Leon went scrambling across the deck, trying to collect up the rifles. The waves made it look like he was on a trampoline.

"Don't even bother!" Vargas yelled. "If they catch us, we're dead. No matter what."

Leon sat down on the deck and held onto the rail. The sky grew darker, the waves picking up to six feet. It was slowing us down to under twenty knots. We could only hope it was slowing down the boat behind us just as much.

By the time we made it to Whitefish Bay, they had closed the gap to a half mile. I kept waiting for the first bullet.

Then I saw my second beautiful sight of the day. It was a Coast Guard patrol boat, forty feet of nautical authority, in gleaming white with the distinctive orange stripes. There was another boat right next to it.

Bennett.

"We have to dump these weapons!" Leon said. Before we got any closer, Leon and I rounded up the four taped-up rifles, along with my revolver, and slipped them off the back end of the boat. As we did, we could see Isabella's boat doing a quick U-turn. They were close enough for me to see two men at the rail, looking right at us. They were both dressed in black, with black sunglasses.

"I never thought I'd say this," Vargas said, "but thank God for the U.S. Coast Guard. If you don't mind, I'd rather not thank them in person. Those boys can get a little nosy."

He set a new course to the southwest, tracing a

mile-wide circle around the two boats. When the Coast Guard boat finally pulled away and headed for the river, Vargas took us closer to Bennett.

He was nowhere to be seen. It was just Ham and Gill, calmly sitting at the controls, waiting for us to pull up to them. The rough water made it hard to get close.

"What happened?" I said to them. "Where's Bennett?"

On cue, the cabin door opened. Bennett poked his head out, his forehead wrapped in bandages. "Are they gone?"

"We ran out of gas," Gill said. "We had to radio the Coast Guard. We were afraid you might miss us coming back in. Bennett went down below so they wouldn't ask too many questions. As it was, we had to explain this shattered windshield."

"We just got ourselves a first-class reaming, too," Ham said. "All the time they're filling us up, they're bitching at us about being out here in the open water, with the weather turning bad, and running out of gas. They must think we're the biggest fucking idiots on the lake."

"I'm not sure I'd argue with them," I said. "Come on, let's go home."

We headed down the bay, toward the river. With nobody chasing us now, we could take our time. I went in and checked on Jackie. He was wrapped up in the blankets, and snoring.

"Are you telling me he slept through all that?" I said.

"As soon as the bouncing stopped," Jonathan said. "That's when he went out."

"We'll be home soon."

"When do I start thanking you, Alex?"

"Next time you pull out my bar tab."

He gave me a tired laugh. I slapped him on the shoulder and went back up to the deck.

Leon had taken over the wheel. Vargas was sitting by the back rail now, rubbing his left shoulder.

"You're gonna be hurting tomorrow morning," I said.

"Yeah, well, considering the alternative, I'll take it."

"How much of a problem are you gonna have now? With Isabella, I mean."

"I think I'm done with that gig now," he said. "I just retired."

"Will they let you do that? Just walk away?"

"They'll have to. I'm done."

"All that talk about building houses up here, the new Bay Harbor—Isabella was behind that, too, wasn't he?"

"He was. I think that's done now, too."

"Maybe that's for the best."

He looked at me. "Yeah, I suppose it is. It obviously wasn't doing me any good. All it did was make me a target."

"I don't know how this day would have gone without your help. I don't think it would have ended well."

"I figured it would be in my best interest to keep you all alive. *Somebody's* got my money, after all.

You promised me the full story, Alex. I'm waiting."

I told him what I knew, about Bennett and his son, about the money being long gone now. "You're gonna have to take this up with Bennett," I said. "I don't know what else to tell you."

"We'll have a little chat about it."

"When we get back to his place, why don't you come in and have a drink?"

"I'll catch up to you later," he said. "Maybe tomorrow I'll stop by."

"You sure?"

"I want to go home and let Miata out. He's been inside all day. Cynthia just will not take that dog for a walk."

"Maybe you should go somewhere else," I said. "You know, lie low for a while. Hell, maybe you should hire Leon again. After today, I think he can take care of anything."

"I appreciate the thought," Vargas said. "But don't worry about me. I can take care of myself."

When we got to Bennett's place, we all climbed down off the boats. Jackie was awake now, and none too happy about making his way down a ladder wearing only a blanket. When we were all on the dock, Vargas gave us all a long look, nodded once, and then pulled away.

"Hey, Alex," Bennett said. "Whatever happened to the money bag?"

"Excuse me?"

"You know, the bag with the two thousand dollars in it?"

"I must have dropped it in the lake, Bennett. I'm real sorry about that."

"Don't even worry about it, Alex. I'm not saying you should've held onto the bag. I was just asking."

"I need a drink," I said. "I think we all do."

I was the last one off the dock. I looked down the river, saw Vargas at the wheel of his boat, just before he disappeared around the bend.

It was the last time I'd see him alive.

Chapter Twenty-three

We had our drinks. We had Margaret's world-famous beef stew. I looked at each man, one by one—Jackie sitting there wearing some clothes Bennett had given him, the sleeves a good six inches too long. Jonathan, sitting next to his father, his left hand on Jackie's back. Gill, who had come along to help his friend, without ever questioning us. Leon, his orange hair in complete disarray from the wind and the spray off the lake, still wearing his black windbreaker, sitting there with a weary smile on his face. My partner.

I couldn't help feeling something for everybody there, even Bennett, the jackass who started this whole mess—sitting there with his head in bandages, telling Margaret all about the rescue, getting just about everything wrong. I could only imagine what the story would sound like a year from now. Bennett kept looking up at Ham, who was pacing around the room, still riding his adrenaline high. The look on

Bennett's face made me almost forgive him. Whatever was going through his mind when he started all this, none of that seemed to matter much now. Bottom line, Bennett did this for his son—his other son, Sean, the one who had gotten himself into so much trouble. It was a stupid, dangerous thing to do. But I didn't have a son. Maybe there's no way I'd really understand it unless I did.

The sun was going down when we finally left. I took Jackie and Jonathan home in my truck, with Jackie in the middle, falling asleep once again. We practically carried him up the back stairs, took Bennett's oversized clothes off him, and put him in bed.

Jonathan and I went downstairs to the bar. We had another drink together.

"Tell me something," I said. "Did Jackie ever tell you about his father?"

"Oh sure. My grandfather Eli. I never got to meet him, of course, but I've heard some of the stories. He had a million of 'em, I guess. Those years out on the north Atlantic, hunting U-boats."

"He's out there right now, huh? In that lake?"

"My father never told you any of this?"

"No," I said.

"You should ask him about it."

"I'll do that."

I watched him drain his glass. He looked so much like Jackie, on this night more than ever. At least to my eyes.

"What do you say?" he finally said. "Think he'd mind if we didn't open for business tonight?"

"Just tell him it was my idea," I said.

We kept the "Closed" sign on the door. Jonathan went up to his bed. I went home to mine.

I drove down to the end of my road, got out of the truck and looked at the ashes. I stood there in the dying light, trying to feel something, but I had nothing left. I went back to my cabin and crawled into bed. I could still feel the pitch and roll of the water as I fell asleep.

The phone rang. I sat up, my heart racing. For a moment, I was back on the boat, trying to find my gun. Why was it dark?

I found my bearings, took a breath, and looked at the clock. It was just after midnight. The phone rang again.

"McKnight, this is Chief Maven."

"Chief?"

"I'm at Winston Vargas's house. He's dead. Get over here now."

"Vargas is dead?"

"That's what I said. Get up, get dressed, and get over here."

"Why?"

"Because I want you to see him, first of all. And because I want to ask you some questions. I'll see you in thirty minutes."

He hung up.

I drove in the darkness, from Paradise to the Soo, the second night in a row I had made this trip. There

were four Soo police cars in the Vargas's driveway.
I parked on the street, went up to the door, and rang
the bell. A Soo officer opened the door. I told him
Chief Maven had called me. He showed me in and
had me wait in the living room.

I sat there for a few minutes. While I waited, I
tried to work out just how I was supposed to feel
about Winston Vargas. It was no surprise he was
dead. And yes, he had brought it upon himself. This
would have happened to him eventually, one way or
another. But not tonight. Not if he hadn't been out
there on the water with us.

I could hear the camera snapping pictures in the
next room. I could see the light of the flashbulbs on
the hallway floor. Finally, Maven poked his head
around the corner. He looked tired.

"Come here," he said.

I got up and went to the other room. It was the
entertainment room, the same room where everything had started. Vargas was lying face first on the
carpet, not four feet from where he was lying the
night of the robbery. But this time, he wasn't getting
up, at least not until the coroner got there and zipped
him into a bag.

I'd seen men with the backs of their heads blown
off. None of them were bald like Vargas. Somehow
it made the whole thing that much more sickening.
There was no hair to soak up any of the blood, or
to hide any of the grim details, like where the bullet
went in or how much of the skull was destroyed. I
had to look away.

"I suppose we should go back to the station," Maven said. "Frankly, I don't have the energy right now. I'm just going to ask you straight out, right here. Do you know anything about this?"

"I don't know who did this," I said. Technically, it was the truth.

"Do you have any idea why Vargas would be planning on a long trip? He's got two suitcases packed upstairs."

"We don't exactly hang out together, Chief. How would I know?"

"Do you know anything about Vargas's boat? Why, for instance, there'd be thirty high-end appliances packed into the cabin?"

"He was obviously into something pretty shady, Chief. Sort of sheds light on what happened here, doesn't it?"

He looked at me. "It's hard to believe you never made detective. You're a natural."

"I'm not trying to be a smart-ass, Chief. I'm just saying—"

"Do you happen to know anything about two men named Marcus and Derrick Forsythe?"

I hesitated. If I denied it outright, it could come back to hang me. "I think I know who they are," I said. "Somebody's been threatening me, along with Bennett, Jackie, and Gill. They thought we had something to do with the robbery, that maybe there was more money involved, and that we had it."

"Why would they think that?"

"Because you arrested three of us," I said. "And I was guilty by association. It was all a mistake."

"Caused by our mistake in making the arrests?"

"Chief, this is no joke. I'm sure they're the ones who set my cabin on fire yesterday."

"Yeah, well, you won't have to worry about them anymore. We heard their boat washed ashore in Batchawana Bay a few hours ago. There was nobody aboard, just a lot of blood and about a hundred bullet holes."

"So those are your three robbers," I said. "These two Forsythe guys and this other guy, Danny Cox."

"Uh-huh. It ties up pretty nicely, eh? All three robbers are dead."

"And one of them," I said, "I guess it had to be Cox—he was holding out on the other two. He set up Bennett, Jackie, and Gill just to cover himself."

"So the DA should drop all the charges."

"That's up to him," I said. "But I can't imagine he'll want to push this too hard."

"No," Maven said. "Knowing him, I don't suppose he will."

"Where's Mrs. Vargas? And for that matter . . ." I looked around. Come to think of it, something else was missing. "Where's the dog?"

"Mrs. Vargas is at the hospital," he said. "She's in shock. She saw the whole thing, apparently. She said two men walked right in, told her not to worry, they didn't shoot women or dogs. They did him right here on the floor, one shot, and then they left. When we got here, the dog was practically foaming at the mouth. Damned little thing put up quite a fight when we tried to remove him."

"So where is he now?"

"He's in the garage. He just stopped barking a few

minutes ago, must have run out of gas."

"Can I see him?"

"What the hell for?"

"I just want to see him."

"You go right ahead, McKnight. He'll tear your face right off."

I went through the kitchen, opened the door to the garage, and prepared myself for the attack. It never came.

"Miata," I said. "Where are you?"

I turned the light on, saw Vargas's Saab parked in one spot, his wife's blue Miata in the other. I didn't see the dog.

"Miata, come on out. I don't need a sneak attack tonight."

I walked around both cars. No sign of the dog. Finally, I got down on my hands and knees. The dog was under Vargas's car. He was shivering.

"I know you've had a tough night," I said. Hell, he'd seen his master's head get blown off. "Just come here."

When I reached for him, he bit me. I pulled my hand back, looked at the little drops of blood forming between my thumb and forefinger.

"You really got me," I said. "Do you feel better now?"

I reached in again. This time he nipped the end of my ring finger.

"Miata, there's something you should know about me. We're actually a lot alike. If I know I'm right, I'll fight anybody. You can bite me all you want,

I'm not going to give up until I get you out of here. So give us both a break, huh?"

I reached for him again, gave him a little fake this way, then that way, and finally grabbed him by the collar. He was all teeth and claws when I picked him up and held him against my chest. I kept holding him tight while he fought me for a good five minutes. Then he gave up. When I took a step, he fought me some more. I held him. Five minutes later, I was back in the house with him.

"What are you doing with that dog?" Maven said. "Are you crazy?"

"Probably," I said. "I wanna take him. Otherwise, he'll just go to the pound, right?"

"We'd hold him until Mrs. Vargas was ready to claim him."

"I don't think she will," I said. "If she does, just tell her to call me, okay?"

He shook his head. "Fine, McKnight. The two of you deserve each other."

When I got to the truck, I expected Miata to put up another fight. Instead, he just curled up on the far corner of the front seat.

"I know how you feel," I said. "I feel the same way. Tell you what, instead of you coming home with me, I've got an even better idea."

I drove south to Rosedale. It was after one in the morning now, but I knew Leon was a night owl. I saw a couple of lights on inside the house when I pulled up. Miata let me pick him up this time. When Leon opened the door, he took one look at the dog and said, "Vargas is dead."

"They got to him," I said. "He had his bags packed."

Leon shook his head. "You wanna come in?"

"No, that's all right," I said. "I couldn't leave the dog there, so I was wondering if maybe your kids could look after him for a while."

"You don't want to?"

"We sorta got off on the wrong foot," I said. "Besides, he's too much dog for me."

Leon took Miata, scratched his head, and said, "No problem, Alex. Between the four of us, we should be able to keep up with him."

"I appreciate it."

"Come on in, Alex. One drink."

I went in and sat at his kitchen table, had a drink with him.

"I'm packing up the office tomorrow," he said. "I'm giving up the private eye biz."

"You don't think you can make it?"

"I had one customer. Look what happened."

"You saved Jackie, Leon. You came up with the whole thing."

"Even more reason to retire," he said. "Go out on top."

"I can't thank you enough," I said.

"That's what partners are for."

We drank to that. I said good night to him. I left Leon with his family, and his new dog, and drove home alone.

It wouldn't go away.

Everything else went back to normal. The charges

were officially dropped. I spent most evenings
having dinner at the Glasgow Inn, watching the Tigers on his television set. Jackie and I didn't talk
much about what had happened. One night, he asked
me when I'd be ready to play poker again.

"I'm ready when you're ready," I said. "Just do
me one favor."

"What's that?"

"Keep the game right here in the bar. We don't
play at some stranger's house."

"Typical," he said. "You never want to go anywhere."

That's how I knew Jackie was getting over it.
Every day, he was acting a little bit more like his
old self again. Whether I liked it or not.

The summer passed. It got colder at night. The
sunsets came earlier. They kept working on the golf
course down in Brimley, but nobody was talking
about major development. The new money hadn't
found us yet.

For now at least, our secret was still safe.

I worked on the last cabin every day, making runs
to the dump with half-melted bed frames and black-
ened pipes, clearing away all the charred wood, getting the site ready. In another couple of weeks they'd
deliver my load of white pine logs. I'd rebuild the
cabin by hand, doing it the right way, the way my
father had taught me back when I was eighteen years
old. I'd use the original foundation, and my father's
stone chimney, and I'd rebuild the whole thing from
the ground up, no matter how long it took me.

All that work, out in the sun, it should have

cleared my head. It should have helped me get over it.

But it kept coming back to me, usually at night. Just as I closed my eyes, I'd be back on the boat. I'd see the same scene, played out over and over, hear the same words spoken.

Then one day, one of the last warm days of the summer, I was breaking up the one corner of the old cabin that hadn't burned. I would use it for firewood. I had sharpened my ax, and was swinging it in the air, splitting the logs in half, and then into quarters.

Swing. Chunk. Swing. Chunk. Swing.

I stopped.

The ax hung in the air. I dropped it to the ground.

I stood there and thought about it, played it back again and again, just the one piece of it, one small loop out of the whole episode.

I got in my truck and drove.

Bennett was sitting at one of the tables when I walked in. Ham was behind the bar. I didn't see Margaret anywhere.

"Alex!" Bennett said when he looked up at me. "How the hell are you? I'm glad you stopped in! Ham, pour the man a beer."

I sat down. Ham brought the beer over. He put his hand on my shoulder as he put the beer down in front of me. "On the house," he said.

"Damned straight," Bennett said. "This man never pays for another drink. Not in this bar."

I didn't drink the beer.

"Tell me again," I said. "How did he get the money out of the house?"

"What?"

"Your son, Sean. The one who took off with all the money. How did he get it out of the house?"

"We were assuming he had it under the bag—you know, those black plastic bags they were wearing."

"Seven hundred thousand dollars," I said. "Minus thirty thousand for his partners. He had all that money under that bag?"

"He must have, Alex. How else would he have gotten it out of the house?"

"Exactly," I said. "How else?"

"Alex, what are you talking about? What's the problem here?"

"I'm just wondering," I said. "Maybe he did something else with all that money. Maybe he threw it out the window. It would explain why he broke the window in the first place."

Bennett looked at me. He raised his hands in the air. "I don't get it."

"If he threw it out the window, somebody else must have picked it up."

I looked over my shoulder. Ham was pouring another beer. He stopped.

"How did it work, Ham? Were you on the shoreline? Or on the river?"

"Hold on one minute," Bennett said. "Surely you're not accusing Ham. You can't come in here and say that about my son, Alex. Not my *good* son. Not Ham."

"It wasn't just Sean and Ham, your good son," I said. "It was *you*. You were in on this from the beginning, Bennett. And you know what the best part is? That little speech you gave me on the boat. Remember? 'There's no good money, Alex. It's all bad. I hate money, Alex.' "

"Alex, you are so out of line right now. I know you helped us out, but . . ."

"When your friends got arrested, you kept lying about it," I said. "When Jackie got fucking *kidnapped*, you kept lying about it."

"All right, that's enough. You're gonna have to leave, Alex."

"What are you gonna buy with that money?" I said. "A nice new SUV to drive around? An even bigger television?"

"Alex, out."

"Don't you want to know how I figured it out?"

Bennett sat there with his arms folded. He didn't say a word.

"When we were on that boat, before Vargas's boat got to us, I was telling Blondie to take the money. You remember that? I was saying, 'Here, take it. Give us Jackie. Take the money and run before Isabella's men get here.' You were behind me saying, 'Don't be a fool, take the money.' And I was just thinking, Bennett, shut up for God's sake. I wasn't really paying attention to what you were saying. It didn't come to me until today, as a matter of fact. You told him there was seven hundred thousand dollars in the bag. You used that exact figure."

"That's how much we were talking about," Bennett said. "You just said so yourself, when you asked me where Sean had put the money. You said seven hundred thousand dollars. That's how much Vargas had in his safe."

"You didn't know that," I said. "At the time, you had no idea. Or at least you *shouldn't* have. First you told me there was only thirty thousand, and Sean got nothing. Remember? Then you told me there must have been more after all, and that Sean had disappeared. You never could have known how much money was in that safe, Bennett. Unless you were in on it yourself."

I could hear Ham coming back out from behind the bar.

"How long has Jackie known you?" I said. "Fifty years? A half a century of being your best friend?"

This is what the whole summer had come down to. This summer of secrets. The biggest secret of all was what a bag full of money could make a man do.

"It's all on you, Bennett. Everything we had to go through. Vargas dead, your son's friend dead. Jackie almost dead. It's all on you."

Ham was right behind me. Bennett was standing up. They were both a hell of a lot bigger than I was.

I didn't care.

It's like I told the dog. If I know I'm right, I'll fight anybody.

A few hours later, I stopped in at the Glasgow Inn. It was cold that night. It was cold and the wind was blowing hard enough to drive three-foot waves against the rocks. The sound was familiar to me. It came to me as soon as I turned off the truck and listened.

Summer was over, that's what the sound said. No matter what the calendar said, the lake was turning the page to fall. For the last ten thousand years, the lake has always had its way.

When I walked in, I saw a nice fire going. It was a welcome sight. I sat down in one of the big, over-stuffed chairs and put my feet up. Jackie took one look at me, then brought over an ice bag and a Canadian.

"Now what?" he said.

"My face is having a hell of a week," I said. I held the ice bag over my left eye.

"You gonna tell me what happened?"

"Sit down."

He sat in the other chair and put his feet up next to mine.

"First you gotta tell me something," I said.

"What's that?"

"You gotta tell me about your father."

"Come on, Alex."

"I'm serious. I want to hear it. Start at the beginning."

"It's a long story," he said. He looked into the fire.

"My evening is free," I said. "Tell me."

So he did. While the wind blew outside, I sat by the fire and listened to the story of Elias Connery, how he came to Lake Superior when he was twenty years old, how he fell in love with a girl in a bar, and also with the lake itself. He went to war, he had a son, he came back to the lake, and now he was a part of it. And would be forever.

I didn't want him to finish, because then it would be my turn. I'd have to tell him what had happened over at O'Dell's place. After fifty years, he was about to lose his best friend. Meaning he'd be stuck with me now. Alex McKnight would be his best friend in the world.

Talk about a big job. I hoped I could handle it.

I sure as hell was gonna try.

**Keep Reading for an Excerpt
from Steve Hamilton's Next Alex McKnight Mystery**

BLOOD IS THE SKY

**Available in Hardcover
from St. Martin's Minotaur!**

I saw a lot of fires when I was a cop in Detroit. I was supposed to help secure the scene and then get the hell out of the way, but sometimes I'd stick around and watch the firefighters doing their work. I saw some real battles, but when they were done, the building would always still be standing. That was the thing that got to me. The windows would be blown out, and maybe there'd be a big hole in the roof, but the building would still be there.

Years later, I watched a Lake Superior storm taking down a boathouse. When the storm let up, there was nothing left but a concrete slab covered with sand. It wasn't surprising. Anyone who lives up here knows that water is stronger than fire. Water wins that one going away. But at least water cleans up after itself. It does the job all the way. When water destroys, it makes everything look new. It can even be beautiful.

Fire doesn't do that. When a fire is done, what's

left is only half destroyed. It is charred and brittle. It is obscene. There is nothing so ugly in all the world as what a fire leaves behind, covered in ashes and smoke and a smell you'll think about every day for the rest of your life.

That's why I had to start rebuilding the cabin. Maybe I was fooling myself, but it was something I had to do. Even though the days were getting shorter. Even though the pine trees were bending in the cold October wind. No man in his right mind would have started rebuilding then. So of course I did.

I had already taken away most of the old wood, those logs that would have lasted another three hundred years if they hadn't burned. I had hauled them away along with the pipes burned black and the bed frames twisted by the heat. There was nothing now but the stone foundation, stripped of the wooden floor, and the chimney, the last thing my father had made with his bare hands before he died. I knew that the snow would come, and it would cover the black stains on the ground, and the chimney would stand alone in the cold silence like a grave marker. I wasn't going to let that happen.

The rebuilding didn't start well. The man who said he'd be there on Monday with my white pine logs rolled up on Wednesday morning, acting like he had nothing to apologize for. He had one of those long flatbeds with the crane on it, with enough lifting power to set every last log down as gently as a tea-cup. But it took him all morning to clear the truck, and he damn near knocked over the chimney in the process. Then he stood around for a while, trying to tell me about his own cabin down in Traverse City. "The cabins I passed on the way in," he finally said. "You built those?"

"My father did."

"Looks like you had a big one here," he said. He hitched his pants up as he looked around the clearing. "What happened? Did it burn down?"

"It did."

"Hell of a thing," he said. "You gotta be careful with those wood stoves."

"I can't argue with that."

"Looks like you learned the hard way."

I let a few seconds tick by. "It wasn't a wood stove," I finally said. "Somebody burned it down."

"You're shittin' me."

"This gentleman and I, we had a little disagreement."

It took a moment for that one to sink in. "Are you shittin' me, man? You gotta be shittin' me."

"You don't have to believe it."

"I suppose you're gonna rebuild this all by yourself, too."

"I'm gonna try."

"Seriously, where's all your help at?"

"If I need help, I'll get it."

"It's October," he said. "You're not thinking of starting this now, are you?"

"I'd have to be crazy, you mean."

"Is what I'm saying, yeah. Unless you're just shittin' me some more."

"Well, I appreciate your concern," I said. "And I

appreciate you bringing up my logs. You were only two days late. Have a good trip back home."

He was still shaking his head as he drove away. I listened to the distant sound of his truck as he rumbled onto the main road and headed south. When he was gone, there was nothing left to hear but a steady wind coming off the lake.

"Well, Pops," I said to the wind, "let's see if I remember how to do this."

This was the cabin he had built in the summers of 1980 and 1981. I helped him for a few weeks in that second year. I was already out of baseball and working as a police officer in Detroit, and this was my last attempt to make peace with him. The days were hot. I remember that. And as I helped him peel and scribe the logs, it brought back yet another summer, back in 1968, the first time I had ever been up here in Paradise, Michigan. I was only seventeen then, with one more year of school ahead of me before heading off to single A ball in Sarasota. He wanted me to go to college, but I had my own ideas. Thirteen years later, he finished this cabin, his biggest and best. His masterpiece. Six months after that he was dead.

The cabin may have burned to the ground, but at least we had those summers.

Twenty years later, on a cold October day, I started all over again. I cut the sill logs first, the logs that would run along the bottom of each wall, then secured them to the foundation with J-bolts. I cut a groove along the outside edge with the chain saw, just as he had taught me. When it rained, the water would collect in the groove and drip away instead of running down the foundation. Then I cut the grooves for the floor joists. I put rough plywood down for the time being—I'd put the nice hardwood floorboards down when the outside was finished.

That was the first day.

When the light was gone, I went down to the Glasgow Inn for dinner. My friend Jackie owns the place. If you ever find yourself in Paradise, just go to the one blinking light in the center of town, then go north another hundred yards or so. It'll be there on the right. When you step into the place, you won't see a typical American bar—there are no mirrors to stare into while you drink, no smoky dark corners to nurse a bad mood in. The chairs are comfortable, there's a fire going in the hearth every night, regardless of the weather, and there's a man there named Jackie Connery who looks like an old Scottish golf caddie. If you ask him the right way, Jackie will even risk his liquor license and give you a cold Canadian beer.

I take that last part back. Those Canadian beers are just for me.

I felt like hell the next morning. My hands were sore, my arms were sore, my legs were sore, and my back was sore. Aside from that I was fine.

I had my coffee and looked up at the dark clouds.

Rain was the last thing I needed, because today was
the day I'd start building the walls.

I scribed each log the way my father had done. I
did most of the heavy cutting with the chain saw,
stopping every half hour to sharpen it. I used an ax
to cut the notches, keeping both hands together as I
swung it, like a baseball bat. That much he didn't
have to teach me. You can't be accurate with your
hands apart.

Of course, cutting the scarf just right is the hard
part. Or as the old man liked to say, this is where
you separated the men from the boys. The idea is to
cut it so perfectly that one log will rest on top of the
other with no daylight in between. If you do it right,
you don't need any chinking. If you don't do it right,
then God help you. You've got no business building
a cabin in the first place.

The first log I tried cutting that morning, I didn't
get right. The second log was worse. The third log
you could have put in a carnival and charged people
five dollars a head to come laugh at it.

The wind picked up. It looked like rain was coming. I kept working. I was halfway through the fourth
log when the hornets attacked me.

The nest was hanging from one of the birch trees.
They had already been smoked out the night of
the fire, the nest partially caved in by the spray
of the fire hoses. They were trying to rebuild, just
like I was, but they had run out of time. Now half-
crazed by the cold weather, most of them near the
end of their natural lives, they saw me moving
around below them, rattling around with my chain

saw. They decided to go down fighting.

I slapped two off the back of my neck, another off my arm. "Crazy fucking things! Get away from me!" The next one caught me right on the cheek and that was it for me. The day was already going bad enough.

I had my extension ladder there, figuring I'd need it eventually, so I braced it up against the birch tree and climbed up with my ax. I was just about to swing at the branch. I was going to take the whole thing down with one good whack, and then I was going to soak the nest with gasoline and set it on fire. Knowing me, I would have emptied the can, a full two gallons of gasoline, and then I would have thrown a lit match right in the middle of it. All the leaves on the ground would have gone up at once and I'd be running around with my pants on fire and both eyebrows singed right off my face.

I stopped myself just in time.

I took a deep breath and climbed back down the ladder. I dropped the ax.

It wasn't worth it. Watching the nest burn, sending the rest of those hornets to hell. They'd all be dead in another week, anyway.

It was a lesson I had taken most of my life to learn. Sometimes you have to let things go.

The rain came. The dark clouds stayed in the sky. I went back to work.

I had come back up here in 1987. My marriage was over and I was off the police force, with a dead partner in the ground and a bullet in my chest. I came up here intending to sell off the land and the six cabins my father had built, but I didn't do it. Somehow the Upper Peninsula was just what I needed. It was cold and unforgiving, even in the heart of summer. There was a terrible beauty to the place, and I could be alone up here in a part of the world where being alone was the rule and not the exception. I moved into the first cabin, the cabin I had helped him build myself, back when I was seventeen years old. I stayed up here and lived day to day and never thought I'd have to face my past again.

That didn't work. It never does.

Hours after I called it a day, I could still feel the buzz of the chain saw in my hands. There was a deep ache in my shoulder, right where they had taken the other two bullets out.

"What was it this time?" Jackie said. He slid a cold Canadian my way.

He was talking about my face, of course. There was a nice little swollen knot under my eye. Whenever something goes wrong, I end up wearing it on my face.

"Hornets," I said.

"How's the cabin going?"

"It's a little slow."

He nodded his head. He didn't say a word about how late it was in the season or how much of a fool I was. Jackie understood why I needed to do this.

"You know who could help you," he said.

I knew. I took a long pull off the bottle and then

set it back down on the bar. "I've got to get some sleep," I said. Then I left.

I was just as sore the next morning, but somehow everything felt different. It was all coming back to me, the way you let the chain saw and the ax do the work, the way you work with the grain of the log instead of fighting against it. The logs starting fitting together the way they were supposed to. I had the walls two logs high by lunchtime. Of course, that meant it was getting harder and harder to wrestle the logs into position. I'd have to start using the ramps soon, and eventually I'd have to set up some kind of sky line. That would slow me down.

Hell, maybe Jackie was right. There was one man who could really help me.

But I'd be damned if I was going to go ask him.

My father had bought all the land on both sides of this old logging road, nearly a hundred acres in all. He built the six cabins and lived in each one of them off and on over the years, renting out the others to tourists in the summer, hunters in the fall, and snow-mobilers in the winter. When I came up here and moved into the first cabin, I kept renting out the rest of them. It was a good way to stay busy without having to go anywhere.

A few years after I moved in, somebody bought the couple of acres between my father's land and the main road. I was a little worried about what the new owner might do to that land. I had visions of a triple-decker summer home, with every tree knocked down so they could maybe get a view of the lake. But it didn't happen that way. It was one man, and I watched him build his own cabin by hand. If my father had been around to see it, he would have approved of this man's work.

I got to know him eventually. You don't live on the same road up here with one other person without running into each other. I'd plow the road for him. He'd give me some of the venison from his hunts. He didn't drink, so we never did that together, but we did share an adventure or two. I even played in goal one night for his hockey team. The fact that he was an Ojibwa Indian never got in the way of our friendship.

Until one day he had to make a choice.

I didn't hear his truck pull up. With the chain saw roaring away, I wouldn't have heard a tank battalion. I happened to glance at the road and saw his truck parked there. Vinnie Red Sky LeBlanc was standing next to it, watching me. He was wearing his denim jacket with the fur around the collar. I had no idea how long he'd been there.

I shut the chain saw down and wiped my forehead with my sleeve.

"You're gonna go deaf," he said. "Where's your ear protection?"

"I left them around here someplace. Just can't find them."

He shook his head at that, then walked right past me to the stacks of logs. Like many Bay Mills Ojibwa, you had to look twice to see the Indian in him. There was a little extra width to his high cheekbones, and a certain calmness in his eyes when he looked at you. You always got the feeling he was thinking carefully about what to say before he said it.

"White pine," he said.

"Of course."

"Where'd it come from?"

"Place down near Traverse City."

"I thought I saw a truck going by," he said. "That was what, Wednesday?"

"He was supposed to be here Monday."

"Couple of these logs I wouldn't use on a doghouse," he said. "Like this one right here."

"I know. I was gonna put that one aside."

He slipped his hands under the log and lifted it. He was maybe three inches shorter than me, and thirty pounds lighter, but I wouldn't have wanted to fight the man, on the ice or off. He carried the log a few steps and tossed it in the brush.

"That'll be your waste pile," he said. "I see another one right down here."

"You don't have to do that, Vinnie. I know which ones are bad."

He went over to the cabin, knelt down, and ran his hand along one of the logs. "You know which ones are bad," he said, "and yet this one right here seems to be part of your wall already."

"When did you become the county inspector?" I said. "I didn't see it in the newspaper."

He let that one go. "Can I ask why you're doing this by yourself?"

"My father did it by himself."

"Did he start building in October?"

"I know I'm not going to finish it," I said. "I just had to start. I couldn't wait until spring."

He smiled at me as he stood up. "Patience was never your strong suit."

"Vinnie, you always loved this cabin. You told me once you'd buy it off me for a million dollars. You remember?"

"I do," he said. "This was the best cabin I've ever seen."

"Put yourself in my place," I said. "If somebody burned this down, what would you do?"

"First of all, I'd kill whoever did it." He thought about it for a moment. "Did you kill him?"

"No," I said.

"But he's dead."

"Yes."

"Okay, then. The next thing I'd do is rebuild the thing, as close as I could to the original."

"Exactly."

"But I wouldn't do it alone," he said. "Not with a friend down the road who knows twice as much about building cabins as I do."

"Excuse me, twice as much? Since when?"

"Make that three times as much. I was trying to be kind."

"Yeah, well, if you'll excuse me, I've got work to do."

"You'll never even get to the roof," he said. "You want the snow to pile up in here all winter?"

"What are you saying? You really want to help me?"

"Your father's spirit sent me," he said. "He knows what this thing would look like if you did it yourself."

"Ah, Indian humor," I said. "I've really been missing that."

"Let me go get my stuff," he said. "I'll see if I have an extra pair of earphones, too."

"Yeah, get me those earphones," I said. "I have a feeling I'll be needing them now."

That's how I got my help. That's how we started being friends again.

We worked until the sun went down. I offered to buy him dinner at the Glasgow, but he took a pass. He said he was going over to the reservation to see his mother. The next morning, he was on the site before I was. He was spot-peeling logs with his drawknife.

"Let me ask you something," I said when I pulled up. "Aren't you supposed to be out in the woods this month?" Vinnie's regular job was dealing blackjack over at the Bay Mills casino, but every fall he'd make extra money working as a guide for hunters.

"I'd rather be doing this," he said.

"And your day job?" I said. "You're still dealing, right?"

"I asked for some time off."

"Vinnie, you don't have to do this."

"I needed a break anyway, Alex. Okay? Don't worry about it. Just help me peel these things."

"Those are already peeled, Vinnie."

"By what, a machine? Here, let me show you the right way to do it."

Somehow, I managed not to kill him that day. When we got to work, we found a good rhythm and added three more rows to the walls. We didn't talk much about anything except what log came next, and where it should go. There was not a word said about what had happened between us.

When we had run out of daylight, I invited him to have dinner at the Glasgow again. He seemed to hesitate for a second before saying yes. "If you've got a hot date or something, just tell me," I said. "I won't be offended."

"I've been over on the rez a lot lately," he said. "They can do without me for one night."

There was a whole story behind that one—Vinnie moving off the Bay Mills reservation and buying his own land. I knew it didn't sit well with the rest of his family, even though he made a point of spending most of his free time there.

"Come on," I said, "I'll buy you a steak."

Jackie did a double-take when we walked into the Glasgow together. "Well, look at this," he said.

"Two steaks," I said. "Medium rare. You know the rest."

"Good evening to you, too," he said. "I'm just fine, thanks for asking." If he was genuinely mad at me, it didn't stop him from opening a cold Canadian and sliding it my way.

"It's good to see you," Vinnie said. "It's been a while."

"Don't tell me," Jackie said. "You're showing Alex how to build his cabin. Am I right?"

"It was too painful to watch," Vinnie said. "I had to step in."

"You guys are hilarious," I said. "Just keep it up."

That's the way it went, on a cold October night.

It had been another cold night, not that long ago, when the woman had come to me. She was an Ojibwa, someone Vinnie knew, someone he had grown up with on the reservation. She was in trouble and I did what I could to help her. In the end, Vinnie was involved, and that's when he had to make his choice—whether to trust me or his own people. I had no good reason to blame him, but the choice hurt me just the same. And it had stayed there between us ever since.

Until this night. We sat by the fire and talked about the cabin and what we would work on the next day. We pretended that nothing had ever changed. Maybe that's how you get past it. You pretend until it's real.

He was there to help me the next day, the day after that, and then the next. I bought him dinner every night. Hell, it was the least I could do. We were putting those walls up so fast, we actually had a shot at getting the roof on before it snowed. That's what I thought, anyway. And then, of course, it did snow. It wasn't much, just a few flurries overnight that turned to rain in the morning, but it was enough to knock us out of the game for the rest of the day. Vinnie ran off to do something on the rez, and I checked on the renters in the other cabins. It was bow season in Michigan, so I had all the usual men from downstate, the men who appreciated the fact that my land was right next to the state land, and that I'd leave them a cord of firewood outside their door and otherwise leave them alone. Bow season was easy, because bow hunters are the true gentlemen of the sport. They don't make a racket, and they keep the cabins clean. Firearm hunters were usually okay, although I'd still get my share of drunken clowns.

Snowmobilers, of course, were the worst of all. Just one more reason to dread the winter, and to hope like hell that the snow wasn't coming for good.

It wasn't. Not yet, anyway. The next morning the sun came out and melted away the thin traces of snow on the ground. When I got to the cabin site, I was surprised to see he wasn't there yet. An hour later, I started wondering. I was doing as much of the work as I could on my own, but it was getting harder and harder to set the logs. Without Vinnie to help me, I'd have to set up the sky line. Of course I wasn't even paying him, so what right did I have to complain?

By lunchtime I thought I'd head down the road and check on him. His truck was gone. I couldn't help but think of another day, when I had sat in this exact same spot, looking at his empty driveway, wondering where he was. It turned out he had spent the night in jail, having taken a hockey stick to the face of a Sault Ste. Marie police officer. That was the beginning of a very bad week.

Good God, Vinnie, I said to myself. I hope to hell you weren't out finding trouble last night.

I went down to the Glasgow for some of Jackie's beef stew and a Canadian. "Where's your man?" Jackie said as he served me.

"You got me. He didn't show up today."

He gave me a look. "Whattsa matter, trouble in Paradise?"

"No trouble. I just don't know where he is."

"Last time you ended up in the hospital."

"Jackie, he's been helping me all week, okay? Don't you think he deserves a day off?"

"If that's all it is, fine," he said. "I'm just saying, the last time Vinnie got in trouble, you're the one who ended up almost getting killed."

"Okay, I hear you."

"Okay, then."

"Okay."

Vinnie walked in just then and saved us. He came to the bar and sat down next to me.

"Give the man some beef stew," I said.

"No thanks," he said. That's when I knew something was wrong. If you have any appetite at all, you don't turn down Jackie's beef stew.

"What's going on?" I said.

"I'm sorry I wasn't around today. Something sort of came up."

"You don't have to apologize," I said. "Hell, it's not like I'm paying you anything."

Vinnie thought about it. "You realize," he said, "that I'm the one paying you. For what happened. This is how I'm settling my debt to you."

"You don't owe me anything," I said. "We've been through this, remember?"

I sure as hell didn't want to go through it again. Not when we both seemed to be finally getting over it.

"I remember," he said. "But still—"

"For God's sake," I said, "are you gonna tell me what's wrong?"

He sat there for a long moment, while Jackie

looked back and forth between us, clearly expecting the worst.

"It's Tom," he finally said.

"Your brother."

"Yeah."

I didn't know a hell of a lot about Tom LeBlanc. I knew he was a few years younger than Vinnie, and that he had caused his family enough trouble to make Vinnie look like the golden boy. There was one incident at the Canadian border that Vinnie never wanted to talk about. I had to read about it in the *Soo Evening News*. That was the last time I had seen Tom, in fact, right before had gone off to serve his two years at Kincheloe.

"What's the problem?" I said. I knew he was out on parole now, and saying all the right things about staying straight. But hell, if he was in trouble again, it wouldn't exactly shock me.

"He was on a hunting trip in Ontario. He was supposed to be back a couple of days ago."

"And he didn't make it back?"

"No."

"You don't think—"

"What, that he's passed out in some bar in Canada? Is that what you mean?"

"Vinnie, come on."

"It's different this time, Alex."

Here it comes, I thought. He's been going to the meetings; he's a changed man. The whole speech. That's what I expected.

That's not what I got.

"This time," Vinnie said, "he's me."